HELL BENT ON SUCCESS

Copyright © A M P Mills 2019

Third Edition

The moral right of A M P Mills to be identified as the author of this work has been asserted by him in accordance with the Copyright, Designs and Patents Act 1988.

This book is a work of fiction. Names, characters, places, and incidents are either products of the author's imagination or are used fictitiously. Any resemblance to actual events or locales or persons, living or dead, is entirely coincidental.

A catalogue record for this book is available from the British Library.

For my wife, Diana, and my sons, Cameron & Finley.

1

'*This is the life*,' thought Gordon. '*If I died now, I'd die happy.*'

A broad, satisfied smile creased his face, blissfully unaware that in eight minutes' time he would be dead and far from pleased with his demise.

Behind the wheel of his silver 1954 Porsche Spyder convertible, Gordon was in a buoyant mood. Since being appointed Chief Financial Officer of the world's most powerful and feared hedge fund — Sheol Trading — he had struggled to find time to indulge his two life passions: His beautiful car and, the game of gentlemen, golf. However, this trip to St Andrews, courtesy of the company, provided him with a rare opportunity to enjoy both.

The Spyder glided across a medieval stone bridge as the sun's final rays lapped over the car. His girlfriend, Sarah, relaxed in the passenger seat, her chestnut brown hair whipping around in the breeze. Whenever they drove anywhere, Sarah pleaded with Gordon not to drive with the roof down, but he ignored her pleas; he didn't appreciate the fact she would spend an hour washing, brushing and blow-drying her hair into the elegant coiffure that greeted him at the door. And, no matter how short their journey, by the time they reached their destination her hair would always resemble a bird's nest.

Secretly, Gordon fancied the dishevelled look.

The car pulled into a quaint service station. A small decrepit shack, a poor excuse of a shop, cowered in the corner. The car stopped beside one of two old-fashioned pumps, the type before digital displays.

Gordon grinned impishly at Sarah as she struggled to recreate her hairstyle, then hopped from the car, and landed with a splash. He lifted his foot, disapprovingly clicked his tongue, and frowned at the sight of the water stains marking his camel-hide loafers. His eyes strayed to the drenched forecourt and the multi-coloured film shimmering on its surface. He flinched as he inhaled the distinctly noxious fumes.

A buzzing from beneath his suede bomber jacket distracted him from his thoughts. He reached inside his coat and retrieved the latest smart phone.

'It's Oliver, the COO,' he announced with a flamboyant wave. 'I've been away from the office for one day and already they need me. I swear that place would fall apart without me.' He rolled his eyes with a smile, revelling in how invaluable to the company he apparently was.

Sarah smiled warmly, appreciating his seeming importance.

His fingers glided across the device, flittering up and down. He beamed with pride as he read the message aloud: 'Despite your opinion and to the contrary, it is with deep regret we must inform you; your services are no longer required. Please consider yourself terminated.'

Gordon's lips quivered. Sarah stared, absent of expression.

'This must be a joke,' Gordon laughed nervously. 'And not particularly funny I must say.'

His phone buzzed heralding the arrival of another message. Gordon stared perplexed as he read the latest message: 'Perhaps we were not clear. We do not make jokes. This is quite serious. Your employment is terminated. Effective IMMEDIATELY!'

Gordon's jaw flapped about, suddenly lacking muscular control and the ability to close.

'Why… This… This is ridiculous,' stammered Gordon.

Sarah remained quiet, instead searching Gordon's face for a clue as to what the right reaction would be in such circumstances. Only last year, as head of Human Resources for an investment bank, she notified five hundred staff of their redundancy by text message but dismissing executive management in a similar fashion she felt was a step too far.

The smart phone sprung to life again.

Gordon raised the screen to eye level, his fingers swished, and he read the new message: 'On a personal note, I would like to say it has been a pleasure having your acquaintance over the past three years. All the best, Oliver.'

'This can't be serious. It must be…' His words trailed off.

The phone began to emit a hissing noise. A flash from the rear of the device briefly illuminated Gordon's palm. He turned it over gingerly and noticed smoke seeping from the inside. The phone quickly heated up, and tiny flames escaped, licking the casing. Gordon's hand immediately reddened, and he released his grip on the device, watching it tumble towards the ground.

It all happened very quickly. While only a mere second passed, for Gordon it would be the longest second of his life and, ironically, the last.

As the phone collided with the liquid surrounding his feet, huge flames, resembling stampeding horses launched across the forecourt. An inferno raged around him. His skin blistered and a juddering commotion welled beneath his feet, followed by a loud explosion — the fuel storage tanks beneath the ground, long in need of replacement, surrendered to the intense heat and detonated.

Gordon's beloved Spyder hurtled skywards, pirouetting, before landing, top down, in a field a few hundred metres away.

The ground-shaking smash interrupted a cow's grazing. It cocked its head and contemplated the smouldering wreck before dismissing the car falling from the sky as an everyday occurrence and continuing with its meal.

Suffice to say, Gordon was dead, and he wasn't the slightest bit happy. All happiness and contentment instantly disappeared, instead replaced by anger and resentment as Gordon fumed at the way his life had ended so abruptly; so undignified and hardly befitting a man of his stature. A simple heart attack would have been sufficient. Surely there was no need for this sledgehammer approach, with his crispy, blackened and shrivelled body parts resembling that of the sausages he had served at last summer's barbecue. Where was the justice in that?

****

Meanwhile, somewhere above the Atlantic Ocean, a private jet — the size of a regular commercial aircraft — winged its way to London, its tail fin emblazoned with an exotic logo of dancing flames.

The plane, originally built to transport two hundred and fifty passengers, had been converted to allow a few to travel in a style that only the incredibly wealthy were accustomed to. To describe this flying palace as merely comfortable would be to say that World War 2 was a minor altercation. The interior was breath taking, decked out with plush carpeting, fine woods, leather chairs and gold fixtures. The only reminders that this was an aircraft and not a seven-star hotel were the constant dull hum of the engines and the uniformed flight attendant; the attendant who did, nevertheless, continually top-up the passengers champagne flutes whilst offering caviar, foie gras and lobster.

Sheol Trading's Chief Executive Officer reclined in the beige leather chair. The long fingers on her exquisite hand slithered across the dark wood table in search of her champagne glass.

Sitting opposite her, a balding and generously proportioned man grinned as he pressed the end call button on his phone.

'Tragic news, I'm afraid. Gordon has been killed in an unfortunate accident,' said the man.

'How… unfortunate,' the woman replied in a voice of indeterminate accent.

The back of her seat slowly inclined as she firmly pushed her finger down on a black button embedded in the arm of her seat. A dulcet ringing tone played.

'Yes, Ms Smith,' answered a voice a few seconds later.

'Hello, Wesley. Please prepare a press release for general publication. It begins: "Sheol Trading is today in mourning at the news of the tragic passing of its Chief Financial Officer, Gordon McBride. His contribution to the success of the company is well known and all within the Sheol Trading family feel his loss. The board of directors extend their commiserations and heart-felt condolences to his family and friends. Our thoughts are with each of them during what must be a very difficult time". End it with the usual blurb and company statistics.'

'Should I have the marketing department review it before release?' asked Wesley.

'For what purpose?' she snapped. 'I am perfectly capable of stringing a few words together!'

'Of course, Ms Smith. I will see to it right away.'

The woman shuffled in her seat, readjusting her position, and ran her finger around the rim of her glass. 'I think now would be a good time for us to approach Gordon's replacement.'

The man nodded his agreement with a sickly smile.

'Be a dear, Oliver, and arrange the meeting with Mr Bottomley.' The woman flicked a switch and her chair reclined.

***

Tucked away in the backstreets of Clapham Junction lay a small run-down cemetery. It was a sad sort of location which was once a site for mourners, with their considerate thoughts and flowers, but now frequented by drunken teenagers, drug addicts and those attempting to spice up their sex life.

Three sides of the cemetery were bordered by a brick wall, with the fourth lined by a small wrought-iron fence, separating it from a narrow road, and on the other side of this road a row of terraced housing overlooked the graveyard. Dominating the landscape of decrepit headstones was a mausoleum, square and bold with grand columns on each corner. Its pitched copper roof had once reflected the moonlight, but now a green patina was draped across the surface after years of exposure to the elements. Aided by the full moon, the surrounding headstones cast elongated shadows across the road.

In the darkness, a man leaned against a Celtic cross tombstone, doing what seemed to be his best impression of an inconspicuous plank of wood. Dressed in a long dark coat, he wore the collar up for protection from the elements and on his head a bright orange hat with an excessively large brim. Had it not been the middle of winter, people would have sworn it was a sun hat.

With his eyes flitting left to right, scanning the road, he mumbled some indiscernible words.

'Speak up, will you!' commanded the Celtic cross.

'Easy for you to say,' said the man. 'Look, is this really necessary?'

'You're the one who prefers not to visit the office.'

The man's head tilted backwards in a faux yawn, exposing his pockmarked and diseased face. The moonlight always brought out the best in his lacklustre greying skin; it made it appear almost alive.

'The same old excuse,' said the man's voice from the Celtic cross. 'Look, I'm a little busy. What do you want, Ballsy?'

'Balthasar. The name is Mr Balthasar, or Balthasar if you must!' boomed the man's voice.

'Whatever. What do you want?'

'Where are you, Gilgamesh?' asked the voice.

'What do you mean, where am I? I am in a cemetery talking to a tombstone because you are too cheap to provide mobile phones. No, that would be far too sensible. Instead I have to look like a complete moron.' Gilgamesh sighed with exasperation.

'It's the way we have always done things; I see no reason for it to change just because you're feeling precious,' said the voice. Gilgamesh's back straightened and his hands tightened into balls. 'Have you approached Duncan Bottomley yet?' the voice demanded.

'No, I haven't!' snapped Gilgamesh. He paused to breathe in deeply before continuing in an even tone. 'As I said in my last report which, unsurprisingly, you haven't read, I have him under surveillance but the right opportunity to speak with him has not presented itself.'

'I do tire of your excuses, Gilgamesh. All of us in Purgatory have work to do. Why don't you do us all a favour and try to do some yourself?'

Gilgamesh looked heavenwards. And under his breath, loud enough for only the wind to hear, he grumbled: 'Immortality sucks!'

2

Every Friday at 6.00 p.m. it was the same. The usual hush in the office gave way to a din of excitement as the weekend and its possibilities loomed. The sense of urgency and anticipation enveloped everyone in the office, with only one exception — Duncan Bottomley who was oblivious to the noise.

Lowering the phone from his ear, he slowly rested it into its cradle and sank back limply into his chair.

Duncan's life was remarkable for being unremarkable. With the exception of his work, where he toiled over company accounts by day and took them home by night, he had little to show for his thirty-seven years of life; with few friends to his name and a life lacking in social activity, he preferred the company of numbers.

The firm's head partner had phoned Duncan with extraordinary news, news that left Duncan flummoxed. His reaction to the news was akin to the discovery of fire by his early ancestors, in particular the ancestor who first burnt his finger.

The head partner explained how, moments earlier, he had received a personal phone call from the Chief Operating Officer of Sheol Trading, arguably the world's largest hedge fund, to advise him that on Monday they would be announcing the appointment of their firm as the auditors for Sheol Trading. This was most unexpected and a considerable achievement for a mid-sized accounting firm like Wollenwal & Wollenwal, or the 'two Wallys' as it was known to its competitors. None of this piqued Duncan's interest but what was inexplicable and most surprising, and what perplexed Duncan the most, was their specific request for Duncan to personally manage their account — Duncan, a mere senior manager. The head partner finished the call by congratulating Duncan and, as an afterthought, mentioned the small detail of how he was required to meet with Sheol Trading's management on Monday and it was subsequently in both the firm's and Duncan's best interests if he prepared over the weekend.

He sat silently, absorbing the news.

Sheol Trading was one of those trendy hedge funds which regularly dominated the news headlines, normally accompanied by the words 'record bonuses' and 'greed', yet nobody could explain what they did or how they made their record-breaking profits. They prided themselves on their obscurity, for the more obscure they were, the more talked about the company was, the more exposure they received from the press, and the more powerful they were subsequently perceived to be. It was a never-ending cycle. With no other company opaquer and more incomprehensible than Sheol Trading, it was little wonder that banks the world over salivated in their presence.

Other hedge funds and competitors praised them for their ruthlessness and insatiable appetite for money, similar to how one serial killer would defer to another.

Duncan's fingers tapped away at the keyboard; the click-clack sound a love song to his ears. His search for 'Who is Sheol Trading?' returned several results: One source labelled it an 'investment phenomenon'; another described it as a 'modern day colossus'; and a small newspaper in the middle of England, the Skegness Squeak, described it as a 'bloody large company'. While this latter description had outraged the Squeak's readership, which consisted predominantly of families and retirees, the editor defended their use of strong language, arguing they had spent far too many hours considering other approaches and if they had spent any longer, they would have missed their dinners.

'Hey.'

The voice startled Duncan. A head bobbed above his cubicle wall. It was Nick from three cubicles away.

Nick gave a crooked grin. 'We heard the news. That's sick. You must be so happy. Um. We're going to the Honey Pot for a pint, and were wondering if you fancied joining us? You know, to toast your good fortune?'

'Umm, thanks, but I have work to do.' Most unexpectedly, Duncan paused, before shrugging his shoulders. 'Um, actually, why not? Yes. A drink would be good.' He gave a rare smile, as rare a sight as his wallet, and grabbed his coat.

To most people those two words 'why not' are innocuous in their use but for Duncan it was as if he had suddenly developed the ability to speak Mandarin. He had never used them before. Why, after all these years, he would suddenly use those specific words was a mystery he would ponder in the future, along with why teenagers allowed their trousers to sag exposing their boxers. As soon as he had uttered those two words, he regretted it, for he knew they would lead to change. And Duncan despised change.

Duncan's life was deliberately absent of controversy, variety, spontaneity, or any word ending in 'y' — anything which could, in one way or another, foster change. He constructed routines which governed every aspect of his life, ensuring he left nothing to chance. Every morning he left for work at the same time. His attire followed a set schedule of routine: If he was not wearing a dark blue suit, he would instead opt for a cardigan in either brown or grey, except in warm weather when he chose a classic navy polo shirt. Even his hairstyle remained as it had been since high school — brushed from left to right and swept back, which unflatteringly exposed an example of an unwelcome change: his receding hairline.

Duncan and his colleagues left the office in a long straggly line which seemed to get longer as they threaded their way through the streaming crowds. The streets were a hubbub of people, clashing in various directions.

The Hungarian Public House, or the Honey Pot as its regulars affectionately referred to it, was famous for its distinctions. First, it was an authentic English pub, nestled down a cobbled stone lane; a rare find and a hidden jewel in the city of London. Traditional English pubs in the city bordered on extinction due to the grotesque proliferation of trendy bars that only sold bottled beer and encouraged their patrons to consume champagne or cocktails. The Honey Pot had no time for such pretensions — it was home to alcohol-infused rose-patterned carpets, an abundance of dark wooden fittings, and that unwelcome but nevertheless homely, stale, smoke-ridden air which still permeated the pub years after the introduction of the smoking ban. Adding to its charm was the bar manager, a genuine brassy East Ender with her distinctive cockney accent and confident welcome. And then, there was the food menu which had lost its way in the seventies, with the chef's two specialities being scampi and chips or a ploughman's lunch which, to the uninitiated, might have sounded quite cultured: A wedge of cheese, a dollop of pickle, a few slices of onion, bread coated in butter and a sprig of wilted parsley on the side (as if that made a difference).

However, the Honey Pot's greatest distinction was that it excelled at providing reasonably priced drinks in the city.

'Awright love,' the bar manager, Peggy greeted Nick. 'What can I get you?'

Nick relayed the orders to Peggy.

'Would you Adam and Eve it? Oi! Marky! Get off the dog,' bellowed Peggy at one of her staff. Duncan, who was standing behind Nick, was taken aback by Peggy's rather loud outburst, but was relieved to see the bartender end a call on his mobile phone rather than extricating himself from a canine.

Peggy continued to operate the hand pump, skilfully filling a pint glass before handing it to Nick who duly passed it on to Duncan for distribution.

Duncan accepted the final pint and shuffled to the rear of the group, slightly apart from the circle of his colleagues. He inspected the rim of his pint glass for lipstick then took a large gulp. His eyebrows raised in surprise at how good it tasted.

Four pints later, three more than he planned, Duncan found himself lolling against one of the many fruit machines littered throughout the Honey Pot. The trill of the machine acted as a mating call to any punters in its vicinity and although it was irritating, it wasn't sufficient to move him on.

Around him a discussion raged on the harmonisation of regulations and procedures on the presentation of cross-border financial statements. Duncan, uncharacteristically bored by the conversation, found himself staring at the corner of the bar or, to be precise, at a couple who were busy fondling each other: The man's hand caressing the woman's breast beneath her blouse was a magnet for his eyes.

'Last drinks,' hollered the bartender as he rang the brass bell overhanging the cash register.

Duncan held the pint glass level with his eyes and tipped it slowly from side to side, confirming it was indeed empty. And it was then, through the glass, that he first noticed the blurred figure standing before him. His brow creased and his eyes narrowed as he studied the shape. While he could tell the person was a she by the sizable chest, he was nevertheless puzzled by other factors, such as age, which were indeterminate.

The edges of the figure drifted in and out of focus.

It suddenly struck Duncan that this coincided with the swaying of his body. He glanced at his colleagues and noticed they were in focus. And suddenly, as if the light bulb above his head had been turned on, he experienced a moment of clarity and lowered his pint glass. An attractive woman stood before him, staring intently, admittedly with a vacant expression. She couldn't have been taller than five foot with shoulder length strawberry blonde hair, with a little twist at the corner of her mouth which, while it wasn't an attractive smile, Duncan did find cute and enticing in a baby gorilla kind of way.

'Hiya. I'm Shannon,' she said in a lilting voice. She smiled as she clasped his hand tightly and tugged him towards her. 'Let's go.'

Duncan's nerves shot up, as would a chicken's when confronted by a fox:

'*Is she going to eat me alive or toy with me?*' he wondered in a haze as his head bobbled.

It seemed an eternity before he finally spoke: 'You must have me confused with somebody else.'

'Let's go.' She pulled on his arm again, more forceful this time.

Duncan swallowed loudly. 'Would you like a drink?' He turned and waved a desperate finger towards the bartender.

'Sorry mate,' the bartender replied with a broad Australian accent, 'we've stopped serving drinks.'

'What?' Duncan squeaked.

The lights in the pub brightened until fully illuminated. He noticed how angular Shannon's features were. They made her appear wicked like a temptress; perhaps that was why he found her attractive.

'Let's go,' she said again.

Duncan remained rooted to the spot, confusion weaving and winding its way through his mind. Whilst it was true, she was suggesting they leave, could he have been misinterpreting her signals? He was certainly no Casanova.

Over the years he had gone out on the occasional date, but the prospect of dating terrified him; in particular the possibility of having sex afterwards caused such anxiety in him, he decided it was simply better to avoid women. On the few occasions in his life where he had engaged in sex, he had found the whole experience a tad dull, and if he found the whole scenario boring, then he could only imagine what the woman thought of the experience; it was a horrible thought. Nevertheless, he looked forward to the day when he would meet a woman with low expectations when it came to sex — those, he might just be able to fulfil.

His brow dotted with perspiration.

Ignoring his apparent apprehension, she grabbed him by his wrist and pulled him towards the exit. His feet scrambled as they searched for secure ground. It was clear she was determined and focused on what she wanted — a woman possessed.

Once outside, she pulled Duncan into a passionate embrace that left no doubt of her intentions. His mind swirled with shock and questions as her fingers crept to his belt buckle. He took a sharp intake of breath and instinctively stepped backwards but she seized the buckle on his belt and towed him down a narrow alleyway leading away from the Honey Pot.

He looked the slightly sized woman up and down, and then down and up just in case it made a difference. Her curvaceous body clad in a tight-fitting black cocktail dress, belied her impressive strength; she certainly didn't have the build of somebody who would possess such a level of strength.

Duncan's protestations, which grew in volume the further she dragged him, were ignored and the more he struggled the tighter her grip became.

They turned into a city square.

Duncan, desperate to halt their progress, reached out and seized the distinctive bright red pillar mailbox which stood guard at the entrance to the square. His hands clung to the top of it, his body outstretched and suspended in the air. Fighting for a secure hold, his sweaty palms slid helplessly across the smooth pillar, offering no resistance and, with little effort, she wrenched him free.

In the shadows of the Bank of England, by a statue of Paul Julius Reuter, Duncan made another bid to escape her grip. Frantically, he fumbled with the prong on his buckle. His belt swung free, slapping his chest as it unfurled around him and without the weight of Duncan to provide resistance, Shannon reeled forwards, tumbling to the ground with a sickening crash. Duncan winced at the sound of bone and gristle crunching.

Duncan bent double, his hands on his knees, gasping for breath.

A few metres away the crumpled figure stirred. With surprising dexterity, considering the severity of her fall, Shannon picked herself up and released her grip on the belt. As Duncan watched it fall to the ground, she turned and strode towards him.

Duncan's face fell as he met her gaze. His eyes overflowed with incredulous terror.

Each step Shannon took was accompanied by a loud splintering noise. The source of the unusual noise became clear as her shinbone visibly protruded at a nasty right angle from a gaping wound where her knee had once been. Blobs of blood beaded across the wound's surface and popped, splattering red droplets over the surrounding area and down her leg. He cringed.

'Your… Your knee. I think it's broken. You need to get to a hospital,' said Duncan, his voice shaking with shock and panic.

Shannon stopped. She bent over, placed her hands on either side of her leg and, in one sharp movement, forced the bone back into the void of her knee. She continued to stomp towards Duncan.

'Stop. Please… Please stop,' he pleaded.

Her mood abruptly changed. Her lips curled into a twisted smile. Fluttering her eyelashes, she ran her fingernails lingeringly along his extended forearm. Her other arm crawled around his waist, pulling herself towards him. Instinctively, Duncan raised his arms for protection. Without the support of his belt or his hands, his trousers slipped to the ground, and he could feel the cool night air on his bare legs. She softly kissed his neck, arousing a tickling sensation over his body. Her fingers crawled up his spine, a pleasant shivering followed her fingers. Her lips tenderly touched his.

SLAM.

His head crashed backwards. A blood-curdling scream tore the silence of the night asunder and, as he weaved in and out of consciousness, he realised it was his screaming permeating the darkness. Shannon bit hard on his lips and warm blood trickled down his chin. Her fingers raked his back, tearing through his jacket and shirt.

Pain skewered his body.

She forcefully steered him backwards until his legs collided with a park bench, buckling beneath him, and she released her grip. He collapsed onto the bench. Powerless, confused, disorientated, he stared up at her. The streetlight behind cloaked her face in darkness and created a halo-like effect around her head. Duncan grimaced and pawed at the remaining shreds of clothing on his back. He could feel his blood drizzling over his fingers.

'Please... Please stop. I'm really not into kinky stuff,' he stammered.

The veins in Shannon's neck were like a street map, visibly bulging and pulsating. Her eyes blazed red. Duncan gulped.

Her hands were a blur now, ripping at the remains of his clothes. By the time she stopped, his body felt like it had been dragged through a forest of thorns, with his chest marked with thick wounds and trails of blood.

'I think you've got the wrong idea,' Duncan panted. 'I'm boring. I'm a missionary kind of guy.'

Duncan had seen magazine articles discussing the increased popularity in S& M but had never experienced it. Where before, he had held no opinion of this activity, and there was even a remote chance that he might have been tempted to experiment, he now considered it to be highly overrated and not in the remotest bit pleasant.

A deep guttural rumble emanated from Shannon, silencing his protests.

She hitched her dress around her waist and lowered her hips to straddle him. Using her thumb and forefinger she pulled his chin towards her. The glow in her eyes illuminated the bridge of his nose.

'Time to die,' she hissed with a twisted smile lingering at her lips.

Her eyes bulged and her cheeks swelled. Duncan tilted his head backwards and shut his eyes, any ounce of strength lost to the pain. Surrendering, he steeled himself for the torture to follow.

There was a faint noise, no louder than the popping of a

champagne cork, and then silence eerily echoed. He felt the bench beneath him shudder. A thunderous roar reverberated around him and an intense flash seared the back of his eyes. A multitude of colours exploded before him, merged and formed a blinding corona. He felt a slapping sensation across his bare chest and the distinct smell of burning flesh and sulphur tantalised his nostrils. The explosion rumbled on, and then abruptly stopped.

Duncan's head collapsed onto his chest. In spite of the cold night air, sweat dripped down his brow, and everything went dark.

3

It felt like hours but, in reality, only a few minutes had passed. Duncan stirred and groaned. The smell of burning flesh was like smelling salts, and his eyes snapped open.

A circle of murmuring bystanders stood at a distance; their gaze fixed on him. There was no mistaking their disgust.

His head throbbed as he lifted it; he let it fall and waited for the pain to subside. He waggled his head to shake off the veil of confusion draped across his senses. His eyes darted left to right, scanning the crowd, only stopping for the briefest of moments to examine each face for familiarity. Relief fell over him, he had survived, Shannon was nowhere to be seen. He threw his head back, smiled and exhaled loudly.

With his head throbbing with pain and reality a haze, it took a few moments for Duncan to consider the scene before him, and it was as his surroundings registered that his jaw fell like an out of control elevator and his eyeballs strained against their sockets.

The city square, which had been quaint and welcoming when he had entered it, now resembled a bombsite replete with strewn body parts. The storefronts appeared to have been redecorated with a scattergun using blood for paint.

As he spun from side to side, absorbing the chaos, he glanced down at his boxer-adorned body, and he baulked, instinctively leaping to his feet. His skin was covered in blotches of blood, shards of bone and globules of what he assumed to be flesh. His arms flailed about like an out of control wind turbine, swatting his chest in an attempt to remove every trace of gag-inducing matter.

Two police constables, alerted to his sudden consciousness, inched their way forward. Each held one hand outstretched towards him, while the other remained on their truncheons.

'Stay calm and don't move,' commanded one of the constables.

Duncan froze. For the briefest of moments, he considered ignoring their request but a little voice deep down inside him chose that moment to speak up and caution him, perhaps driven by self-preservation: *Don't do anything you might regret. You don't exactly look innocent.'*

'*But I haven't done anything*,' Duncan reminded himself.

'*Why don't you tell them that while you're trying to explain your blood-splattered torso?*'

Duncan frowned and glumly looked at the constables. He hated it when his inner voice was right. He dropped to his knees and interlocked his fingers behind his head. The constables shuffled through the carnage towards him.

The wail of a siren grew in volume, announcing its imminent arrival.

He could sympathise with the police and the outraged public congregating before him. It was hardly what you expected to see on a Friday night, and the whole scene must have been all the more surreal by the sight of this near naked man covered in blood, kneeling in the midst of what would later be reported as 'a scene from a horror film'.

His arms were swiftly handcuffed.

A police car followed closely by a van squealed to a halt and its sirens fell silent. The car's beacon cast an oscillating beam of blue over those gathered. Duncan flinched each time the light fell upon him.

Life couldn't get much worse than this. His spirits sank to the dark depths of his being, then found a room, locked the door and refused to come out — enough was enough.

From the rear of the van emerged three forensic scientists dressed in white overalls. They slipped plastic covers over their shoes, covered their hair with shower caps, not the frilly colourful ones Duncan's mother used to wear but clinical white ones, and stretched gloves over their hands which slapped against their flesh as they sprung into shape. They immediately went to work on Duncan, picking at him with their tweezers like chickens to their feed.

With his head bowed, Duncan felt cold, confused and embarrassed in equal measures. His shoulders and head remained slumped as the square overflowed with revellers who had spilled out of the nearby clubs and pubs, attracted by the flashing blue lights and the buzz of gossip.

There was a firm pat on his shoulder. One of the police officers, irradiated by the blue strobes, gestured for him to stand then ushered him towards one of the many vans parked beside the square. The grills on the darkened windows of the van were ominous. His protests of this all being 'one big misunderstanding' were ignored as he was thrust inside. The doors slammed shut behind him with a metallic thud.

The crowd of onlookers had swelled and were engrossed in the scene before them, intently watching the forensic experts pick and prod at every object in the square.

'This is better than television,' one observed.

It was fortunate the crowd were distracted by the gruesome scene of bloodshed, otherwise they might have noticed the man standing in their midst, wearing a ridiculously oversized sunhat and a long coat with high collar; a man who was peculiar to say the least. The last thing this man wanted to happen tonight was to be noticed; it tended to make his job difficult.

He cast his head about the square and watched the police van disappear down the road. Beneath his hat's oversized brim, he frowned before stepping backwards and melting into the surrounding shadows.

4

Gilgamesh stood at the centre of a tiny well-lit room, which offered no more space than a phone booth, holding a rather large sunhat. From the rear corner, above his right shoulder, a gentle, bland instrumental arrangement emanated from a speaker. For a few seconds he gazed at the speaker as he pondered the music. He recognised the tune, '*The girl from Ipanema*'. He despaired at the depths his employers had stooped to.

The lift door interrupted his despondency with a ping, and the door slid open.

He stepped into a large reception room glowing with warmth. Plush brown leather sofas lined the right and left walls as he stepped out of the lift. A metallic and glass oval desk at the far end. Above the desk mounted on the wall, framed in a perfect circle of light, in simple clear typeset, were the words 'Welcome to Purgatory — Part of the Tellus Limited group of companies'.

An elderly woman, neatly dressed, with her grey hair styled into an elaborate coiffure, staffed the desk. She had a sophisticated aura, with everything about her in its correct place; not a strand of hair out of place, not a crease in her skirt suit. Clearly, she prided herself on her preciseness.

Gilgamesh, or Gilly as he preferred, avoided the office whenever possible. In fact, given the choice, he would have preferred a root canal treatment, if he still possessed teeth, to visiting the office.

Millennia ago, when he first joined the corporation, it was an idealistic start-up, but since then it had morphed into the behemoth of today. Back then, the office had a simple open-plan format, and the employees thrived on the buzz of being part of something that promised greatness. But as the years rolled by and millenniums passed, the number of employees required to administrate the burgeoning bureaucracy increased exponentially. As the company matured it lost touch with its original simple values. Staff no longer felt they were part of a family; they were another number in a corporate juggernaut. Dissatisfaction grew and consequently staff left in their droves, seeking improved job satisfaction elsewhere.

In an attempt to stem the flow and to attract new staff, management implemented an ambitious modernisation programme. They revamped the office, removed the battery hen conditions, and introduced computers to help people in fulfilling their roles. They added other numerous little touches: Paintings and fresh flowers, plush carpets and extravagant furnishings. The office surroundings and atmosphere were an instant success, with queues of prospective recruits immediately forming in unlimited numbers. It seemed like everybody who died wanted to join Purgatory. Management congratulated each other, praised their respective brilliance, and rubbed their hands with glee at the prospect of the sizable bonuses they would receive in return for turning the company around.

But, before their celebrations had reached a climax, their dreams and ambitions were deflated, as if a pin had been taken to a balloon. The pin was Pope John Paul II. Traditionally he and the occupants of his role were considered to be the company's biggest advocates amongst the living; they were an essential backbone, a strong, supporting fabric, and so it came as a complete shock when he sermonised to the living that Purgatory was 'a condition of existence and not a place'.

Staff numbers plummeted. Insecurity swelled and staff rejected Purgatory en masse, instead flocking to Limbo. Nobody wanted to spend their afterlife working for a figment of their imagination.

With insufficient staff to dispense the reams of bureaucracy, Purgatory descended into gridlock. It took an eternity, well not quite that long but still a long time, for decisions to be made.

It wasn't only the red tape Gilly found frustrating, there was the sycophantic senior management who were as effective at their jobs as a waterproof teabag. These deluded self-important managers were under the ridiculous impression their job functions were more interesting than counting from one to 3,650,000,000. Incidentally, these are the odds of being struck by lightning on a particular day of the year that you personally nominated, and as far as Gilly was concerned, being struck by lightning was eminently preferable to visiting Purgatory.

'Welcome back, Sir. I trust you have been well?' said Ms Fairchild from behind her desk.

'Ah. Ms Fairchild. You are a vision of loveliness. It makes coming into the office such a pleasure,' replied Gilly, beaming in her direction.

She frowned and peered down at the large red appointment book resting on her desk. Her manicured fingers traced across one of the entries. 'Your appointment with Mr Balthasar was four days ago, Sir.'

'Ah yes. Alas, I was regrettably detained attending an incident involving Duncan Bottomley.' He gave her a knowing nod. 'I'm sure Ballsy won't mind.' He smiled sweetly and would have fluttered his eyelashes if they hadn't already dropped off his decay-ridden body.

'I see. One moment.'

Ms Fairchild's hand hovered above the old-fashioned red phone as she stared crossly at Gilly. He looked at her and followed her gaze to his arm. Immediately, he drew himself erect, removing his arm from the desktop where it had been perched. As she picked up the receiver she motioned with her eyes to the far wall of the room. Gilly retreated to one of the leather sofas and carefully lined his back with the chair, then fell backwards. He rested rather uncomfortably on the sofa, like a wooden plank would if it had been invited to lounge.

Several hours later, Ms Fairchild coughed discreetly and informed Gilly that Mr Balthasar was now available.

He threw his arms backwards to propel himself forward, staggered a few steps before steadying. In the corner of the room, to the left of the desk, a door suddenly appeared. In fact, it had been there all along, but nobody ever noticed it until they needed to use it.

This habit of items appearing from seemingly nowhere and only when required was the recommended approach for utilising space and storage in Purgatory. Centuries ago, management tackled the issue after noticing the piles of paperwork being routinely generated were quickly transforming into papered hills and were rapidly approaching land mass status in their own right. The Chief Strategy Officer, Gabriel, devised the solution to this problem: Vanishing Storage Facilities (VSF units). Essentially, the office remained dotted with filing cabinets but when they were not in use they vanished, only to reappear when somebody required something stored inside a cabinet.

The VSF units were a huge success, though they were not without a few negative effects. First, it made locating documents harder, for once the document was hidden, its existence was soon forgotten, which inevitably made it difficult for staff to retrieve the document if they could not remember it even existing in the first place. There had also been a sudden increase in accidents within the office due to staff colliding with the suddenly appearing VSF units. Management dismissed these issues as teething problems and immediately expanded the programme to include water fountains, stairs and doors, which created a whole additional array of problems.

Gilly smiled, inclined his head towards Ms Fairchild and walked through the newly visible door, stepping into a brightly illuminated corridor. He shielded his eyes and waited for them to adjust to the light.

At the end of the long, bright corridor, there was a passageway to the left which ended at an elegant circular glass staircase; it spiralled and swooped upwards, leading to a large glass-fronted office. On the right-hand side, someone disappeared through a set of double doors not dissimilar to those in a hospital wing. They swung backwards and forwards until fully closed.

Gilly took the left passage and limped up the stairs using the railing for support. Through the glass staircase below him, he squinted at the large expanse of cubicles which stretched out to the horizon. A desk, a set of drawers and a member of staff occupied each cubicle. He watched the bustle of people, working, and hunched over their computer terminals. Gilly groaned. The battery hen conditions remained, though under a sleeker, modern guise.

At the top of the stairs, from behind his desk, Ballsy spied Gilly's approach, and beckoned him to enter. The glass door slid open.

A large oak desk dominated the room. On one side of the room, floor-to-ceiling windows provided a view of the world below, while the opposite wall was handsomely panelled in light oak. Ballsy sat in a large black leather chair occupying the far side of the desk. In front of Gilly was a basic swivel chair minus arm rests. Without raising his eyes from the desktop, Ballsy indicated for Gilly to sit in the swivel chair.

Ballsy remained engrossed in the screen embedded in the top of his desk. His fingers slid across its surface, inputting instructions. As always, he was conservatively presented, dressed in a pressed grey suit with a dark purple tie, attire befitting his status of Chief Executive Officer of Purgatory. The only possible concession to individuality was his long grey ponytail which reached down to the middle of his back. Soon after Gilly started work in Purgatory, he realised the ponytail was not an expression of individuality, as all the senior male executives had ponytails. It was a symbol, a warning: Staff knew that if the person thundering in their direction had a ponytail, they were management.

Gilly lowered himself stiffly into the chair. It rolled back several feet as his weight fell onto it. He shuffled the chair back to the table with his feet. Ballsy watched from the corner of his eye, the line of his mouth to curled into a lopsided smirk. Gilly had no evidence of any malicious behaviour but the conspiracy theorist inside him believed Ballsy deliberately placed this particular chair in the room whenever he visited, aware of the physical problems it posed.

'Gilgamesh. Perhaps this hasn't cascaded to you yet, so let me confirm something: We're running a company here with unique challenges. With that said, it would be appreciated if you could be timely for meetings, especially those which you have personally requested.' Ballsy frowned and leaned back into his chair. The chair squelched as he nestled into the leather. 'So, what is so urgent that it could not wait a decade?'

'Ah, lovely. No small talk. Straight to the point, eh, Ballsy?'

'How many times do I need to tell you? The name is Mr Balthasar! If you insist on being disrespectful you may call me Balthasar. Nothing else!'

Gilly ignored his protestation with a curt wave. 'Of course, Ballsy. I have been monitoring Duncan Bottomley and —'

'It's Balthasar!' interjected Ballsy. 'Is this in regard to the demon attack this evening?'

Gilly's brow furrowed. 'You know about it?'

'Of course. It was on the Living Channel's news bulletin.'

'You don't seem concerned?' Gilly asked dubiously.

'And why should I be?' Ballsy mocked. 'Demon attacks happen all the time!'

'This wasn't just any demon! It was a Succubus!' Gilly paused to allow his words to sink in. 'It was about to kill Mr Bottomley when it spontaneously combusted. Now you may not find a Succubus attack odd, but have you ever heard of one spontaneously exploding?'

Ballsy smiled a response, it oozed smugness.

Gilly sighed and then continued. 'Do you know what the odds of being attacked by a Succubus are? There is a reported Succubus attack roughly every twenty years and the Earth's population is seven billion, give or take a couple of hundred million.' Gilly stared intently. 'So, the odds of a Succubus attacking Mr Bottomley are about 1 in 3.6 trillion. That's an impressive coincidence, wouldn't you agree?'

'Not really. Somebody has to be attacked, just like somebody has to win the lottery,' said Ballsy with a dismissive wave of his hands.

'This isn't a case of six balls popping out of a machine. Don't you think it is odd that, just as I was about to approach Mr Bottomley, a demon attacked him?'

'Not at all. Is there anything else?'

Gilly shook his head in disbelief. 'This is unbelievable,' he took a deep breath. 'I think in light of this evening's circumstances it would be prudent to reconsider our decision, Ballsy.'

'Gilgamesh!' Ballsy slammed the table with his fist. 'It should not be necessary for me to remind you that I am your superior, and as such you will address me by my name and not some common moniker. I am owed some respect.'

'Come on Ballsy. I'm an old man set in my ways. You know, you can't teach an old dog new tricks. Blah blah blah. Let's agree to disagree.'

Ballsy, lost for words, muttered sounds instead as if he had regressed to that of an infant.

'Anyway Ballsy —'

'Balthasar!' interjected Ballsy.

'I appreciate your time is precious, and trust me when I say I can think of a million and one things I would rather be doing, but with regards to Mr Bottomley, can you arrange for the decision to be reconsidered?'

Ballsy laced his hands together behind his head. 'Absolutely not. I see no need for such action. You do not seem to appreciate that these decisions take centuries to be made and formalised, not to mention the considerable planning. Decisions, plans and strategies cannot be changed on a whim. This is merely yet another example of you feeling too precious to complete a day's work.'

'You can't be serious! You think I'm lazy?' Gilly struggled to his feet and leaned across the table towards Ballsy as if he had just launched himself off a ski jump. 'This corporation would have been taken over centuries ago if it wasn't for me, and you know it! You would be nothing more than a defunct CEO sitting in Limbo, boring souls with your recollections of the glory days.' He tutted his tongue in disgust and, with a flourish of his coat, he spun round and stomped towards the door.

'Oh, Gilgamesh,' called Ballsy with a grating lilt in his voice.

As if jerked to a standstill by a rope, Gilly stopped mid-stride.

'There is a recently deceased in After Death Services with a grievance. See to it on your way out,' said Ballsy.

Without looking back Gilly gestured good-bye over his shoulder, which consisted of only the middle finger being fully extended while the others remained comfortably in his palm.

'Charming,' remarked Ballsy.

5

'Spread your legs, squat and sway your hips forward and back until we tell you to stop,' ordered the police constable. He pointed with his torch toward the centre of the room.

Duncan hesitated, shifting his weight from side to side, overtly conscious of his nudity. His hands, free of the cuffs, were clasped together and hung below his waist in a feeble attempt to protect what little modesty of his that remained.

'Really, officer, this isn't necessary. I don't do drugs.'

The constable, his patience dissipated, shoved Duncan into the middle of the room. 'Squat!'

Duncan sighed, widened his stance and slowly lowered himself. He rested his elbows on his splayed knees for support. His naked bottom, inches above the cold concrete floor, and swayed backwards and forwards. He could feel the police constable's torchlight examining his nether regions.

His gaze wandered to the doorway and the room's only chair beside it. His blood-stained boxers hung over the back of it in a heart-sinking reminder, jerking him to face up to his reality and exactly why he now stood exposed and degraded.

The constable shone the torch in Duncan's face. He flinched.

'No drugs, Sir,' the police constable advised the senior officer standing to one side, before replacing the torch in a metal cabinet bolted to the wall.

The senior officer tossed Duncan's boxers to him. Words could not possibly describe the humiliation; Duncan struggled to recall any point in his life which could even come close to being as low as this. If it wasn't for the shock and how he was still trying to come to terms with what had happened, he would have taken solace and descended into despair and had a good old-fashioned crying session. Instead, he numbly obeyed the barked orders, and tried to ignore the blatantly obvious fact: This was his new reality.

With his boxers on and a blanket draped over his shoulders, Duncan was escorted through a maze of brightly lit corridors. With the constant weaving and twist and turns, he had long lost track of where in the building he was, though he hadn't taken any stairs, so he knew he was still on the ground floor. After countless identical corridors and doors, they finally entered another windowless room where a plain-clothed detective waited inside the doorway. The detective dismissed the police officer with a curt nod before directing Duncan to a pair of chairs, and what looked like an old school desk. Duncan cautiously seated himself in one of the chairs, while the detective sunk into the other. Above the pocket of the man's short-sleeved light brown shirt was a nametag, which read, 'DSI Sergeant Malloy'.

Detective Superintendent Malloy had been in the force for close to twenty years and, according to his colleagues, suffered from an image problem: He never smiled. Jokes and mocking comments constantly circled the police station, some stating how he had been caught smiling a few months prior, and that based on this current trend his next smile was due in roughly two years' time. His face etched with crevices, his hair cropped, and his lean jaw line was sharp enough to cut bread. He was in his early forties but appeared much older. The job had taken its toll.

Malloy shuffled the papers stacked on the table and read through them for a few moments. The silence in the room was loud and unnerving; it echoed around the room as seconds ticked by like hours. Without raising his head, Malloy spoke in a clear, loud voice. 'Your name?'

'Um,' Duncan's voice trembled. 'Duncan Bottomley.'

'Occupation?' Malloy continued his rapid-fire questioning.

'Um, accountant. Actually, I'm an auditor.' Malloy glared at Duncan through the top of his eyes.

'Your employer?' continued Malloy.

'Um, Wollenwal & Wollenwal.'

'The girl's name?'

'Sorry? What?'

'Who was the woman you carved up tonight?' snarled Malloy.

Duncan vigorously shook his head. 'No, no. You don't understand. I don't know her. I was having a beer when she dragged me out of the pub… I knew it was too good to be true, nothing like that happens to me. I don't think I get out enough. My brother says I should get out more often, but I think he's being funny.' He paused to catch his breath then continued at breakneck speed. 'I didn't do anything. She was dragging me through the streets. Then she fell and broke her leg then… Well, she started to attack me, tearing my clothes off. I thought she was being kinky. Sorry, can I say that word? But I'm not kinky. She tore my clothes off, ripped my back. Then… Then her eyes caught fire. And there was this loud bang, like a sonic boom.' He exhaled. 'I don't know what happened. It all went black. I must have passed out and when I woke up, she was gone.'

Malloy smiled wryly. 'Let me see if I have this right. She attacked you, there was an explosion and you passed out?' He glared at Duncan who was frenetically wobbling his head up and down like one of those car dashboard ornaments. 'But somehow you end up covered in what is presumably her blood and flesh. I'm sure that will be confirmed by my forensics soon, but for now, let's assume that's the case.'

Duncan frowned, shaking his head. 'I can't explain it.' He paused and then his eyes opened wide in sudden realisation. 'Wait. I know what happened. She was one of those suicide bombers. She blew herself up.'

'Do you appreciate the seriousness of the charges you are facing?' Malloy asked.

Duncan nodded po-faced.

'And, to be clear on this, you're saying her eyes caught fire?' asked Malloy, referring to his notepad.

'I know how it sounds. It's the truth!'

Malloy rose, crossed the room and knocked three times on the door. He glanced back at Duncan. 'By any chance, do you have a history of medical problems, Mr Bottomley?'

'No. None at all. This is all a misunderstanding,' implored Duncan. 'I know it sounds crazy, but you have to believe me!'

The door opened and Malloy exited. A police constable shepherded Duncan out of the room and through numerous corridors, flanked on either side by windowless walls. The constable deposited Duncan in a cell and, before slamming the door shut, explained breakfast was provided, not served, at 7 a.m. This was not a hotel.

The cell was as Duncan had seen in the movies. A small bed with a thin plastic mattress, covered in a cotton sheet with a rough blanket for warmth, rested against one wall. The steel legs of the bed were bolted to the concrete floor. In the middle of the far wall, opposite the door, a solitary sink and next to it a metal toilet, minus the seat. A fluorescent light, protected by a wire cage, was the sole source of light, and he could see no way of switching it off. Duncan lowered himself to the bed and curled into the foetal position. He desperately wanted to sleep but everything conspired against him — where the blanket contacted his skin, he was sore and itchy, and the air resounded with a mixture of drunken singing and groans from the nearby cells.

He lay there in the cold and isolation, not quite asleep or awake. His mind ran rampant as he considered all possibilities to explain the evening's events.

Lost in a swirling of confusion, fear and pain, he eventually fell into an uncomfortable, nightmare-ridden sleep.

6

Gilly fumed as he shambled through the brightly illuminated corridors, scowling at anybody who ventured a friendly greeting.

After all these millennia, he should have been used to Ballsy's attitude. He should have known Ballsy would never agree to anything he suggested.

It all started when the corporation's Chairperson decided to take a sabbatical to focus on his next venture, Gorf Limited, and during his absence, he subsequently decided to appoint somebody to represent his interests. After an exhaustive search, the decision was made to offer the role to Gilly, much to the apparent vexation of the board of directors — the board which Ballsy headed up.

The Chairperson had long suspected somebody was accruing stock, and that it was only a matter of time before a hostile takeover was launched. The board repeatedly tried to quell his fears. They did not subscribe to the Chairperson's opinions, fears or concerns, and dismissed them as idle conjecture and rumour mongering. Despite their attempts to reassure him, or maybe because of them, the Chairperson proceeded with his plan, and Gilly joined the company.

Since that day, the board had gone out of their way to provide as little assistance as possible in the hope their inaction would lead to Gilly's failure, and then the Chairperson would have no choice but to terminate his employment. Considering the bureaucracy and the truculent behaviour of the board, Gilly could be forgiven for avoiding Purgatory whenever possible.

He rounded a corner and stopped outside a plain wooden door with a sign: 'After Death Support'. He sighed and leaned against the door to push it open.

He entered a small square room replete with clinical décor and hospital ambiance: chilled air, and the aroma of pine disinfectant tickled his nostrils.

A reception desk occupied the left corner of the room, with a bored looking albino man staffing it. A barefooted man, with slicked back hair, clad in a linen shirt and trousers combination, lounged on a metal bench bolted to the adjacent wall. As Gilly approached the desk, he spied a pair of the stained loafers beneath the bench.

The existence of 'After Death Support' always surprised those who passed by its front door in the corridor for the first time. No doubt their interest piqued by the use of the word 'Support'; after all, what support does a dead person require?

By Purgatory's standards it was an infinitesimally small department. It consisted of one employee, the albino, and this tiny room which doubled up as a cloakroom during special events.

'What seems to be the problem?' enquired Gilly.

The albino ignored the voice from the opposite side of the desk in the hope its owner would go away. The albino hated providing customer service, and, despite having specifically requested a non-customer facing role, he had nevertheless been assigned here. He complained to Deceased Resources, but they politely explained it was a requirement of their PYD scheme[*] Unfortunately for his career prospects, he had been assigned to a department which nobody visited, and as the centuries passed, he was forgotten — yet another file lost in a VSF unit.

'I hate to be a pain, but people to see and things to do,' said Gilly. His bony fingers impatiently rapped the desk.

The albino lifted his head and glared at Gilly. He was as white as the proverbial sheet, with pink eyes as you would expect from an albino rabbit. 'Oh, I am sorry. I didn't realise you were in a rush. Why didn't you say? Perish the thought the funny looking man behind the desk might be busy, or that he might prefer to be doing something else or be anywhere other than this cloakroom. No. Let's forget all about the funny looking man. Everybody does.' He sighed with frustration.

'I'm sorry,' said Gilly, looking around him perplexed. 'Maybe I've made a mistake. Is this After Death Services?'

'Why? Do you need the cloakroom? Are they holding another party? Oh, wonderful!' He clapped his hands in mock glee. 'Once

---

[*] Authors Note: The PYD (Promising Young Deceased) scheme is a new initiative introduced by Purgatory to retain talented souls. Participants of the scheme are moved to new roles in different departments every century or two until they have a thorough understanding of the organisation, where they are then moved into management positions.

more, I'm not invited. I remember the last time: People came in here and mistook me for a coat stand.' He paused; his bottom lip quivered. 'Is there another party on? Can I go this time? Please.'

'Sorry? There's no party, at least not that I know of.' Gilly rubbed his bony fingers along the thin deteriorated skin of his forehead. 'I was told there was a deceased with a grievance here and I should deal with it. Am I in the right place?'

The albino blinked rapidly; his eyes flew wide. 'Do you mean you're here about my memo? My memo requesting assistance?'

'I guess.' Gilly threw his palms into the air.

'You mean, somebody read my memo? It wasn't filed in a VSF unit and forgotten about? You mean… My memo was read?' The albino's posture straightened.

'Yes. I wouldn't be here if it hadn't. So, the problem?'

'Of course, Sir. Over here, Sir. Right this way, Sir.' The albino sprung to his feet; an excited buzz illuminated him. He motioned to the bench and its current occupant. 'This recently deceased refuses to accept he is dead, Sir. He claims to be a victim of "duplicitous behaviour" and insists on lodging a formal complaint.'

The man slowly untangled himself from the bench and stretched out.

'When one has a complaint, one expects it to be taken seriously and handled promptly. I have been waiting for a week! It is hardly what any reasonable person would describe as "service"!' The man's languid diction sounded like he had stepped straight into Purgatory from the pages of a Jane Austen novel.

'Actually, by Purgatory's standards, that would be considered instantaneous service,' corrected Gilly.

'My name is Gordon McBride, and I have been a victim of a travesty of justice,' he announced in a grandiose voice. His chest puffed out like a pigeon.

'Oh well. You're dead now, you'll get over it,' said Gilly.

'Bloody hell, man!' Gordon stormed. 'Do you appreciate the magnitude of the situation we have here? Do you even know who I am? I am the Chief Financial Officer for Sheol Trading, the world's most powerful financial services company. If Sheol Trading sneezed, the rest of the world would catch a cold. I am a stratospherically important person!' Gordon's head angled upwards, a deliberate attempt to look down his nose at Gilly.

'That doesn't mean much when you're dead.' Gilly scratched his head and his large hat shifted from side to side. 'You may not have noticed this, but you are in Purgatory. Who you were when you were alive, doesn't matter here. I hate to be the one to break this to you but, just in case you've miraculously failed to realise this, you are dead.'

'Oh, my Lord. Really? Snap out of it, man! Clearly, I am aware of my current predicament! Why else am I complaining?'

Gilly raised an eyebrow, then turned to the albino. 'Has he been processed and cast his vote?'

The albino nodded enthusiastically. 'Yes, Sir. Absolutely. There were no exceptions. His vote was placed via straight through processing while he was amongst the living.'

'Lovely. Do I need to guess who his vote was assigned to?' gnarled Gilly.

'Hell, Sir,' replied the albino.

Gilly shook his head and clicked a disapproving tut with his tongue.

'Extraordinary. I do have a name you know… It is Gordon. This voting matter is the crux of my grievance. Try to understand this: I signed a contract whereupon in exchange for my vote, I was to receive certain compensation while I was alive. My unscheduled death represents a fundamental breach of this contract and I intend to seek restitution for damages. At the very least there should be an immediate injunction on my death until my complaint is heard.'

Gilly's jaw fell like a drawbridge. 'Sorry. Did I hear right? You want an injunction on your death?'

'As an absolute bare minimum! While I was alive, I entered into a contract that promised to pay certain benefits in exchange for my vote. Those facts are not in dispute. However, the other party to the contract terminated my life prematurely. It is reasonable to believe that if I had never entered into this agreement then I would still be alive. Nowhere in the contract, not even in the fine print, is there any mention of the apparent fact they had the option to terminate my life. If I had been aware of this possibility, then I would never have signed the blasted contract, and in that event I would still be alive.'

'Let me guess, the other party to this contract was Hell?'

'Absolutely.'

'So, if I understand you. You made a deal with Hell, our competition, but because *they* ended your life you now want to sue *Purgatory*?'

'If I must. This is all quite simple. If somebody trips over a crack in a footpath and breaks their leg, they don't sue the person who broke the pavement and they don't blame themselves for not watching where they are walking. No, they sue the council for not maintaining the footpath. Therefore, it follows that as Purgatory is responsible for the maintenance of death then my illegal termination is Purgatory's responsibility. This is a classic negligence lawsuit.'

Gilly slowly shook his head, his mouth agape.

'Come.' Gordon placed his hand on Gilly's shoulder and ushered him to the other side of the room. 'You seem to be a nice chap, but you need to understand this situation from my perspective. My death was… extremely inconvenient, and any court would agree that it was wrongful. Under such circumstances, my request for an injunction on my death is perfectly reasonable.' Gordon took a deep breath and straightened his posture. 'Now,' he continued. 'The last thing either party requires in this situation is a spectacle and not to mention the publicity a court case of this magnitude would surely garner. Wouldn't you agree?' Gordon whispered.

'Publicity?' spluttered Gilly.

'Indeed. It would be positively bad for business. I think, considering the circumstances, it would be in all of our best interests to settle this rather distasteful situation amicably, and avoid the need for an expensive lawsuit and undue publicity. I am nothing but reasonable. So, if Purgatory agrees to cancel my death then I will agree to forget this entire incident. I promise to return to the living quietly, without kicking up a fuss. Nobody will be any the wiser. I have a stupendous amount of money stashed in the Cayman Islands that will facilitate my disappearance, allow me to retire if you will. Nobody needs to know about this, it will be our little secret.' A broad smile cleaved Gordon's face in two.

Gilly stared at Gordon in disbelief. 'I don't want to labour this point, but you do realise you're dead?'

'I appreciate that it is probably not an easy thing to arrange. But I am a reasonable man. Perhaps I could offer some charity in return? How about, upon my return to the living I arrange for a sum of money, shall we say a million pounds, to be deposited into your personal bank account? Or perhaps there is a loved one you left behind who would appreciate my *donation*? You could consider it as my way of thanking you for your efforts in resolving this unfortunate incident.'

Gilly frowned and turned to the albino. 'Could you please send a memo to Deceased Resources and ask them to arrange for a counsellor to visit Mr McBride? He is clearly delusional and in denial.'

The albino furiously scribbled the message.

'Very well. Shall we say five million pounds then?'

'You're deluded,' muttered Gilly.

Gordon stood by the bench and frowned at the sight of his loafers. 'I don't think you appreciate the gravity of this situation. My life was terminated prematurely. Any settlement made by the court would be sizable in this situation. I would have to be compensated for damage to my reputation, loss of income, my car, which was completely destroyed, and look at my shoes! Do you know how expensive they are? Made of camel-hide and now look at them — they're ruined! Oh, and if you think *I* have an issue with being dead, you should meet my girlfriend. She is far from pleased. Now she should definitely sue. She wasn't even party to the agreement.'

Gilly anxiously cast about the room. 'There's another one?'

'Alas no,' said Gordon. 'She's in shock over her unexpected death — and that's to put it mildly. She isn't actually dealing with it very well. I have tried to explain to her about the contract which subsequently led to our unlawful deaths, but she did not take it well.' Gordon nervously fidgeted from one bare foot to the next. 'Not taking it well at all.'

'Not taking it well?' enquired Gilly.

'She's not very happy, to say the least. I believe she screamed, "you're a prick" and stormed off. Harsh words indeed, and completely uncharacteristic of her. I tried to buy her flowers to apologise, but seemingly there are no florists here!'

'That's because you're in Purgatory, Mr McBride, not a

shopping centre,' answered Gilly.

Gordon fell onto the bench. 'I hope you realise I intend to engage the best legal representation available. I will exhaust all legal avenues to rectify this situation,' he paused for a minute. 'Just out of curiosity, how would one acquire legal representation here?'

'This is Purgatory! There are no florists and there are no law firms!' snapped Gilly. 'You are wasting your time. You didn't enter into any contract with Purgatory. You entered into a contract with Hell, or one of their representatives, so you probably deserved to die. You can't sue Purgatory!'

'I can so,' riposted Gordon.

'No, you can't.'

'I can so.'

Gilly sighed and turned to leave. His departure halted by the flailing body of the albino who had, at that moment, lunged forward, sliding across the floor. He locked his arms around Gilly's leg as he collided with them.

'What are you doing?' asked Gilly as he tried to shake him off.

'I am so sorry, Sir, but I need to thank you. I can't begin to tell you how happy I am, knowing my memos are being read. You have given my death purpose.'

Gilly grimaced at the sight of the prone albino. 'Right. Um. Well, why don't you get off the floor and... perhaps you could send a memo to Deceased Resources and mention to them you need to get out of here. Tell them to sort it out as a favour for me.'

'Oh, thank you, Sir! You have answered my prayers.'

Gilly extricated his leg from the arm lock and padded over to the door.

'This is your last chance to avoid legal action,' boomed Gordon's voice. 'I will get that injunction!'

'Righttttt. Good luck with that,' Gilly replied sarcastically as he exited the room.

7

Duncan was woken by a resounding clang of a key turning in a lock. For the briefest of moments, Duncan expected to be waking up in his warm bed at home. It was only when he moved, and pain splintered through his body, he was reminded of his current whereabouts.

A police constable strode into the cell carrying a tray of food. He mumbled a morning greeting before laying the tray down at the end of the bed.

Breakfast, as Duncan soon discovered, consisted of bland looking reconstituted scrambled eggs served alongside a rubbery sausage that contained excessive spice, presumably to compensate for the lack of flavour, and a piece of extra crispy bacon which slid around the plate like a surfboard on a pool of oil.

Duncan's stomach belly-flopped at the prospect of eating it. As he tried to cut the sausage, the knife bent sideward. Eventually, he dismissed the knife and stabbed the sausage with the plastic fork and nibbled on its end. It tasted worse than it looked. He replaced the sausage and pushed it to one side before using his fork to poke at the springy surface of the eggs. He grimaced and moved the tray to the floor in disgust.

Hours passed.

A glint in the corner of his eye distracted him from his contemplation of the featureless concrete walls. The caged fluorescent light above sparkled on a pool of liquid that had formed on his breakfast plate.

Duncan leaned over; his curiosity piqued by the liquid which had appeared from nowhere. Without any logical explanation, the scrambled eggs had begun to weep, and the plate filled to the brim with the mysterious fluid. The sausage floated around the plate like a piece of driftwood.

He found himself intrigued by this phenomenon.

The last time he had been this interested in food was when he discovered a green congealed ball residing at the rear of his fridge. He had become aware of its existence after noticing an unpalatable odour emanating from the fridge whenever he opened the door. This glob of unidentifiable substance bristled in defiance, almost menacingly, at his attempts to remove it. Eventually he conceded defeat and decided they could co-exist happily. Shortly after making this decision Duncan purchased a new refrigerator so as not to disturb the occupant of the other fridge.

An hour later, with every second spent analysing the contents of the plate, Duncan could not think of a satisfactory explanation for the sudden appearance of the liquid.

He recalled reading about religious symbols taking the form of food — a piece of toast in America had come out of the toaster with Jesus Christ's profile burned into it. Perhaps these eggs were an example of food stigmata? Maybe his incarceration was actually a blessing and it had been his destiny to find these sacred scrambled eggs. Maybe he had been blessed with a rare opportunity and he now had to bring this to the world's attention. He would be forever known as Saint Bottomley, Defender of the Scrambled Eggs.

'Stand at the rear,' a voice commanded from behind the iron door, interrupting his thoughts. The hatch on the prison door banged open to reveal a set of eyes. As instructed, Duncan moved to the back of the room.

The hatch slammed shut, followed by a rattling of keys. The door swung open and collided with the tray, scattering its contents. Duncan stared at the toppled plate, the pool of liquid, the strewn eggs and the sausage. He was crestfallen. His Sainthood had dissipated through the cracks in the tiled floor.

Malloy marched in and, with an abrupt movement of his arm, gestured for Duncan to vacate the cell. He stood to one side, waiting impatiently.

As Duncan made his way through the concrete hallway, still dressed in only his boxers, he fleetingly sneaked glances behind at Malloy who followed closely. All attempts to engage Malloy in conversation were ignored.

'Sir. Can we talk about this? I'm innocent.'

'You're a pervert!' snapped Malloy.

'I'm an accountant!'

Malloy grabbed his elbow and shoved him through a sliding door secured with a lattice of iron bars, and into another corridor.

Up ahead, the corridor opened up into a more pleasant room. Desks, occupied by people in plain clothes, filled the room. At the front a large unattended counter stood in bold view. A vase of sunflowers decorated the far end of the counter. The walls were painted pastel blue and lined with notice boards displaying various posters. A beautiful blue sky and swaying trees were visible through a door on the other side of the counter. Duncan's lower lip trembled, he longed to be outside and free. He turned on his heel to face the people at their desks. They all sat glaring at him, and not in a happy to see him kind of way.

'It's your lucky day,' muttered Malloy.

'I don't understand,' said Duncan in a soft voice, almost breaking with relief.

'We received an anonymous tip last night that the remains we found weren't human.' Malloy thrust a form in front of Duncan, handed him a pen and pointed at a cross on the page. 'The forensic tests confirmed they belonged to a goat, but you knew that already, didn't you? You sick—'

'I don't understand.' Duncan's jaw flopped open.

'We're dropping all charges except for disorderly conduct but, in the meantime, you can go. We'll be in touch. You're a lucky man. I have no idea what you were doing to that goat, but it's tantamount to cruelty.' Malloy scowled at Duncan.

'Disorderly conduct? I don't understand,' said Duncan, shrugging his shoulders.

'What's not to understand? You were in a public place, wearing nothing but your boxers, and you were covered in goat entrails. Need I say more?' He smiled without humour.

'But… I didn't do anything.'

Malloy didn't bother to reply. He stabbed the form with his index finger and waited for Duncan to sign it. Once signed, he lifted a panel in the front counter to reveal a gap large enough for a person to sidle through. He pointed at the front door, waited for Duncan to squeeze through, and let the board fall back into place with a loud bang.

Duncan exited through the door and stood at the top of the stairs dazed, still wearing nothing but his boxers.

His life unrecognisable compared to a mere twenty-four hours earlier. The appointment at Sheol Trading, last night an attractive woman trying to have her wicked way before exploding, and now, just over twelve hours later, he stood on the doorstep of a police station in his underpants.

'Why is life so unkind?' he lamented to nobody in particular.

He shook his head as he pondered what he had done to deserve this, and briefly entertained the idea of praying for this nightmare to end but even if God did exist he considered it futile praying, for how would God, the very God who had created the universe and everything in it, have the time or the inkling to do him a favour? He would be far too busy, probably off creating the next universe. With no answers from the sky, Duncan could not understand what he had done to deserve this horrible unfolding of events.

Duncan squinted as the sun shone through the thin layer of clouds sailing across the blue sky, herding his stray thoughts back into line. It was an unseasonably warm day, a contrast from the day before.

He regarded the tree-lined road. Sunlight dappled gently across the branches at the top of the trees. Two vans were parked in front of the station. A police car drove down the road, turning into the car park adjoining the station. He gazed skywards; his face bathed in the sunshine.

'*Finally, things are looking up,*' he thought.

Plop.

A sizable pile of pigeon droppings splattered across his shoulder. Without thinking, Duncan swiped at it, only succeeding in smearing it across his chest so it resembled a disgusting white sash.

'*I was wrong.*'

No longer was this arguably his worst day, it definitely was; the pigeon had put that beyond doubt.

'It wasn't a goat,' said a voice disrupting his melancholy.

His eyes traced down the flight of steps to the footpath. Standing next to the road, and to one side of the pavement, stood a peculiar looking man. Dressed in a long coat with a huge sunhat, he looked out of place, and seemed to emanate a strange, indescribable aura. His attire, with even the unusual weather conditions taken into consideration, was optimistic for this time of year.

Duncan slinked down the stairs, watching the man as he absently played with his left ear.

The man hobbled towards him with the gracefulness of a clog-adorning ballerina.

Duncan lifted his head. A noxious smell pummelled his nostrils. Fearing his armpits to be the source of the odour, he clenched his arms to his sides.

'Rough night?' asked the man with a nod of his head.

Duncan initially planned to view the comment in a harmless light, knowing his somewhat dishevelled appearance would be a clear indicator; after all he had spent a night in prison, and he was wearing only a pair of boxers. But nevertheless, he silently mulled over the comment, and as he did, he became more self-conscious. Was the comment intended as a reflection of his current, out of the ordinary appearance, or was it a suggestion that he always looked rough? This is how complexes start.

'What do you mean?' Duncan asked.

'I've been told I need to be more understanding. I was trying to sympathise with you,' explained the man. 'I thought it was a good effort. I did sound sympathetic, didn't I?'

'Sorry. I've had a bad day… bad night. I don't have time for this. I don't mean to be rude but have a nice day,' said Duncan. He looked up and down the street and mentally pleaded for a cab to appear.

'Why don't we walk and talk? You can tell me about what happened last night. I'm a good listener.'

Duncan studied the man shambling towards him with a strange stiff walk. His eyes narrowed. 'Why? Who are you? Are you with the police? I didn't do anything.'

'Whoa,' the strange man held his palms up. 'There's no need to be paranoid. I'm on your side.' He stopped his erratic hobbling. 'It was me who made the anonymous call to the police last night.'

'You called the police?'

'Hallelujah! The light is on and somebody is home!' exclaimed Gilly as if he had discovered religion.

Duncan stepped backs and lowered himself onto the bottom step. His head slumped and he began to nurse his head, as if he was suffering from a hangover.

'This is… too much. What have I done to deserve this?'

whined Duncan.

'Well, that depends. If you were a bureaucratic, pompous and out-of-touch CEO, then you might say it was all one big coincidence. Me, on the other hand, well, I have no idea, but I do find it all a little concerning.'

'Who are you?' Duncan tilted his head but could only see the deathlike pallor of the man's lower face under the oversized brim. 'Who are you?' he repeated.

'I'm not surprised you don't recognise me, but you probably know my name: Gilgamesh? Yes? I was once a King. A very famous King I might add.' He paused. 'You don't know me, do you? Why is it that nobody knows me these days? If I said Hannibal or Nero you would know them, but nobody remembers me. Why is that? Personally, I blame the education system,' the man lamented. 'Story of my life — sorry, I mean death.' The man shook his head.

Duncan stared blankly in response.

'Typical! I wish somebody knew me, just once. I don't think I am asking for too much.'

There was a long silence. The man looked down at Duncan, earnestly awaiting a response. Duncan squinted as he regarded the man and his strange persona.

'I'm sorry. I really don't have time for this. I have to go.'

'What's the rush? Look, my name is Gilgamesh, but my friends call me Gilly. You may call me Gilly.' The stranger doffed his hat, but his face remained obscured.

Duncan's nose pinched and his brow furrowed as he inhaled a distinctly unappealing and rotten aroma. He squeezed his arms tighter against his sides.

Gilly tugged on the fingers of his glove, each finger in turn, until his hand popped free like a champagne cork escaping its bottle. Duncan's gaze was immediately drawn to the hand. It was dotted with lesions, almost lifeless, with only two fingernails remaining — both stained black from dead blood. Duncan grimaced. Gilly dug his hand deep into his pocket and energetically rummaged around. He removed a plain silver card case, then in one swift movement flicked it open, and squeezed out a business card.

Duncan glanced over his shoulder at the police station and

mentally noted it was only a few steps away if he needed to run. He accepted the proffered card and stared at it. It was beautifully textured, ivory in colour and delicate, and almost sensual to the touch. Inscribed on the top line it read 'Gilgamesh', and directly underneath in bold gothic embossed font was one word: **DEAD**.

He turned the card over in his hands. The reverse side blank.

'What's the meaning of this?' asked Duncan in an irritated voice. His eyes still on the card.

'Ah. Yes. I probably should explain. My job title isn't "dead" per se. That wouldn't make sense. No, I'm more of a trouble fighter, but I can't really say my occupation is "trouble fighter". I'd sound like one of those dodgy mercenaries. So, I thought, seeing how people remember me for being dead, that would probably be the most appropriate way to phrase it. You know, "Did you meet Gilly?", "Oh, you mean the dead guy?" It used to bother me, people saying I'm dead but in my line of work you get used to people being deadist.'

'Dead? Sorry, I don't understand.'

Gilly raised an eyebrow, absent of most hair. 'Okay. I'm not dead in the conventional sense that you know, but I am dead.' It was a well-rehearsed line Gilly had repeated many times over the centuries. It irritated him how people refused to accept he was dead just because it didn't equate to their understanding of being dead.

Duncan's mind performed several somersaults. 'You're dead?'

'Yes. Dead as a door nail. Biologically challenged. Terminally inconvenienced. Or if you prefer the politically correct line my employers insist on using: I am living impaired.'

Duncan raised his eyes from the card and stared wide-eyed at Gilly. 'You're dead?' he said with a quavering voice.

'Um, yes. Why is this so hard for you? It's just a word! Dead. Dead. Dead.' Gilly fiddled with his left ear.

'Is this some sort of joke? Who are you?'

'Doesn't my business card explain it?' Gilly bent at his waist and pointed to the card in Duncan's fingers. 'I've only had them for a few months. They're a new initiative I'm trying out. It's part of this trying to be sensitive and "in touch" malarkey work is pushing on me — as if I don't have enough things to worry about.

Look, if you don't like them, let me know. I can always change them or lose them.'

'What? No, it's not your business card,' said Duncan, his face contorting in confusion.

'Then what is your problem?'

'You… You can't seriously expect me to believe you're dead?'

'Why? Because I'm dead? Do you have a problem with minority groups?'

'No. That's not —'

'Oh, I get it. You're another deadist. Why is it such a problem for you?' Gilly ranted about the injustices the living inflicted on the dead: The blatant prejudice, the stereotyping and discrimination he regularly had to endure; how the living continually derided him, as if being dead somehow made him a lesser person than they were. In short, he felt his life — death — was one of continual persecution.

'Look. I… I don't understand,' muttered Duncan.

Gilly sighed and his shoulders slumped.

'I… I'm sorry. This is one joke too many. I'm not in the mood for this. Look at me,' said Duncan. 'I'm wearing my boxers!'

'If you don't mind, I'd rather not look. It's not a pleasant sight.'

'I don't have time for this.'

'This isn't going as I hoped. Let me try again. My name is—'

'Please leave me alone or I… I'll call the police.' Duncan backed a few steps closer to the police station, his arm held out in a warding off gesture.

'I appreciate this is a bit of a shock, but we do need to talk. It's very important. You see, that wasn't a woman — or even a goat — that attacked you last night,' implored Gilly.

'What do you mean?' Duncan shuffled his feet.

'You see, last night, you were attacked by a demon, a Succubus actually. Nasty critters. Very anti-social.'

A black cab motored up the road, its yellow vacant light a beacon for Duncan's attention. Duncan plunged down the few steps, leapt over the footpath and tottered into the middle of the road, his arms outstretched in the hope that if the cab didn't stop in time his hands would somehow prevent the cab from running him down. The cab screeched to a halt. Duncan exhaled in relief, glanced in the direction of Gilly then inched his way around the vehicle.

The cab driver greeted Duncan with a grin that all but said 'big night last night', apparently unfazed at being hailed by a man covered in dried blood and wearing only boxers, as if this type of thing happened all the time: *Darling, don't you know, wearing faux blood and underpants is all the rage on the catwalks this year*.

The front passenger side window wound down and the cabbie leaned across. 'Awright?'

'Clapham Junction please, driver,' instructed Duncan.

'Awright Guv'nor,' the cabbie replied.

Duncan fumbled at the handle, flung the door open and slid into the seat. It squelched as he sunk into it. It reminded him of a comfortable leather sofa. His shoulders sagged as he soaked in the comfort then, remembering Gilly, he leaned forward, pulled the window down and whispered. 'Please. Please leave me alone.'

The cab drove away. Duncan fell back into the seat, surrendering to some much-needed comfort. At once, his mind and body felt like shutting up shop and going on holiday.

'We really do need to talk! Your future depends on it.' Gilly bellowed at the receding black cab, before turning and shuffling in the opposite direction.

⑧

The juddering of the cab ensured Duncan drifted off to sleep soon after hopping in.

It was just after four in the afternoon when Duncan pulled up outside his house. The sun had already begun to retreat on the horizon, causing the sky to quickly darken. The temperature noticeably cooler than earlier.

The cabbie glanced at the cemetery opposite and shuddered. 'Must be quiet around here.'

Duncan grunted his agreement, instinctively reaching for a pocket which wasn't there. He patted around for a few seconds before the realisation hit him that he had no pockets, which subsequently meant he had no wallet or keys. He collapsed back into the seat.

'Twelve pounds twenty, Guv'nor,' said the cabbie.

Duncan looked up and could see the cabbie smiling in the rear-view mirror. 'Can you wait here. I just need to get the money. I'll be right back.'

As Duncan stepped out of the cab, he shivered in the cool evening air. Wrapping his arms around his torso, he ran up the footpath which led to the front door of his building. Next to the door, plugged into the brick wall, was a rusting panel with two black buttons. Beside each button a piece of brown mould which had once displayed the flat owner's name belonging to each button. Duncan pressed the bottom button.

Several minutes later the door eased open a few inches. A single eye, dominated by its pupil, appeared in the gap and greeted Duncan's sullen look.

'Hello. Wadda ya want?' the eye asked tentatively.

'Err. Hi, it's me. Um, from number two upstairs,' muttered Duncan, like an embarrassed child asking for their ball back.

The door opened a few inches more, revealing the eye's sibling.

'Oi. It's me bruv from upstairs. Check it,' the eyes wandered down to the lower half of Duncan's body. 'You know you in your underpants, bruv?' The door swung open to reveal his downstairs neighbour, dressed in a black t-shirt with an oversized pair of jeans sagging around his buttocks, and his less-than-white Calvin Klein boxers pulled up to his waist. His hair, a multitude of colours, stood on end as if he brushed it by sticking his fingers in a power-point.

'It's a long story. I'm sorry to bother you but I don't suppose you have my spare keys?' The desperation in Duncan's tone was obvious.

His neighbour patted his trouser pockets, disappeared into his flat and eventually returned dangling a dust-encrusted set of keys between his fingertips.

'These them, bruv?'

Duncan exhaled loudly, took the keys and muttered his thanks. His neighbour almost spun three hundred and sixty degrees as Duncan pushed past.

His neighbour stretched over the banister in time to see Duncan reach his front door and nonchalantly asked, 'You want a spliff?'

'Um, no… Thanks.'

'Respect.' His neighbour thumped his chest and disappeared from view. Duncan waited for the sound of his neighbour's door to close before entering his flat.

Two minutes later Duncan emerged from the building dressed in a white terry towelling bathrobe and a pair of threadbare slippers. He hurried to the cab and mumbled sounds rather than words as he pushed the exact fare into the cabbie's hands. He stared up at the bay window of his flat and sighed a remorseful sigh.

His flat wasn't the type of home people looked forward to returning to after an exhausting day at the office, and it was far from a welcoming sight after spending a night in jail. The atmosphere in his flat was lacking, with even that of a funeral parlour more inviting. It was absent of any personal touches, apart from a lone cushion sat neatly on his sofa, something an ex-girlfriend had once explained would act as the room's focal point and give people something to look at. He neglected to mention to her it wasn't necessary as she was the only person who ever stepped foot inside his lonely rooms.

Duncan didn't see the point in trying to make the flat 'feel like a home' for it had been a short-term investment, a stepping-stone for something bigger, without a cemetery view. Unfortunately, that had been several years ago, and he was no closer to moving anywhere bigger or better.

Duncan slumped into the sagging, well-worn sofa and snatched the phone resting by his feet. If other people found themselves in a similar situation their first phone call might have been to a loved one or to a friend in search of comforting but not Duncan, his first call was to his bank.

An efficient sounding woman answered his call and immediately challenged him when he announced he was Duncan Bottomley. She asked his date of birth, his mother's maiden name and details of his last purchase on his credit card; a question that flummoxed him, as he couldn't remember when he last used his credit card.

'How may we help you today, Sir?' asked the operator.

'I've lost my credit and debit cards, and I need to have them stopped,' said Duncan. His tone suggested he had been naughty and was feeling guilty.

'*Big night last night*,' thought the operator.

A moment passed. 'Your cards have been cancelled, Sir. You should receive your new cards within the next five to seven working days. Is there anything else I can help you with today?'

'Um, yes. Have there been any withdrawals or payments made on my accounts recently?'

'One moment, Sir.' Duncan could hear the frantic tapping of a keyboard through the phone. 'No, Sir. The last withdrawal from your account was on Wednesday and your credit card was last used…' There was a pause. 'August, four years ago.'

'Thank you.'

'Is there anything else we can do for you today, Sir?' asked the operator in a friendly and efficient tone.

'No, thank you,' said Duncan.

'I hope you have a lovely day, Sir.'

'It couldn't get much worse,' quipped Duncan.

'Have you had a rough day, Sir?' the operator enquired in her friendly fashion.

'If you call spending the night in prison because a girl you have just met explodes in front of you a "rough day", then yes.'

'Ah… I see.'

Duncan could hear the faint sound of paper shuffling on the other end of the line.

The operator rapidly flicked through her instruction manual entitled "Acceptable responses to Customer comments". The manual was the bible for call centre staff. Handling customers was a delicate matter, and this manual ensured that, regardless of a customer's comment, there was a politically correct response. For example: "Your fees are outrageous," to which the manual declares the acceptable response should be, "Thank you Sir/Madam (delete as appropriate) for your comments. Your comments are important to us and we will raise your concerns with management". If the customer was to say, "I'm feeling hungover," the manual states the correct response should be, "That is terrible, but we all need to let our hair down. I hope you feel better soon".

Strangely enough, the manual failed to cover the situation whereupon the caller makes the comment of "spending the night in prison because their partner exploded". But, a year after this conversation, the manual was updated to include this comment and the acceptable response was deemed to be, "That is unfortunate, Sir/Madam (delete as appropriate), we do hope she/he (delete as appropriate) will be fine".

However, as no acceptable response existed at this point in time, the operator closed her eyes, opened the manual at a random location and stabbed at a random spot on the page.

'I know what you mean, Sir, but the weather can only get better. Just remember to take your Wellington boots with you. Thank you for calling.'

Click.

Duncan glared at the phone and let it slip from his fingers. He pulled the curtains closed, grabbed a blanket from the top of the sofa, discarded his bathrobe, and crawled on to the sofa. Wrapping the blanket over his cold and aching body, he realised that he couldn't recall the last time he felt this exhausted.

***

When Duncan awoke the living room was draped in the dark of night. The luminous digital display of the DVD player provided the only source of light in the room, displaying the time as 5.21 a.m.

Like a cat, he unwound himself and stretched out. He briefly allowed himself to hope the recent events had been one long nightmare, but his body provided stark reminders to the contrary in the form of severe aches and pains.

He rose to his feet, allowing the blanket to fall to the floor in a heap and, using his hands, he patted his hair down into a semblance of neatness. With his hands on his waist, he rolled onto the tip of his toes and paused as he considered his next action. A sickly odour, reminiscent of whatever was residing in his second fridge, permeated the air. Duncan sniffed a few times. Slowly, he lifted his arm, lowered his nose to the exposed armpit, and inhaled deeply. The smell overwhelmed his lungs; a shower was definitely top of his to-do list.

Duncan exited the shower feeling refreshed and alert. He sauntered into the kitchen to make himself a much-needed cup of tea. Spying his laptop on the kitchen table, he reached across and switched it on. It glowed to life accompanied by an annoying jingle which served no purpose other than alerting other people in its vicinity to the fact a computer had just been turned on.

He opened his mail folder and scanned through the inbox and found nothing but reams of unsolicited emails and spam. Next, he opened his Internet browser and perused the latest news headlines, which consisted of the usual: Asylum seekers; knife victims; recession fears; credit woes, and so on.

Moving his attention from the headlines, Duncan's attention reverted to the tiny line of text at the bottom right of the screen. He blinked twice, and then a third time. According to his laptop, the time and date read 5.43 a.m. on Monday morning — and not Sunday morning as he had presumed. In the desperate hope his laptop had suddenly developed the capability of playing practical jokes, he visited a few more websites to confirm the date.

'Unbelievable. I've slept for thirty-nine hours straight.'

When it came to calculations, Duncan was very precise, after all he was an accountant. It was never sufficient for him to simply state he had 'slept round the clock'.

Duncan brought himself to reality and instructed himself to be pro-active; he had less than thirty minutes to have breakfast, dress for work, and prepare for his meeting with Sheol Trading.

Like a whirling dervish, he flew into action.

Once ready, with a few minutes to spare, he fell into the seat before his laptop and started scouring the Internet for information on Sheol Trading.

He despaired at the lack of public information and, more importantly, his lack of preparation. He had a valid excuse for being unprepared, but it was probably not in his best interests to share that excuse. He gazed blankly at the laptop. From behind the screen a white piece of cardboard glistened under the kitchen light. He picked up the business card and read the two words inscribed on it: 'Gilgamesh' and 'Dead'. He frowned. With one finger, he typed the name into the search engine.

Several search results appeared. More than several; 2,220,114 to be precise (Duncan is an accountant after all). Apart from a lone reference to a restaurant in London, they all appeared to relate to the same information. Duncan clicked on one of the links.

It was a simple website, intended for fans of Gilgamesh. A simple black sketch of a muscular man dominated the middle of the screen. With long hair and a plaited beard, he stood grasping a small lion to his chest. Duncan considered the possibility the man was actually a giant holding a fully-grown lion to his chest. Underneath the picture was the heading, 'Gilgamesh, hero king of Uruk from Sumeria'.

Duncan's brow furrowed and he clicked on the link directing users to the 'About Gilgamesh' page.

The web page provided fantastical reading:

'According to legend, Gilgamesh was a Sumerian king who was believed to have lived around 2,500 B.C. A harsh sovereign who subjected his people to hard labour and regularly abused his authority. He was renowned for demanding to be the first to have sex with any bride on the day of her wedding.

'One day, Gilgamesh met a great man, Enkidu, who opposed his custom of taking brides. With such strong opposing views, a great battle ensued. Only when both Gilgamesh and Enkidu were exhausted did they realise that they were equally matched and decided to end their battle. They became good friends, sharing many adventures. They even slew a God together.

'Sadly, one day Enkidu died. Gilgamesh was filled with grief for his friend but mostly for himself, as he realised one day he too would die. From this realisation, Gilgamesh began a quest for immortality. It would be a perilous quest which took him through the Land of the Scorpion People, and then to the Land of Night, a Land of Eternal Darkness. After walking for twenty leagues, Gilgamesh found himself in a garden of gems where the trees grew precious gemstones. He crossed the Sea of Death where his arrogance interfered and, as a result, he almost died when making the crossing. However, surviving his journey, he arrived on the other side of the sea, whereupon he met Ziasudra who told him of a powerful flower of life that existed at the bottom of the ocean, and if eaten, it would provide eternal life.

'Gilgamesh tied stones to his feet and sunk to the bottom of the ocean to retrieve the flower. With the flower in his possession Gilgamesh chose not to eat the blossom straight away, but instead went ashore where he would test it on an elderly stranger first. Unfortunately for Gilgamesh, he fell asleep and a snake stumbled upon him, eating the flower. The snake shed its skin as it slithered away. Gilgamesh, distraught he had missed his opportunity to be immortal, returned to his city as a mortal, but wiser for his journey.'

Duncan reread the story. His head pounded.

'You're thinking crazy stuff. Forget it,' Duncan scolded himself.

He shook his head to stir himself from his melancholy mood. He needed to focus on work. He had to be ready for the meeting.

9

Sheol Trading wasn't simply a large company but, according to most financial publications, it was the world's largest and most feared Hedge fund. That company's arrogance and contempt for the market knew no bounds, and they ruthlessly expanded their dominance: They bribed regulators, devoured competitors, and spent hundreds of millions employing lobbyists to convince governments introducing legislation to limit or oversee their activity was bad for the global economy.

It had been a rapid rise from insignificance to notoriety. Five years ago, the company burst onto the scene with an ambitious takeover of one of the stalwarts of the London financial scene. The most curious thing was that, until that day five years ago, not one financial analyst had heard of Sheol Trading; let alone having the financial might to consume such a pre-eminent investment bank. Since then the company had gone from strength to strength, and garnered considerable press attention along the way, most of it negative. Yet, despite this, they quickly established themselves as the darlings of the financial industry. It was the type of company investment bankers salivated and fantasised about.

Sheol Trading's staff regularly appeared in the newspapers in various stages of inebriation, accompanied by articles discussing their penchant for ten-thousand-pound bottles of vintage wine, extravagant meals and largesse tipping. These articles generally frowned on the behaviour, describing it as 'inappropriate given the difficult times people faced', yet it did little to discourage people from wanting to be a part of the Sheol Trading juggernaut.

Graduates queued for hours for the opportunity to be interviewed for places on the company's graduate trainee programme. And there was no shortage of prospective employees, who were attracted by the routine seven figure bonuses, the opportunity to work in an environment of Michelin starred staff canteens, and where employees commuted to their meetings on Segway's.

Initially, Sheol Trading's reputation was due to their ruthless short selling of companies, which to be fair was typical behaviour for a Hedge fund. However, other opportunities soon arose and unlike other Hedge funds, they decided to expand their business into realms commonly occupied by Private equity groups and Investment banks.

They deliberately manipulated and forced the share prices of companies down, making millions in the process, and when the shares of these companies could go no lower, they swooped for the kill, like vultures to a corpse. They would buy the company, strip it of its assets, and sell them piece-by-piece until nothing remained but huge profits. It was a highly lucrative practice. However, all this paled in comparison to their innovative and — some would say — creative approach to investments which literally brought incalculable wealth to financial companies worldwide.

It was this radical new approach that ensured their place in the pantheon of Investment companies.

Two years ago, during the announcement of their third quarter results the enigmatic Chief Executive Officer of Sheol Trading, Lucy Smith, announced to the gathered financial analysts and reporters that Sheol Trading had decided to expand their business in a most surprising, audacious and innovative way.

Sheol Trading's experts had developed their own financial instrument they had dubbed 'CSO', short for Collateralised Search Obligation. In effect, they had converted everyday searches conducted on search engines across the Internet into an object of speculation, a means of creating wealth for its owners. In even simpler terms, an everyday search conducted on an Internet search engine was now the equivalent of such traditional commodities as oil, gold, soybeans, wheat, and mortgages.

It was pure alchemy. The audience frothed at the mouth when they realised how many billions would flood the marketplace and, after quick mental arithmetic, what their commissions would be.

'This is giving me a hard-on,' bawled one analyst at the top of his voice.

The principal behind the securities was a simple one. It was possible for a million searches to be conducted without anybody ever clicking on a sponsored advert, and this would derive an income of zero. But it was equally possible for millions of pounds of revenue to be generated from those same searches. It was this variance in revenue which allowed them to create their object of speculation.

Of course, with any financial instrument there was a considerable amount of risk attached, but the analysts dismissed such concerns, after all the money they were investing wasn't their own, it came from a pension fund, the government or somewhere equally unimportant. Insurance companies sensing the opportunity to line their pockets rushed to provide insurance on the securities, thus providing Sheol Trading with the credibility they required to address all concerns. The success of these securities was assured, as was the billions Sheol Trading would consequently net.

Interestingly, despite so many of the meeting attendees having the word analyst appear in their job title, nobody actually analysed the announcement. Instead, each individual — industry professionals and reporter alike — all behaved as if they were witnessing the second coming of Christ.

The securities had been an instant success with demand far outstripping supply. Financial institutions the world over were falling over themselves in their rush to throw money at Sheol Trading and, in order to gain favour for the next round of security offerings, they pandered to every whim and demand Sheol Trading put forth. The greedy mentality prevalent within the financial industry had taken over, and these firms became willing allies in the growth of Sheol Trading. Immediately upon the release of their CSO securities their revenue leaped ten-fold.

Once upon a time, the press could have been relied upon to highlight Sheol Trading's greed and ambition, but they too had become besotted. The press happily bought into the hype surrounding the company aided, of course, by the lavish press junkets. Whenever Sheol Trading made an announcement they didn't simply issue a written statement like the majority of other companies. Instead, members of the press were flown to exotic locations in private jets. After the announcement, the gathered reporters were then treated to an exceptional dining experience, feasting on gourmet foods prepared by master chefs, washing down course upon course with vintage wines. They were treated like royalty, and they subsequently never had a bad word to say, unless Sheol Trading asked them to.

Sheol Trading's plan for domination had been monstrously

successful. In a few short years, they had gone from a non-existent company to a global financial monstrosity. Yet, despite this success, their grand plan was in its infancy and still to be revealed.

10

'Good morning, Ms Fairchild. A vision of loveliness, as always.' Gilly swaggered towards the desk. His hips creaked and threatened to crack from his willowy movements.

'Welcome back, Sir. I don't mean to be rude, but are you lost? You do know you do have an appointment? There is a board meeting in process,' said Ms Fairchild efficiently.

'Of course, I know. I am here for the board meeting. Ballsy insisted.'

'But you never attend board meetings.'

'Yes, well, that may be true but understandably, don't you think? There are more exciting things in death, and that is saying something.'

'Do you even know where the boardroom is, Sir?'

A door appeared in the corner to the right of Ms Fairchild. Its sudden appearance caused Gilly to recoil. He had grown so used to taking the left door and, even though he knew his way to the boardroom, it had been several centuries since he last treaded that path. He beamed at Ms Fairchild and then padded towards the door. He paused at the entrance to allow his eyes to adjust to the bright light.

A set of double sandblasted doors blocked the end of the corridor. The doors stood out, solely because they were unique to the rest of establishment.

Gilly shoved them open to reveal a cavernous boardroom, darkly panelled with rare woods and dominated by a huge table.

There were twelve people scattered around the table: Six men and six women. All with snow-white hair and attired almost identically in neatly pressed white suits, though each of their ties were different in colour. The men were distinguished, clean-shaven with their hair tied back in long ponytails. The women were elegant with their hair set in a bun at the back of their heads. If he had to guess, he would have placed their ages between fifty and sixty-five, though he knew in reality they were millennia older.

A hush fell over the room and everybody turned in their chairs to face him.

Ballsy coughed discreetly. 'Welcome, Gilgamesh. What a... surprise. Nice of you to grace us with your presence.'

'Thanks, Ballsy. I thought I would slum it for a change,' said Gilly.

'The name is Balthasar,' scowled Ballsy. 'If Gilgamesh has no objections, perhaps we can continue.'

Gilly shrugged his shoulders and lumbered to the far end of the table and occupied the only empty seat. The chair was noticeably smaller than the others; his head barely cleared the table top.

The meeting dragged on inexorably, much to Gilly's distress. The topics discussed ranged from the implementation of speed humps around the VSF units with a view to reducing the number of collisions, through to the burgeoning infrastructure requirements for processing the recently deceased. Nobody seemed to be in any hurry.

Gilly's hand shot skywards.

'This is not a school, Gilgamesh,' said Ballsy.

'Sorry, my mistake, Ballsy,' said Gilly.

'Balthasar. My name is Mr Balthasar or Balthasar if you must. It should not be necessary to remind—'

'Yes. Yes. Yes. While it is fascinating listening to you all, I do have a slightly more important issue to deal with, Mr Bottomley.'

'If I was you, Gilgamesh, I would be more concerned with yourself and your future with the company,' said Ballsy. The line of his mouth began to curl itself into a lopsided smirk.

'What are you talking about?'

Ballsy straightened his tie and nestled into the back of his leather chair. 'Perhaps it would be prudent of me to offer you a chance to resign before word of your latest fiasco is leaked.'

'Resign?' asked Gilly in a voice of mild concern.

'It is what one does when one diligently underperforms and creates a mess.' Ballsy locked his hands together behind his head.

'Now what have I done?' chided Gilly.

'To be precise it is what you haven't done, Gilgamesh. You were asked to deal with a grievance from a recently deceased,' said Ballsy.

'And I did!' snapped Gilly testily.

'Oh yes, you certainly did. According to the complaint I have received from Deceased Resources, after your visit with the recently deceased, a Mr Gordon McBride. He has decided to start his own law firm with the intention of suing Purgatory for gross negligence and discrimination. He is demanding compensation and,' Ballsy looked around the table at each board member in turn, 'he is also seeking an injunction on his death.'

The occupants of the room gasped, then frowned at Gilly.

'So, what is the problem?' Gilly asked defensively. 'It's not like he can recruit lawyers.'

'Lawyers!' exclaimed Ballsy in a raised voice. 'We have more lawyers here than we do staff!'

'Um, well actually, Balthasar,' said a small voice from four seats away. 'According to the recent survey conducted by the Living Relations department, that isn't strictly correct.' The board member shuffled in his seat.

Ballsy shot him a steely look. The board member sat with the expression of a teenage boy who just had his mobile phone confiscated by an angry, bill-waving parent.

Gilly chuckled.

'What may I ask is so amusing, Gilgamesh?' asked Ballsy, his tone calm again.

'You have to laugh. This is moronic. We all have better things to do than waste time having this conversation. Gordon McBride can't sue us. This is Purgatory. We don't have a legal system, we're the original dictatorship. His grievance is with Hell, not us. And this injunction, are you serious? He is dead, so what is the point? And how exactly was he discriminated against?'

Ballsy waved his hand airily, and a filing cabinet appeared behind him. He reached into one of its drawers to retrieve a manila folder from the cabinet. 'Now. Let me see. Did you refer to him in his presence as delusional? Oh wait.' Ballsy continued without waiting for a response. 'Yes, you did. Here is the memo. In actual fact, the memo states you described Mr McBride to be "clearly delusional and in denial".' He slammed a piece of yellow paper onto the table then thrust it in Gilly's direction. Despite there being no breeze in the room, the paper fluttered towards him, up and down, before landing before him within easy reach.

Gilly quickly scanned the document. 'But he clearly is deluded.'

'So, now you're a psychiatrist? How many times have we told

you, Gilgamesh? You are no longer a king who can do as he pleases. You are senior management, not royalty, and, whether you like it or not, you must behave accordingly. You cannot cast dispersions on another's character! Purgatory operates a policy of equality amongst all deceased. When you refer to somebody as deluded, it is a clear violation of their deceased rights,' said Ballsy gruffly.

'This is ridiculous. You have had this equal rights policy for over a millennium, and it has never been used. Even if somebody did pursue a complaint there is no such thing as a tribunal or court to hear it. This is crazy!'

'We thank you for your expert opinion, but the fact remains you cannot go around commenting on the mental state of the recently deceased. It reflects poorly on this company. Deceased Resources already have their hands full with our recruitment dilemma without having to deal with your ham-fisted attempts at diplomacy.'

Gilly groaned and threw his head back in despair.

'Wait till the Chairperson hears about this,' muttered Ballsy.

'I don't see how this is a problem,' replied Gilly.

'This is so typical of you, Gilgamesh. You fail to understand the severity of your actions. We cannot afford for a precedent to be set. What would happen if the shareholders learned of these actions? As it is, we have insufficient resources to cope now and if we have to devote resources to addressing billions of complaints then we would have chaos. We would no longer be able to process the deceased. And if that happened, we would have no choice but to suspend all deaths until we dealt with every complaint. It is essential for Mr McBride's grievance to be dealt with in a professional and dignified manner, qualities you clearly lack.'

Ballsy returned the file and waited for the cabinet to disappear as quickly as it appeared.

'So, Gilgamesh, I would like to kindly ask again for your resignation?' Ballsy smirked, like a mischievous child in a sweet shop.

'I'm sure that would make your day. If the Chairperson wants my resignation then so be it, otherwise some other time.'

'Very well. Let's see what the Chairperson says. In the

meantime, until DR cleans up this mess with Mr McBride, please ensure you avoid him. We would hate for his list of claims to get any longer. Now, unless you have something constructive to add, I believe we can conclude this meeting.'

Gilly wrapped his hands around the edge of the chair's seat and thrust himself forward. He tottered for a few seconds until his balance was restored. He shot a sharp look at Ballsy.

'Is there something else, Gilgamesh?' Ballsy asked dismissively.

'The Succubus attack on Mr Bottomley,' said Gilly.

'Gilgamesh, this is not the time. We have discussed this already and there is no cause for concern.'

'I disagree,' bristled Gilly. 'What if our competition knows about our plans for Mr Bottomley? What if there is somebody within the company who is working for Hell?'

'Preposterous,' sputtered Ballsy. The board members whispered amongst themselves as they digested the possibility in Gilly's words. 'Absolutely preposterous. Are you inferring we have a traitor in our midst?'

'It wouldn't be the first time, Ballsy.' Gilly smiled.

'That was a completely different scenario.'

'This is one coincidence too many. This has to be related to the hostile takeover attempt on our company.'

The mood in the room instantly lightened. Ballsy smiled at each of the board members knowingly. 'Ah, I see. How many times are we going to cover this ground, Gilgamesh? There is no physical evidence of a takeover. Only rumour and conjecture.'

Gilly stared incredulously. 'Are you serious? Why was I appointed in the first place?'

'That is something you will have to ask the Chairperson and, when you do find out, please tell us. We would all love to know.'

'How do you explain the turnover of shares? The transfer sheets show somebody is accumulating an enormous block of our stock and we all know who that is. It is obvious to everyone that this company is the subject of a hostile takeover. The only people in denial is this board who have clearly lost touch with reality!'

Aghast mumbling rolled through the assembled, increasing in volume. Ballsy slammed the table with his fist, silencing the room. 'Enough!' he roared. He gave Gilly a withering look.

'Don't try my patience, Gilgamesh!'

It was a waste of time for Gilly to pursue this discussion. The board refused to admit the company was in a precarious position, and Gilly considered the board inept, while the board viewed him as an inconvenience.

Gilly continued in a reasonable, almost placatory tone. 'Fine. What about an internal investigation then? It would stop me from having to conduct my own.'

Ballsy stroked his chin in a regal manner and cast a thoughtful eye towards Gilly. 'I find it highly irregular and believe it will be a complete waste of resources, but if that's what you want, I'll acquiesce to your request. We will inform you once our investigation is concluded. Is there anything else?'

This surprised Gillly, and rarely did Ballsy or the board surprise him. Lost for words, he shook his head.

The heads around the table bobbed up and down, happy Gilgamesh's business in the boardroom was at an end.

Ballsy waved his hand dismissively as Gilly headed towards the door. 'Oh, Gilgamesh, please don't forget to complete form ND69701217S. In triplicate, using only black ink, and capital letters.'

Gilly's head wilted. 'I'm not familiar with that form.'

'Hardly surprising.' Ballsy turned his head and looked mockingly at Gilly. 'All staff are required to record any interaction with our competition or any of their representatives — whether direct or indirect, intentional or unintentional. As you have stated this encounter with the Succubus was the work of our competition, then you are required to complete the form unless, of course, that is you do not believe it was the work of our competition?'

Gilly's mouth opened in protest but Ballsy waved his hand curtly, signalling their conversation was at an end.

Gilly stumbled out of the room, muttering indecipherable curses. Hushed giggling accompanied his exit.

As Gilly was the only person who ever interacted outside of Purgatory, he knew the form had been introduced with the sole purpose of irritating him, as if being dead wasn't sufficient.

As he walked through the reception, Ms Fairchild must have sensed his aggravation. She smiled warmly, reached beneath the desk and handed him a mug, its contents the consistency of thick dark syrup. Steam rose from it and bubbles formed on the surface before bursting and causing slight ripples. Gilly gratefully accepted it with a smile.

'Ms Fairchild. Do you know how truly wonderful you are? Nothing better than a hot mug of tar.' He pulled the drink away from his mouth, strands hung like tightropes between the mug and his lips, until they snapped and flopped down his chin. They quickly disappeared with a slurp and a lick of his pock-marked tongue.

'Hmm. A hint of charcoal… and dirt. And an aftertaste of freshly burned rubber. It warms my heart,' gushed Gilly.

With Gilly's death, his need for food and drink died too, though he still revelled in the familiar smells of cigarettes and alcohol. However, once he started to haphazardly lose body parts after many millennia of decay, the corporation's doctor advised him he should have a cup of tar five times a day — the grittier the better.

It had been scientifically proven that tar provided numerous tangible health benefits for the walking dead; it filled perforations in the skin before they became gaping slashes, and it also helped to reinforce the bone structure. It was generally accepted to be the perfect cure for body rot.

'Will you require anything else, Sir?' asked Ms Fairchild.

'No, thank you, Ms Fairchild.' Gilly gave a toothless smile.

She again reached beneath her desk and produced a large leather-bound document, as thick as an oversized phone book, and dropped it on the desk with a thunderous thud. She then produced another tome of the same size, and then another.

Gilly gazed po-faced at the documents.

'I have been advised you need to complete form ND69701217S in triplicate, using—'

'Black ink and in capital letters.' Gilly interrupted. 'Yes. I know.' He heaved a sigh, picked up a black pen, and hauled the first book across to one of the leather sofas where, after lining his back with the sofa, fell backwards, landing rather stiffly. He flipped open the bible sized form and started to scribble.

Ms Fairchild busied herself preparing further mugs of tar for Gilly, which she served to him with her usual warm smile.

Hours later, documents complete, Gilly sat pleased with himself despite his fingers aching. He handed the last document to Ms Fairchild and thanked her for her hospitality.

'When will we see you again, Sir?' enquired Ms Fairchild.

'Ah, well, that depends on Mr Bottomley. And who knows? He may be dead already.' He bade her farewell, turned and trundled into the waiting elevator.

11

Duncan Bottomley's official job title may have been 'Senior Account Manager' but, during most days which passed by in a haze of numbers and solitude, he felt 'Cubicle Dweller' would have been more apt.

Duncan spent his days facing a computer monitor which was buried in the corner of two desks, flanked by uninspiring and bland walls. Above his desk and to the left, a laminated date planner which was conspicuous in its absence of entries. Not a photograph in sight; not a gadget or humorous desk ornament. It was just Duncan — the Senior Account Manager / Cubicle Dweller.

He settled into his daily routine. The first task of the day being to check his emails. Occasional spam made it past the filters: Emails advertising cheap but 'genuine' Rolexes, another promising he could be a tiger in bed with Viagra, and another from the wife of a General in an African nation he had never heard of asking him for help laundering the General's ill-gotten income. He deleted the junk mail.

His phone rang. The external line indicator flashed incessantly prompting him to answer it.

'Wollenwal & Wollenwal. Duncan Bottomley speaking.'

Silence.

'Hello?'

Nothing.

A shiver inexplicitly sprung to life, starting at the small of his back, tracing up his spine before ending at the base of his neck where his hairs stood to attention. His shoulders shuddered.

'Hello?' he said in a voice that was at once haughty and hesitant. Again, only silence. He raised an eyebrow and returned the receiver to its cradle.

As the morning progressed the frequency of the mute calls increased. Each call the same as before, with silence echoing down the earpiece. Sometimes the sound of a breeze sailed down the line, but no words were spoken. Finally, he stood erect, sighed loudly and allowed his head to droop. He stomped into the break room for a well-deserved cup of tea. A freshly brewed cup of tea was Duncan's antidote to stress and worry; homely and warm, it was like a soothing medicine, allowing him to recoup and prepare to face his world of woes again.

The break room had been a stroke of genius by management, introduced with a view of improving productivity. Staff interpreted the room as a generous act by management, with the endless supplies of food and drink available throughout the working day. However, the reality was motivated by profit, with executive management deciding that with the availability of such a break room, no employee would ever need to venture out of the building at any point during the day. The room acted as mechanism in keeping staff chained to their desks.

According to the management-hired consultants, who were responsible for this idea, the implementation of the break room would generate an additional output of forty-five minutes per employee each and every day. In exchange the company incurred an approximate cost of twenty pounds per employee per week in order to fund the room and its refreshments. However, the advantages of this idea were abundantly clear: forty-five minutes per employee each and every day equated to an additional five weeks of work per person per year for a total outlay of less than a thousand pounds per employee. Management deemed it a 'no-brainer' — it meant increased revenues, which translated into higher profits, and bigger bonuses for the partners. They loved it.

The break room contained three vending machines: One for soft drinks, another for snacks, and the third machine dispensed sandwiches, soups and microwaveable meals. A counter lined the opposite wall to the vending machines. In one corner of the counter sat an unkempt microwave oven, a kettle and a sink. In the far corner of the counter a radio played inoffensive music, except for those with a disdain for ballads and songs from the previous three decades.

Duncan discarded his tea bag in the swing bin, raised the cup to his lips and blew across the surface of the tea. As he took his first cautious sip, the radio chose this particular moment to fall silent.

He raised an eyebrow, and from the corner of his eye he stared at the radio.

Static filled the room. Duncan lowered his cup to the counter.

The radio was a simple black rectangular box with a chrome dial, which when rotated adjusted the numbers on a luminescent green digital display. His brow furrowed as he willed the music to start. The display was fixed on station 106.6, the home of classic hits. The text flickered and the static faded. And, as he watched, the numbers displayed rapidly decreased, then increased again, until stopping at a seemingly random radio station long enough for the word 'you' to blare out. The numbers rapidly changed again, up and then down, before stopping at another station. The word 'are' resounded out. Again, the numbers changed until a third station was selected and the word 'mine' filled the room with a boom in volume, as if this word was far more significant than the previous two.

The words made their way from Duncan's ears across to his brain. His heart pounded as he considered the mathematical likelihood of such random stations being selected and successfully forming a sentence like that.

With his brow soaked with sweat and his pulse increasing, Duncan realised the radio had spoken to him — and he got the distinct impression, it wasn't being sociable.

Duncan reeled. His flailing arms knocked the cup of tea from the counter. It shattered as it hit the ground, its shards bouncing off his trousers. Tiny beads of sweat leaked down his cheeks, his eyes scoured the room. Nothing seemed out of the ordinary, yet his body felt like it had been struck by a wave and he was walking on jelly. He lurched from side to side. The room spun and his touch on reality disappeared, his legs buckled as he crumpled to the floor.

The radio had said: 'You are mine'. Everything went black.

Slowly he regained consciousness, the sensation of grogginess ebbed. He shook his head and glanced around. His colleagues, were standing over him, gazing down on his prone form. They had heard the smash of a cup followed by a loud thud and, more out of curiosity than concern, meandered to the break room to investigate the source of the noise.

'Are you okay?' one of his colleagues asked in a voice of little concern.

His head lolled from side to side. 'Um… Yes… I'm fine'

'What happened?'

Duncan hesitated then pointed at the radio, 'The… radio… it spoke to me'

His colleagues exchanged puzzled glances. One of them ruffled Duncan's hair. 'No lump on his noggin.'

'What did the radio say?' another of his colleagues asked.

'You are mine. It said, "you are mine".'

There was a moment of uncomfortable silence, finally broken by his colleagues laughing loudly. They slapped him on the back as they returned to their cubicles. The few who remained assisted him to his feet as he massaged the back of his head. One of his colleagues pushed a glass of water into his hand and smiled, before telling him: 'Those words are from the lyrics of the song that's playing.'

Duncan listened to the song. Shania Twain echoed through the room. '*Two hearts, one love beating together, I am yours, you are mine…*'

'No. No. It wasn't a song. It stopped, changed stations, and… it talked to me…' His words trailed off as he realised, he was alone in the room. From outside the break room he could hear voices recanting the event, followed by howls of laughter.

His head throbbed as he scuttled back to his desk.

He settled into his seat, ignored the lingering guffaws and dropped his head onto his folded arms. A yellow post-it note stuck to his computer monitor caught his attention. Content to feel morose he ignored it at first but gradually raised his head. Scribbled on the paper in green pen: 'The partners are waiting for you in the conference room' followed by the date and time. It had been left ten minutes ago.

Duncan rose, tucked his shirt in and hesitantly inched his way to the conference room. The secretary staffing the desk by the door nodded and motioned for him to enter. Duncan's hand, still clammy, slipped from the door handle. He smeared his palms on his trousers and tried again. The door opened to reveal the partners huddled in the centre of the room. Heads turned. Initially, they each wore a 'how dare you interrupt' expression, but as words whispered through announcing the arrival of Duncan Bottomley, their response changed to a warm, well-rehearsed smile. Then inexplicably, the partners applauded. Duncan stood flummoxed.

The managing partner approached. His arm extended to embrace Duncan, but he stopped short, and instead ushered him to the front of the room.

'I trust you intend to change your shirt prior to your meeting?' whispered the managing partner as he guided Duncan.

Duncan glanced quizzically at the managing partner then his shirt. He noticed a damp patch in the middle of his chest and grimaced at the sweat map of Africa under each armpit.

Eventually the applause died, replaced by chatter like a gaggle of excited geese. The managing partner stood to the right of Duncan, his hand resting uncomfortably on Duncan's shoulder. He cleared his throat as he patted the air before him signalling to all to be silent.

'Gentlemen and ladies. Thank you for attending on such short notice. Today is a momentous occasion for the firm. I would like to introduce you to Duncan.' Duncan's hand flopped about in a poor semblance of a wave to the buzzing crowd. The managing partner coughed to silence the room then continued. 'Our priority this morning is to formulate a plan, with Duncan's assistance, as to how we intend to handle the Sheol Trading account. Who wants to fire the first shot?'

The partners set about the task at hand and, after they agreed amongst themselves on each point, they looked to Duncan for his nod of acknowledgement as a token way of including him in the discussions. Once their strategy had been decided, the managing partner rested his hand on Duncan's shoulder, preventing his premature escape.

It was one of those moments where the leader felt the need to address the troops, if for no other reason than they enjoyed the sound of their own voice. The managing partner made a rousing speech on the future of the firm and how its growth was assured with Sheol Trading as their most important customer. At the height of his oratory, he announced that, as an added precaution they would also be appointing two partners to the account to assist Duncan. The managing partner turned to Duncan and assured him the choice of partners would be his but, as time was of the essence, they would assist by making some recommendations. In quick succession, the partner named Richard Steel and Harold Wilson.

Duncan waited expectantly for other names to be offered but none were forthcoming.

Duncan sighed, realising the decision had been made on his behalf, and begrudgingly nodded his head. The managing partner concluded the meeting by mentioning that as long as everything with Sheol Trading went smoothly, then they would look favourably upon Duncan's application to join the partnership. After all, they could hardly have a mere senior manager representing their biggest client.

Duncan returned to his desk and spent the next two hours despondently drumming his fingers on the desktop. His eyes focused on the computer's screensaver: the time appeared every few seconds in a different location on the screen. All of a sudden, interrupting his melancholy, a notification box popped up in the middle of the screen to remind him his meeting with Sheol Trading was imminent. The computer-generated jingle that accompanied the alert was a funeral march to his ears. He growled, grasped the mouse and moved the cursor until it hovered over the "Dismiss Notification" button.

Click.

The red indicator on top of his phone pulsated as it rang.

His hand hovered above the receiver. He glimpsed at the caller display and sighed after recognising the internal number. He gingerly picked up the receiver and held it at a slight distance from his ear and remained silent.

'Mr Bottomley? Hello? Mr Bottomley?' It was Richard Steel's personal secretary.

'Yes?' said Duncan, his voice barely audible.

'They are ready for you in the boardroom, Sir.'

'But… it's not meant to start for another five minutes!' whined Duncan.

'I'm sorry, Sir. I was asked to let you know they are waiting.'

'Thank you,' he whispered in a choked voice, before slipping the handset back on its cradle.

He rose to his feet and slipped on his suit jacket. Every step was heavy, like he was a condemned man walking to his execution. Trudging past the break room, he paused at the doorway and shuddered at the sight of the radio in the corner. Trying to put his recollection of earlier events out of his mind, he rounded the corner. Ahead he could see Richard Steel and Harold Wilson waiting for him by the door to the board room.

Richard licked his fingers on both hands then smoothed down his hair. He studied his reflection in the office window, moved his head from side to side for an improved view of himself. He admired his elegantly swept back, collar-length hair and his neatly trimmed goatee beard which framed his slender features. Canine style, he stretched his lips apart to expose his teeth then ran his tongue across their surface. Briefly he pursed his lips before grinning at his reflection and straightening his tie.

Some time ago, Duncan had worked with Harold on an audit, and found him to be a nice enough man. But he was a serious type, into education and knowledge, and spoke only as and when it was required. Most people confused his reticence as aloofness, but he deliberately spoke little as people found his voice monotone and it had a tendency to grate on the ears of those within close proximity. Harold's shiny round face was dominated by horn-rimmed glasses, which hung crookedly across his nose, either that or his eyes were askew. He wasn't particularly tall, and so many of those who engaged in conversation with him found themselves staring down at his balding crown.

Richard, on the other hand, was an unknown quantity to Duncan. On the odd occasion they spoke he found him to be rather pompous. He had a hooked nose, in his early fifties and, according to office rumours, he was suffering a mid-life crisis. This theory was recently encouraged after the discovery of an affair with one of the secretaries, who had been promptly dismissed after she and Richard were discovered 'snogging' in the stationery room. Coinciding with this, his appearance had also transformed. One day he had arrived in the office and his traditional suit was gone, replaced by jeans and a white linen shirt to accentuate his new tan with a distinctly orange tint. His grey hair was dyed a dark brown and slicked back in the style made famous by *Gordon Gecko*.

Harold shook Duncan's hand, while his left-hand patted Duncan's elbow. 'How are you feeling? We heard about your fainting earlier,' asked Harold, his voice full of concern.

'I'm fine. Thank you. I think it was nerves,' Duncan dabbed the perspiration on his brow with a tissue.

'I tried to call you several times over the weekend to have a word with you about this meeting, but I couldn't get hold of you,' said Harold.

'Um.' Duncan gulped. A bead of sweat ran down his forehead 'I went away for the weekend and I… lost my mobile. Sorry.' He offered an apologetic smile.

'So, you're Bottomley?' sneered Richard once he finished preening himself. 'Why would they choose you? Obviously, a case of mistaken identity. I have no doubt they will realise the error of their ways shortly, and this confusion will be sorted.' He gave Duncan a patronising grin.

Duncan's eyebrows flew high on his forehead and he threw his palms into the air. A tap on his shoulder startled him.

'Sorry, Sir,' it was Richard's secretary. 'They are ready now.'

'Excellent,' shrieked Richard like an excited child.

In a few minutes' time, Duncan's moment of reckoning would be upon him. Unfortunately for him, he absolutely hated client meetings, except for those which exclusively involved accountants. For some reason, when an individual qualified as an accountant, they automatically underwent personality transplants, seemingly donating them to somebody else. Besides, when compared to other accountants his personality could be considered quite gregarious.

Together, in a faux demonstration of solidarity, the three of the men marched into the boardroom.

12

'Welcome, welcome,' bellowed Richard as he bustled into the room ahead of the others. Harold and Duncan shuffled in behind, followed by Richard's personal secretary. She closed the door and took her seat in the corner of the room, her pen and notepad ready for note-taking.

A strikingly tall, slender woman with a thick thatch of neatly styled highlighted hair walked round the table towards them. At first glance Duncan could tell she was at ease in this environment and her clothes reflected her confidence. Dark jeans tightly wrapped her slim legs, and an exotic logo of flames danced on the top of her left front pocket. She wore black heels and a black jumper over a crisp white blouse. She carried her age well, with elegance and poise, with the only sign of aging being a few light wrinkles in the corners of her eyes. If Duncan hazarded a guess, he would say she was in her fifties but in a glamorous movie star way.

Richard's face was consumed by his smile. He stuck his hand out, almost spearing her midriff in the process.

The woman stared at the hand as if he was offering her a used tissue. She rolled her eyes and pushed past to greet Duncan.

A broad delighted smile crossed her full lips.

'You are perfect.' She lent in and kissed the air by Duncan's cheeks. Brief kisses, millimetres from his skin, her breath licked his ears.

'You must be Duncan Bottomley. I have heard so much about you,' she said in a voice of indeterminate accent.

'Hi,' said Duncan hesitantly. 'Nice to meet you.'

A balding and portly man with sloping shoulders, who had remained seated at the table during the exchange, rose to his feet and approached. His two hands cupped Duncan's and vigorously shook it. 'Good afternoon, Mr Bottomley. My name is Oliver Baal. I am the Chief Operating Officer of Sheol Trading. And this,' he gestured to the tall woman, 'is Lucy Smith, the founder and Chief Executive Officer.'

That morning, as his only preparations for this crucial meeting with this worldwide company, Duncan had trawled the Internet in search of information on Sheol Trading's management team. To describe the available information as sparse would be an understatement; Sheol Trading's PR team had done an outstanding job in controlling what was reported by the press. There was an abundance of articles which recanted the official company line, full of canned comments spoon-fed to the press by the PR team. By far the most popularly coined phrase was a description of Lucy: 'The enigmatic engine of the Sheol Trading colossus'. Unlike their celebrity-obsessed contemporaries, and those staff members who regularly courted attention, it was apparent the leadership of Sheol Trading intentionally shunned publicity.

Duncan had determined Lucy had only granted one official interview during her entire career. The finished article, entitled 'From Zero to Hero', had consumed four pages of a magazine and focused predominantly on the company's rapid success and voracious appetite for money. Surprisingly, given the article was on Lucy, it was light on details, and contained the same information as in other articles. The employees interviewed for the article had discussed the tingle they felt at the prospect of coming into work and how they regularly evangelised the company. The article drew to a close by focusing on the passion which evidently permeated the company, oozing from every department, describing it as 'a corporate cult'.

Lucy wasn't what Duncan had expected, although he wasn't really sure what to expect. In many respects, she was a walking contradiction: Matronly and a minx, old and young, shy and brash. It was pointless categorising her, for here was a woman who knew exactly how to be whatever she wanted to be.

'Um, it's a pleasure to meet you both,' Duncan stammered.

After a few seconds Harold, concealed behind Duncan, coughed. Duncan took the hint.

'Sorry. I'd like to introduce two of the firm's partners. This is Harold Wilson.' Duncan moved to one side and gestured to Harold who leaned across and shook hands with Oliver. He offered his hand to Lucy; she looked down her nose at it, her distaste obvious. Harold looked down at his hand, turned it from side to side, before retracting it and shuffling backwards in search of the security of a shadow.

Before Duncan could continue, Richard stepped forward. 'I must say, I am relishing the prospect of working with you and your team.' He tilted his head to the right and bent towards her, his lips pursed, but stopped abruptly when Lucy baulked at his approach and made a noise similar to a cat regurgitating a fur ball.

'And who pray tell are you?' Her disdain palpable.

'I'm sorry. How rude of me. My name is Richard Steel.'

Lucy checked herself from responding. Her brow wrinkled as she pondered something. Then, unexpectedly, her face creased with laughter. Oliver followed suit echoing her sentiments. Duncan and Harold exchanged quizzical glances. Richard stole a look at his reflection in the boardroom window to confirm his hairstyle was undisturbed and his teeth were sparkling and food-free.

'Your name is Dick Steel? How wonderful. Were your parent's fans of porn films? Let me guess, you prefer to be called Steel Dick?' She laughed wholeheartedly.

Richard's face turned crimson and his lips narrowed.

'Is that the line you use on the secretaries? Hi, my name is Steel, Steel Dick,' she said between dignified guffaws.

Richard's personal secretary lifted her head from scribbling notes and smirked briefly. Duncan doubted Lucy would have appreciated the irony of what she had said; after all, it wasn't like she had knowledge of the intimate goings on within the company. Whilst many in the room had thought it, none dared to say it, but it probably was the very line he used on the secretaries after a few drinks.

The ridicule continued for a few more minutes before Lucy and Oliver returned to their seats. Their laughter ceased immediately, and all trace of their smiles disappeared.

They were ready to talk business.

Everybody took their seats, except for Richard who scampered over to his secretary. In a whispered voice he instructed her to delete her notes up to that point and to start over. She obliged and quietly tore the sheets from her notebook. Once Richard turned to take his seat, she folded them with due care and placed them in her pocket; they would provide a great deal of amusement later when she joined the other secretaries for drinks after work — she was looking forward to regaling them with a word for word account. Smiling to herself, she straightened her back and prepared for the meeting to begin.

Richard was as popular with the secretaries as a dose of irritable bowel syndrome. Each of the ladies knew of his affair with one of their colleagues, and they were all of the opinion she had been dismissed on Richard's instructions. When the news of him being discovered in a compromising position with one of the secretaries had seeped out, the firm's partners found his behaviour reprehensible and publicly reprimanded him. They took a dim view of such fraternisation. Richard's ego had been dealt a severe blow, as he was unaccustomed to public humiliation, and he immediately set about arranging the secretary's dismissal, for the last thing he wanted was a constant reminder of his public embarrassment.

After her dismissal, the firm's HR department sent an email to staff reminding everybody of the firm's policy on Internet use and confirming that after an anonymous tip-off they had uncovered what they described as 'downloaded pornographic images' on the secretary's computer. The secretaries were convinced it was Richard, or one of his flunkies, who had planted the offensive material, and the poor woman had subsequently paid a heavy price for making the mistake of succumbing to Richard's charms.

Since then, the secretaries were united in their loathing for Richard, and they joined forces in ensuring they were doing all they could to assist their friend and former colleague in uncovering proof of Richard's actions to strengthen her case of unfair dismissal against the firm.

'So, Dick,' Lucy said, emphasising his name. 'Why are you here?'

Richard sucked in his bottom lip and his forehead wrinkled in disapproval. He opened the folder in front of him and cleared his throat. 'Well, the partner committee felt, as we hold your company in the utmost of esteem, that in all good consciousness we wouldn't be doing justice to your account if we allowed a mere senior manager to manage your account without expert tutelage. The partner committee agreed it would be in your best interests if Harold and I assisted Mr Bottomley in a purely advisory capacity. Unless, of course, you decide the experience we bring warrants a more hands-on role?'

She considered his spiel for a moment. 'I am feeling parched. *Dick*, could you be a darling and get me a cup of tea. Darjeeling if you mind. White with no sugar.'

Richard twisted in his chair and nodded curtly to his secretary who rose to exit the room. Lucy raised her hand, signalling the secretary to stop. '*Dick*, perhaps I wasn't clear enough,' she said sweetly, though it reeked of sarcasm. 'But I do believe I asked you to do it. Please be a dear, I would hate for us to get off on the wrong foot.' She beamed demurely.

'But… Err… Of course.' As he left the room, he exchanged confused looks with Harold.

Once the door closed Lucy leaned towards Harold, her jaw clenched. 'Your name is Harold isn't it?' she raised her left index finger in Harold's direction before calmly clasping her hands together and resting them on the table surface.

'Yes,' said Harold, meekly.

'Please be a dear, Harold, and inform your managing partner we specifically requested Mr Bottomley handle our account. Frankly, I am disappointed your firm has not respected our wishes. I find Dick to be repugnant and not a particularly nice person.' She took a moment to consider her thoughts. 'You see, I can sense these things, Harold, and it truly isn't much fun working with people who are already, how to say… naughty. Now you, on the other hand, you seem harmless, so I have no problem with your ongoing presence in a purely advisory capacity, and only if Mr Bottomley consents.'

They all turned to Duncan who had, until that point, done his best wallflower impersonation in the hope his presence would not be noticed. He quickly nodded his agreement.

'Excellent. Harold, darling, if you don't mind, could you please speak with your managing partner? I promise we will refrain from discussing business until your return.'

In just a short few minutes, there had already been a whirlwind of events. Harold, unfamiliar with this brash behaviour, collected Richard's possessions from the table and left the room. Duncan's eyes followed Harold as he disappeared through the doorway, his eyes pleading in vain for him to stay — or to at least return quickly.

'Duncan— Do you mind if I call you Duncan? Mr Bottomley

is a tad serious.'

'No. I mean yes. No… I mean, yes, yes you can call me Duncan. That's fine.'

'Lovely. I understand you are single?' She sat on the edge of her chair facing Duncan, her back straight and her legs together. She oozed confidence and professionalism, and clearly knew all too well how to handle herself.

He scratched his head in confusion, 'Um, yes, that's correct.'

'Excellent. You will have to forgive my prying, but we would hate for your private life to interfere with business. A business such as ours requires long hours, which has a way of being inconvenient for relationships.'

Duncan's head nodded gently in faux understanding.

'When deciding on a firm to represent our business, it is important to us for the firm to be willing to… How shall I say it? To think outside the box. It is essential they are creative when it comes to our accounts.'

'I can assure you we are extremely creative for our clients,' said Duncan, pleased with his response. He sounded almost sales-oriented and competent.

'Ah. But the question remains, would you exploit loopholes if the legality of such an action was questionable?'

Duncan hesitated to avoid speaking too soon. His instinct was to tell her there was no way he would contemplate breaking the law for a client — it would be disastrous for the firm and not to mention his career! Instead, however, a small voice buried deep within, a voice he rarely listened to, found its confidence and volume again, cautioning him not to answer the question. His inner voice felt it judicious to change the subject.

'Um, sorry. Excuse me, Ms Smith, I hope you don't mind me asking but how do you know me? You said before you had heard of me, but I don't understand how.'

'Oh, you are an absolute treasure. I do enjoy meeting people like you. And please call me Lucy, we're all friends here,' she paused. 'I know you very well, Duncan. Maybe better than you know yourself,' she leaned forward and with the mesmeric gaze of a cobra, continued in a deadpan tone. 'Let me give you a rundown. You live in a small flat by yourself, your work is your life, you have no friends, no pets, no girlfriend, not even a boyfriend, and you don't do drugs. In fact, you could die tomorrow, and I doubt anybody would miss you.' She relaxed back into her chair. 'Yet, despite all of these failings and more, I am your biggest supporter.'

Duncan swallowed.

Oliver chortled to himself, throwing Duncan off his immediate thoughts, which weren't altogether pleasant. 'I must apologise, Duncan. Lucy has a tendency to go off on tangents. Get her near a soapbox and, well, you see what happens.' He smiled, displaying a row of sparkle white teeth. 'But I realise, Lucy didn't answer your question, when the answer is actually quite simple really. Nothing sinister, Duncan, so no need to be nervous. We know you through a competitor, who we overheard praising you. Naturally, business being business, anything our competitor wants, we want. You understand? Business is business. We want the best. We all do. Naturally, with any appointment we undertake due diligence first.'

Duncan flashed a feeble smile and felt a glowing of pride inside him. He had been praised by a competitor! His lips parted as he considered how to best word his thoughts.

'You can't be fucking serious?' a voice boomed.

Duncan spun in his chair, and through the boardroom's glass door, he could see Richard, Harold and the firm's managing partner huddled together. Richard stood red-faced, clearly unhappy and gesticulating wildly.

'But I'm a partner!' roared Richard.

'Someone has quite a temper, Lucy,' said Oliver.

'I think it is a mild form of epilepsy.' Lucy smiled a thin smile.

Duncan turned back to the table and clamoured for the water jug in the table's centre and offered to fill their glasses. It wasn't much of a distraction, but it was the best he could think of on short notice.

Finally, Harold re-joined the meeting. He apologised profusely for the delay and for any profanities overheard. He explained how Richard was unexpectedly struck ill and visibly upset at the prospect of having to leave the office early to recover from his sudden illness.

The meeting began in earnest with no further mention of Richard. Oliver detailed their requirements and asked questions, which were duly answered by Harold, concerning the firm's capabilities to deliver. They then moved into a discussion on Sheol Trading's use of special purpose vehicles, and shell companies based in the Cayman Islands and Panama. Duncan and Harold furiously scrawled notes, which were echoed by the secretary on her notepad. Throughout the meeting, Lucy remained completely silent, choosing instead to absorb and analyse every word. Of great discomfit to Duncan was her conspicuous deliberation of him, he felt awkward and self-conscious as her eyes bore down on him.

A few hours later, Oliver finished his questioning. He slapped his hands together, and asked Duncan and Harold if they had any questions.

'Thank you, but no, I think we have an excellent grasp of your needs. What you have outlined is very comprehensive,' replied Harold.

Duncan reached into his jacket pocket and retrieved a shabby piece of paper. He unfolded it, placed it on the table before him and ran his hands over it to iron-out the creases.

'Sorry. Um, I have a few.' He cleared his throat. 'Um, well, I know this may be an odd thing to ask but… could you tell me what Sheol Trading does to generate its revenue?'

Harold frowned. He sucked his bottom lip in; that was not the question he would ask a new client. They were accountants, and the first thing they should know is what the company does. Of course, nobody in the firm did know the answer and, despite Harold's misgivings, he subconsciously leaned closer to listen to the answer.

Lucy allowed herself a moment of smug delight then happily exclaimed: 'We're a cool company!'

Duncan and Harold exchanged confused glances. They waited for Lucy to continue but she relaxed back into her seat. Duncan straightened himself in his chair and scratched his head. 'Right. I see. Yes, but your accounts. You see, I reviewed your latest accounts and your net profit margin hovers around 95%, which is absolutely extraordinary even for a company in your industry. When I looked closer at the accounts, well, there is a considerable volume of funds flowing through them which I couldn't account for.'

Lucy nodded enthusiastically and giggled. 'Excellent. Excellent. Duncan, let me assure you, it is all very simple. You see, we have a substantial presence in countries others prefer to avoid: Syria, Zimbabwe, Iran, North Korea, to name a few. We need to hedge our transactions with these countries in order to eliminate the risk of currency fluctuations, natural disasters, military coups, wars, and so on. And, of course, as somebody as intelligent as you would no doubt be aware, we undertake complex derivative transactions, which are regrettably unregulated by the authorities and, therefore, are not required to appear on the accounts. The funds you refer to are simply these transactions being unwound and settled.'

'But your net profit margins—'

'Are very high,' Lucy interrupted. 'Of course, I agree. Our gross revenue is higher than the GDP of most nations. Why do you think the company is valued as it is?'

Lucy grew in stature like an evangelist rising to a lectern. Passion filled her voice. 'Make no mistake: The future isn't about gold, oil, or high-tech. The future is Sheol Trading. Just look at Sheol Trading's global footprint. It is an empire where the sun never sets. The best gilt-edged names in European and American banking want to be like us, or at least want us to be their client.' Her tone softened, sounding more feminine. 'Now, I am not one to second-guess the experts — the respected banks, institutions and their analysts. But nevertheless, make no mistake, it gives me a great deal of comfort and security knowing that if we were doing something wrong then these experts and the press would be the first to speak out, to keep us in line, so to speak.' She lowered herself demurely back into her seat.

'I want to thank you for your time today,' chimed Harold, resting his hand on Duncan's forearm as he did.

'Our pleasure,' replied Oliver.

They engaged in small talk for a few minutes. Harold tactfully steered the subject to the discussion of next steps. Did they require additional information or was there anything else they required before signing the contracts?

Lucy and Oliver briefly conferred behind cupped hands.

'Congratulations!' the two chorused. 'Welcome to the Sheol Trading family. We are pleased with our decision, we know it is the right one for us, Sheol Trading, and the company's future,' announced Oliver grandly with a flourish of his hands.

The next thirty minutes passed by in a buzz of excitement and activity. Paper flew in all directions. Signatures decorated the bottom of sheets. The sound of pens scratching paper whirred in the background. The sporadic trill of the phone caused those gathered to flinch. As the meeting drew to a close, Harold moved towards Lucy, checked himself, and then motioned in the direction of the door. Duncan's arms spread across the table as he gathered the scattered papers. It was Harold's responsibility to lead Lucy and Oliver to the partner's dining room for a 'meet and greet' session with the partner committee, which would include the obligatory staged photographs of the signing of contracts. This was to be followed by the partners engaging in unabated shameless 'sucking up', followed by the washing down of several bottles of Bollinger champagne.

Unfortunately for Duncan, his new responsibilities did not include delighting in champagne with the partners. Instead, he had to collect the documents, maintain them in a file, and review the last five years of audited accounts in order to familiarise himself with their newly secured client. Accordingly, he could look forward to a night of work at his desk.

Lucy and Oliver walked towards Duncan, both looking like the proverbial cats with their cream and canary.

As part of his preparation for the meeting, Duncan had scoured the Internet for the correct etiquette for handshakes in business: Should it be firm or submissive? His research yielded two interesting snippets: When greeting somebody in Japan, it is of extreme importance to deliver the greeting with energy and vigour, which was a useless fact considering he was in London and not Tokyo, ignoring the fact nobody present was Japanese. The second nugget of information was of decidedly more use: In western civilisation, a flaccid handshake was considered lazy and regarded with contempt. Thus, Duncan opted for a strong grip, which he practised for at least an hour underneath his desk that morning.

Oliver's hand descended on Duncan's like an eagle diving on a rabbit, capturing it in its powerful talons. It took him by complete surprise and any attempt at a firm handshake evaporated, instead his hand reciprocated limply.

As Oliver moved past, his head inclined towards Duncan's and he whispered: 'I guess this makes you her bitch now!'

Duncan's jaw flapped about like a piece of hoarding in the wind.

Lucy approached. Duncan struggled to find his composure, for at that particular moment it had chosen to flee the room. He gritted his jaw tightly and raised his hand much higher than before, ready to pounce. This time his handshake would speak volumes about his professionalism and, dare he think it in today's politically correct world, his masculinity. As the woman neared, his hand swooped down, his fingers like steel cables ready to clamp on, but then he stopped mid-swoop. With a disparaging glare from Lucy and a flick of her finger his hand drooped despondently by his side as if its purpose in life was now in doubt. There would be no handshake.

She planted an air kiss beside each cheek.

'I think we should start with a breakfast meeting at my hotel, the Ritz. I trust you know where it is. Shall we say 8.00 a.m. tomorrow? Please don't be late. One of my many pet-hates.' She glided out of the room like a ship at full sail, leaving Duncan in her wake.

After a deep, audible sigh Duncan tucked the gathered documents neatly under his arm and lumbered back to his desk, dropping the bundle in his in-tray where they balanced precariously. He slumped into his seat and absently drummed his fingers on the table top.

The meeting he dreaded was over and his weekend from hell a memory, admittedly a bad one. But the meeting had gone well. He had been praised, asked to make decisions, been made to feel important. Yet, despite knowing he should be feeling successful, ambitious and excited, he instead felt as if somebody had taken a vacuum cleaner to his inner being and sucked out all of his energy, strength — and soul.

13

Five hours later, Duncan was still at his desk. He sat uncomfortably perched on his chair, his eyes staring and straining at the computer monitor. The office had quietened considerably. He raised his body from the chair until his head hovered above the wall of his cubicle, as if he were a periscope searching the horizon. He gazed at the panel of clocks at the far end of the room; it was 8.14 p.m. in London, 5.14 a.m. in Sydney and 12.14 p.m. in San Francisco. He sighed loudly and sunk back into his chair. It had been a long day.

His mind wandered as he recalled the events of the past few days. Too many inexplicable and surreal things had happened. Unsurprisingly, he felt emotionally and physically exhausted. He longed to feel normal; not quite vibrant — nobody would ever have described him as that — and back to being the Duncan he knew and loved (sometimes).

Subconsciously he reached out for his phone and dialled a number. A voice answered.

'Hello,' there was a pause. 'Hello,' the voice asked again testily.

'Who is this?' responded Duncan, suddenly aware of this voice in his ear.

'Duncan? Is that you?'

'Yes, it is! But who is this?'

'What do you mean who is this? You phoned me!' the voice snapped.

Duncan listened intently; his eyes widened in recognition. 'Herbert? Is that you?'

'Yes, Duncan. How are you?' said Herbert with an exasperated voice.

Herbert was Duncan's younger brother by twelve years. They had never been particularly close and over the years, since their parents' death, they had drifted further apart. They maintained cordial relations, emailed each other on birthdays, and if time allowed, which it rarely did, they would meet for a pint around Christmas. People who met them both were surprised when they learnt they were related; they were poles apart.

'I'm good. And you?' asked Duncan.

'Fine.'

There was an uncomfortable silence.

'Why did you ring, Duncan?' asked Herbert.

'I rang you?' said Duncan in a surprised tone.

'Yes,' Herbert sighed. 'You rang me.'

'Um, I don't know. I didn't realise I called you. I was at work thinking and…' He scratched his temple. 'Well, I guess I must have called you.'

'I guess you did. Are you okay?' Herbert's tone softened. Despite his best efforts he couldn't remember the last time Duncan had phoned him; their previous communications had always been by email. Herbert's wife would joke that even if they had been in the same room, Duncan would still use email. For Duncan to have resorted to the phone, Herbert knew something must have been wrong.

Duncan lowered his voice until it was barely audible. 'I'm fine. Well, that's not quite true. I'm a little worried. Strange things are happening. Very strange things.'

'Like what?' Herbert's voice raised an octave. 'What is happening?'

'You won't understand,' said Duncan.

'Try me.'

'Okay,' Duncan sighed. 'But bear with me. Just listen. This woman picked me up—'

'What's wrong with that? Sounds like great news. It's good you're getting out,' interrupted Herbert.

'No… You don't understand. She picked me up and then got all kinky and… well, I think she blew herself up. I mean, literally, Herbert. She exploded. The police thought I did it and kept me in jail overnight. Then I met this man who says he is dead, literally, dead. His business card even says he is dead. And today at work… the radio talked to me.'

Silence ensued. You could have heard a pin drop.

Duncan glanced above the walls of his cubicle to ensure nobody was paying any undue attention. He sunk lower into his chair and rested his chin on the desktop. Neither party spoke for what felt like hours. Duncan pictured tumbleweed rolling across his desk.

He removed the receiver from his ear, shook it and replaced it to his ear. 'Hello?' he asked hesitantly.

Herbert sighed. 'Are you still taking work home? Are you stressed? You really need to take a break. We all need a break every now and again. Why don't you go on a holiday somewhere? Get some sun. It would be good for you, sort out your pasty skin.'

Duncan feigned an indignant look at the receiver, pasty indeed. 'No. No. You don't understand—'

Before he could finish his brother interrupted. 'Look, Dunc. I have to go. Leslie and I are about to head out to see a movie. Why don't you call me later this week and we can arrange a catch up? It would be good to catch up. But you really need to take it easy, try to relax a little. Stress isn't good for your health.'

He could tell from the sincerity emanating from his brother's tone he was genuinely concerned. The corner of his mouth raised in the start of a smile.

'Thanks, Herb. I'll do that,' he took a shuddering breath. 'Thanks.'

They said their goodbyes and Duncan pulled himself upright in his chair and rubbed his sweaty palms on the cloth-covered armrests.

Grabbing his suit jacket and long winter coat, he silently made his way towards the lifts.

14

Lucy stepped out from the drab building. Its once whitewashed walls now greyed, from years of pollution and weather. It was raining, not heavily but the light drizzle London was famous for. She waited under the awning covering the exit.

Parked directly opposite was a black Mercedes. Water beaded across its gleaming surface. Standing next to the car, a tall wiry man stood as if a pole had been forced up his back. His black hair and dark olive complexion hinted at his Middle Eastern origin. Spying Lucy, he jogged around the car, opened the rear door closest to the footpath and then ambled the short distance to Lucy's side. He sprung open an umbrella and duly held it aloft. Under its protection, Lucy sauntered to the comfort of her car. Shortly afterwards, Oliver joined her, rain dribbling down his shoulders.

The chauffer closed the car door until it was barely ajar, and with a thrust of his hips the door shut with no noise. He returned to the front seat, buckled his seat belt, adjusted his rear-view mirror, and craned his neck for a view over his right shoulder. The car grumbled out into the congested city street.

The boat-like size of their vehicle made the narrow streets of London difficult to traverse and slowed their progress. It wasn't the most practical of cars, but it was comfortable. The darkened rear windows were impregnable to the stares of outsiders; the luxurious dark leather interior, the abundance of legroom, and the rear heated cup holders. Lucy ordered the car on the strength of the cup holders alone — She liked her coffee black and hot.

Not that the size of the car was the real reason for their snail pace. London had long abandoned its attempts to reduce congestion, not that the city officials would admit to it. The official policy they routinely peddled to the press was that they were actively tackling congestion but, secretly, they encouraged it: Congestion was their 'Osama bin Laden', they could blame everything on it. If they needed more income, then they had no choice but to raise taxes to combat congestion; of course, public transport is overcrowded, because the streets are congested; and the increase of crime was due to congestion — not that Duncan could understand what congestion had to do with crime.

In the back seat, Lucy and Oliver engaged in small talk. Lucy rapped her fingers on her armrest. The chauffeur continually adjusted the rear-view mirror.

'Is there a problem, Sam?' she enquired.

'No, Ma'am. It is as you expected. The Ferrari is six cars back,' he answered.

'Excellent. Now don't go too fast, Sam. We don't want to lose him,' she said with a sly grin.

'No chance of that, Ma'am. This is London.'

The purr of the Ferrari's engine was unmistakable. Pedestrians, hunched and cowering from the light rain, stopped in their tracks to watch as its sleek form crawled past.

Richard Steel loved the response his car generated. Despite his attention being on the black Mercedes ahead, he still allowed himself the pleasure of smiling smugly at the gawking pedestrians.

The Ferrari was cherry red and the exact model which had been featured in the television show, *Magnum PI*. He bought the car a few months ago, just days after he replaced his complete wardrobe with clothes that belonged in the eighties.

The road ahead forked. The Mercedes veered down Queen Victoria Street. Richard changed lanes and, as he approached the intersection, the lights turned amber causing the car in front of him to slow to a halt. Richard cursed under his breath as he watched the Mercedes disappear from view. He stretched forward and slapped the steering wheel, the low-slung seat made it difficult to reach the wheel.

'What's your problem?' He hollered at nobody in particular. 'The lights were amber!'

Sam glanced in his rear-view and side mirrors then suddenly pulled the car over to the side of the road. He turned to face Lucy. 'Sorry, Ma'am. He must have got stuck at the last set of lights.'

Lucy lowered the copy of the newspaper she was reading, uncrossed her leg, and glanced out the rear window. 'Why am I not surprised? Just wait here, Sam; he'll be along shortly.' She went back to reading her newspaper. Oliver continued gazing out the rear window.

'There he is,' said Oliver. Their car re-joined the traffic.

Richard shifted from side to side in the leather bucket seat. His right hand repeatedly thumped the steering wheel as he scanned the surrounding streets for the Mercedes. Up ahead, in the midst of the traffic he spotted the ominous black car. His foot plunged to the ground, the engine shrieked like a banshee, and a few seconds later he screeched to a halt two cars behind. 'Oh yeah, no one can escape the steel,' Richard gloated. 'Well done, baby,' he said, patting the wheel of his beloved car.

That afternoon, Richard had felt more than slighted; he had been personally affronted. The more he dwelled on it, the angrier he became. For hours, he sat in his Ferrari at the top of the exit ramp from the office car park, fuming at his treatment. Behind him a queue of cars had formed and, despite being annoyed at being blocked in, nobody honked their horns to complain: Everyone recognised Richard's car, everyone knew his status as a partner in the firm, and only another partner would ever dare to honk their horn.

Over and over he replayed the events from earlier in the day. His fellow partners, on hearing the outrageous demands made by the CEO of Sheol Trading, had wasted no time in kow-towing to her command.

'They are no better than a stray dog begging for food', he thought.

How dare she ask for his removal from the account? The indignation. The humiliation. Did she not know who he was?

He had been charming. He had been dashing, yet scholarly. He was a partner!

'How dare she', he raged to himself.

He certainly hadn't spent the last three decades working his way from a lowly bookkeeper to the dizzying heights of partner to be treated in such an unforgivable manner.

As the Ferrari's engine grumbled its complaints at having to remain stationery, he came to the conclusion there was only one logical explanation for what had happened to him: somebody had sabotaged him. In his mind, he rapidly formulated a perfectly acceptable solution which rationally explained Lucy's behaviour. Somebody must have spoken to Lucy and spread malicious rumours and lies. He also knew the identity of the culprit; after all, there was only one person who stood to gain from such a heinous act: Bottomley.

It was obvious, when he thought about it. Duncan had no alibi, he had been late in arriving for the meeting, giving him plenty of time to place a call to Lucy and spit his venom. Then there was motive — Duncan felt threatened once Richard had been assigned to assist on the account.

How dare that overpaid, overachieving, ungrateful buffoon sully my reputation for his own gain!

Richard had no intention of allowing Duncan to get away with this travesty. He allowed himself a moment of gratification as he imagined how the events would play out. First, he would produce evidence of Duncan's actions to the partner committee, who would act swiftly in dismissing Duncan. Lucy would learn the truth about this pathetic accountant and, before long, he would be personally responsible for the Sheol Trading account; the way it should have been from the outset.

At that exact moment, he noticed Lucy strolling across the footpath under the shelter of an umbrella towards the parked Mercedes. Instantly, he knew exactly what he had to do.

All he had to do was to speak with Lucy freely. From their conversation she would realise that he is in fact charming and nothing like how Duncan has portrayed him. Then, without hesitation, she would admit it had been Duncan who poisoned her opinion of him. Armed with her admission, he could approach the partner committee and that would be the end of the parasite. An injustice of massive proportions would be corrected, and everybody would feel compelled to grovel and apologise profusely to him.

As his Ferrari pulled out of the car park and into the street, to the relief of those still queued behind, he grinned.

'He has actually done me a favour.'

***

Sam provided regular updates to Lucy and Oliver on the Ferrari's location.

Meanwhile, Richard's brow furrowed with concentration as he tried to remain inconspicuous and at a distance, which was impossible considering his car and the stop-go nature of the traffic. They merged onto Embankment, where the two cars surged forwards for a few seconds, reaching the dizzying speed of twenty miles an hour before stopping at another set of lights. They passed Trafalgar Square: Its lion statues resplendent in the drizzle as they stood guard over Nelson's column. A few turns later they were on Piccadilly.

Richard slowed his car to a halt. In front of him, Lucy's Mercedes turned into the valet parking entrance of the Ritz. He lowered himself in his seat, peered over the sculpted dashboard and watched Lucy and Oliver enter the hotel.

Once sufficient time had passed, he started his car and approached the hotel.

His engine whined as it struggled with first gear.

The low height of the car and a slight case of arthritis in his joints made Richard's exit from the Ferrari anything but graceful. Using his most dismissive tone, he informed the valet of his name and explained he was here for a business meeting with Lucy Smith of Sheol Trading. The valet, oblivious to his rudeness, directed him to the reception desk and gratefully accepted the ten-pound tip with a nod of his head.

Richard strutted into the foyer area. His eyes devoured the sumptuous vision before him: The chandeliers, the gold leaf décor, the rich lush carpet, dark exotic woods, mirrors and ornate carvings. This was a life he could get used to; opulent and extravagant, lavish and luxurious, it was exactly what he wished for.

There was a tap on his shoulder. Richard with his eyes still fixed on his surroundings, inclined his head towards the source of the tapping.

He jumped. It was Oliver, with his hands tucked behind his back he shifted his weight from side to side. 'Welcome, Mr Steel. Lucy has been expecting you.' Oliver gestured towards the elevators.

Richard was at a loss how to reply. He felt like a boy whose hand had been caught in the cookie jar.

The chauffer stood by the lift, his palm resting against the open elevator door to prevent it from closing.

Richard entered and shuffled to the rear of elevator. Everybody faced the door. Oliver leaned across and pressed the button labelled seven. The doors slid closed and with a shudder their lift journey began.

As the floor numbers ticked by, Richard contemplated his situation, and how it might possibly be misinterpreted. Yes, he had been following them, some might even suggest he had been stalking them, but they were not to know that. Even if they had seen his car, it was completely plausible for him to have been travelling in the same direction. He allowed himself some reassurance, knowing he had done nothing wrong. After all, it was Oliver who had approached him in the lobby and invited him to the room; he had been there for a date, yes, he had been there for a date.

In actual fact, this was an ideal situation for him as he could now talk to Lucy without the fear of how she might react to his sudden appearance on their doorstep because Lucy had, after all, been expecting him.

He paused in his deliberations to consider that last thought. *'She had been expecting him?'* he wondered. *'How could she be expecting me?'* The button marked six illuminated, interrupting his thoughts. With only one floor to go, he needed to say something to consolidate his defence.

'What a coincidence meeting you here, Mr Baal. I was... meeting a friend for a drink in the bar. A date in fact.'

Oliver glimpsed at Richard's reflection in the mirrored lift door and grinned. 'What a coincidence indeed, Mr Steel.'

The bell in the elevator tinkled their arrival at the seventh floor. The lift doors moved apart smoothly. Sam exited first, then Richard followed by Oliver. The hall porter tipped his head in greeting as they walked past.

The hall porter was an enduring distinction between the Ritz and other hotels. Their exquisite attire emanated class and sophistication: The highly polished black shoes, the dark pants pressed into perfect folds, the row of polished copper buttons from the waist to the base of their neck, the white glove tucked under their right shoulder strap, and their bellhop cap worn at a rakish angle. The Ritz didn't employ a concierge as other hotels did; instead, they opted to assign each floor its own Hall Porter, whose role was to assist guests on their floor whenever possible. They were the epitome of discretion.

Sam knocked briefly on the door before inserting the security card. The red light beneath the slot turned green, and he twisted the door handle. He stepped to one side to allow Richard to enter the room. The door opened into a small hallway, not much longer than a couple of metres. A partially closed door led off to a bedroom, another to a brightly lit bathroom, and the final door led to a room which was even more sumptuous than the lobby. Edwardian furniture throughout the room, plush antique chairs elegantly placed by the fireplace, chandeliers illuminated the room, highlighting the crisp, golden décor. Richard inched his way into the room.

From a closed door at the rear of this room Lucy appeared. She had changed since their meeting that afternoon, and now wore a white plush dressing gown with ribbon trimming, a silk sash and a plunging neckline. Beneath the gown Richard caught glimpses of a black silken chemise embroidered with a floral lace trim. She smiled before flitting across to one of the chairs beside the fireplace and beckoned for Richard to sit in the chair opposite. She swung her right leg over her left, a diamond-studded sling-back hung loosely from her raised foot.

'Thank you, Sam and Oliver,' she smiled demurely in their direction. The two men bowed their heads and backed into the hallway.

They waited for the sound of the front door closing.

'It is lovely to see you again, Ms Smith,' began Richard. 'I was just saying to Mr Baal what a coincidence it is to see you here. I was here to meet a friend in the bar downstairs. A date actually.' Richard tried his best to look surprised but instead his face hosted an expression of constipation.

'Well, we wouldn't want to detain you from your... date, Dick,' Lucy replied smoothly.

Richard frowned briefly. 'Well, unfortunately, or fortunately, depending on your point of view, as it happens, my *date* was cancelled at the last minute so there is no rush.'

'That is fortunate, isn't it?' The corner of her mouth twitched.

'This is a lovely room.' Richard remarked, looking around. 'Very opulent.'

'Thank you. I hope you don't mind, Dick, but I have pressing business to attend to. So, why don't we cut the small talk. I find it tiresome and such a waste of time.' She smiled absently and turned to face him fully. 'I am interested to understand why you followed us here this afternoon.' Lucy leaned in, her cleavage arresting Richard's attention. He quickly averted his gaze; fully aware he could not afford to taint his reputation further.

Richard feigned indignation. 'I'm sorry. I don't understand. I told you, I was here for a date. In fact, it was your colleague, Oliver, who invited me up here.'

'Of course, you were, Dick. We can continue this charade for as long as you like, or we can get down to business. Try not to disappoint me further, Dick.'

Richard nodded nervously.

'Excellent. Am I correct in assuming you are feeling aggrieved over my earlier behaviour?'

'Well, now that you mention it, yes. Actually, I am pleased you have raised this topic. You see, I am a respected partner in my firm and your behaviour… well, some might misconstrue it as a slight on my character. I am confident this was not your intention and you were merely relaying the mistaken comments somebody else has made to you. I would be—'

Lucy interjected, lifting her finger to her lips, signalling for him to be quiet. 'Please, Dick. Do not belittle me. I know exactly who you are.'

Richard stared in confused silence. She reached over the side of her chair and retrieved a blue folder from the floor. In an exaggerated gesture she licked the tip of her index finger, Richard felt a stirring in his loin, and flicked through the contents of the folder before extracting a page. She returned the folder to the floor and leaned back in her chair. She quietly giggled as she scanned the document.

'Wonderful reading.' She pointed to a paragraph at the top of the page. 'I see at age twenty-one your parents died — I am so sorry for your loss — and clearly you must have been very distraught as I see you used this opportunity to swindle your siblings out of their inheritance. Oh, the poor things. I suppose such an emotional trauma can really affect one's moral standing. But at least you have had the decency not to speak to them since. I am certain they appreciate that.'

Richard sat frozen, unable to speak as Lucy continued.

She ran her finger further down the page and pointed to another section. 'Oh, this is interesting. I do wonder if your fellow partners are aware of your extracurricular investments? I don't think they would be happy if they knew you had been engaging in insider trading. That wouldn't be good for your firm's reputation, would it, Dick?'

Instantly, his eyebrows rose, his lips pursed. 'What is the meaning of this? Are you trying to blackmail me?'

'Oh, Dick. You can be so obtuse.' She crumpled the document in her hand and flipped it over the back of her chair. 'Perhaps now we can be honest with each other, without this moral outrage crap.'

'But—'

'If I wanted to blackmail you, I would have insisted on you being assigned to our account and not having you removed as I did. I have much bigger plans for you.'

'I don't understand,' he responded in a subdued tone, shocked and dismayed at how the conversation had unfolded, in such a black to white contrast of his plans.

'Of course, you don't, Dick. Do you actually think any of this is by chance?'

Richard shrugged; his face contorted into a distressed look of confusion.

'We have been keeping our eyes on you, Dick, and, where possible, we have helped you, encouraged you. Who do you think arranged for pornography to end up on your recent dalliance's computer?'

'You did that?' asked Richard in a voice of mild concern, his mouth parting.

'And there is much more. Think of me as your guardian angel. Now, the reason I have brought you here.

'You brought me here?'

'I have a business proposition to discuss with you.'

Richard's ears pricked. Those words definitely piqued his interest. 'What sort of proposition?'

'The type that will make you rich, Dick. Richer than you can possibly imagine. And, in exchange all I ask is for you to be my inside man at your firm. My eyes and ears, so to speak. Help me to influence certain decisions.'

'Please continue,' he said, with an evil grin.

15

It was a typical winter's night in London. The full moon shone brightly in the cloudless sky, like a pearl resting on a black satin pillow. The lack of clouds ensured the temperature plummeted as soon as the sun sank below the horizon. A hazy fog slowly descended on the city.

Duncan Bottomley exited the misery of the train station. He enjoyed this part of his journey home for it meant his daily experience of public transport was at an end.

The thought of public transport raised the hairs on his neck and chilled his heart. He regarded public transport with cold loathing. It was a modern-day horror story. From the dank atmosphere which saturated your nostrils and the swelling crowds, to the prospect of having your nose crammed against an armpit that reeked of stale sweat and last night's curry. He vehemently believed travelling on public transport carried health implications, and the government should place health warnings on the tickets. All that was required was a skull and crossbones motif emblazoned on the rear of the ticket accompanied by a simple health warning like: 'Taking public transport can harm you and people around you'. For pregnant women, where they have more chance of winning the lottery than being offered a seat, a suitable warning would be: 'Taking public transport when pregnant could harm you and your baby'.

Distracted by his thoughts, he failed to notice the dishevelled man with a cupped hand outstretched blocking his path.

'Any change?' asked the unkempt man in the most pitiful voice he could muster.

The man startled Duncan, not by his words or sudden appearance but by his breath — the smell of bacon infused with alcohol, apple and a hint of garlic.

'Um, sure,' said Duncan morosely.

He made a show of his hand rummaging through his pocket collecting loose change though, in reality he was carefully feeling the size of the coins to ensure he didn't pick any one or two pound coins. He handed over a collection of coins and wished the man a good night then continued his journey.

Other than his bank, there were few things in life Duncan despised more than giving money to somebody else; however, this was overridden by his fear that if he didn't then something bad would happen to him and vice versa. It was his concept of Karma. So, if parting with small change meant he avoided further bad luck, then he would happily hand over the thirty-seven pence (he had counted the coins as they slid from his hand into the man's) if it meant a lack of exploding women and walking dead in his life.

On his journey home he rationalised the recent events and considered the possibility Karma had been the cause of recent events. He must have done something horrible in a past life; he would have had to have been somebody like Vlad the Impaler, or Genghis Khan, to justify the horror he had endured. Unfortunately for Duncan, he didn't believe in reincarnation, so he reluctantly dismissed that notion and accepted he had been extremely unlucky.

Duncan pulled the collar of his coat up around his neck and shivered from the cold. His fleshy features turned a light shade of blue. He breathed into his cupped hands for warmth and watched the steam leak through his fingers.

As it was late in the evening, there were only a few commuters heading in the same direction. Gradually, the other travellers peeled off onto different paths, heading into their warm cosy homes, and only the clip-clop of his footsteps disturbed the stillness of the evening.

He looked both ways, not once but twice, and then ventured across Battersea Rise before rounding the final corner into Trevi Road. It was a narrow street, more like a cul-de-sac, bordered at the end by an empty lot, on the right by a small neglected cemetery with a wrought iron fence, and on the left by a manicured hedge which offered a small measure of privacy to the row of terraced housing.

His pace slowed to a standstill and he shuddered at the sight of the cemetery. It filled him with trepidation. A lamppost overhung the cemetery illuminating the mausoleum in its centre. Regardless of the years spent living opposite the graveyard, it still never failed to send shivers up his spine and back down again.

Duncan grimaced at the cold and reflected on how he would

be returning home to a refrigerator that masqueraded as his home. Of course, the fact his flat was colder than the North Pole was entirely his own doing: While most people programmed their heating to come on at a set time so they would arrive to an invitingly warm home, he, however, considered it thrifty to wait until he arrived home before turning on the heating. On the rare occasion a colleague or a companion accompanied him, he would blame the lack of heat on a faulty timer which he had to get fixed.

The sound of footsteps rapidly approaching interrupted his thoughts. He whirled around with his arms poised like a cobra ready to strike, but the street was empty.

A chilled wind whipped around him, quickly sailing up the road and in between the houses. His nostrils flared as a whiff of rotting garbage trickled by. There was something oddly familiar about the smell. Duncan quickly buried his fists deep into his coat pockets and retreated to his front door.

The front door to his building appeared neglected with its peeling paint and rotting wood, which to be fair it was as neither him nor his downstairs neighbour had the inclination to paint it. He sidled through the door and up the old creaky staircase with its banister hanging loose until he reached his flat's front door. A naked light hung by it, absent of a shade or cover. The staircase groaned with each step he took, its age moaning at his slight paunch — an unwelcome change brought on by age.

Duncan closed his flat door and slumped against it; it was late, yet his day of work was only just beginning.

As exhausted as he was, he had to prepare for his breakfast meeting tomorrow. He couldn't help but smirk at the thought. At long last, he was attending a breakfast meeting. He felt a twinge of pride and allowed himself to briefly smile.

***

It was a little after 2.00 a.m.

Duncan sat at his kitchen table poring over a bland profit and loss statement. His brow deep-set with concentration, and chaos was strewn over the table in the form of various sheets of crumpled paper and a well-thumbed book on corporate governance. Wisps of steam from a fresh cup of tea drifted

99

upwards, teasing his nostrils.

He exhaled loudly and stretched out in his chair. His bones cracked. It had been a long night of work and he still hadn't finished.

All of a sudden, he unwillingly bent double. His head throbbed, his heart raced, his skin bristled and a rapidly escalating intense sense of discomfort rushed through him. It was as if a tannoy system, which only he could hear, had announced 'our apologies for this interruption to your evening's entertainment but we thought you should know you are being watched'.

Slowly he lifted his head.

He took a deep breath and leaned back in his chair, extending his legs out for balance while he gripped the edge of the table with his fingertips, allowing him to stretch his body into the hallway without tipping the chair. He glanced up and down the corridor. There were no signs of movement anywhere in the flat. But a sound became apparent, forcing his heart to race again. He cocked his head and strained his ears, panic building as he prepared for more of that dreaded bad luck.

The noise became clearer; a hissing noise filled the air, somehow simultaneously quiet yet deafening, and sounding like he imagined a snake would, then came silence. Duncan listened and heard the same noise again, but this time he was convinced it had whispered his name.

Gradually, he rose to his feet, panic and apprehension turned his legs to jelly. He tiptoed through the hallway to the doorway of the living room. He gazed around, the darkness of the room slowly gave way to shapes and, before long, he recognised the contents of the room. Sliding down the doorframe he crawled, SAS style, to the curtained bay window, slithering via the coffee table and circumnavigating his aging sofa.

The curtain parted and his head rose cautiously above the windowsill. He peered at the shadowy street below. The full moon illuminated the scene. By the cemetery's fence a strange figure swayed from side to side. Duncan's lips pressed against the window causing the glass to fog.

Allowing the curtain to fall back into place, Duncan scrambled across the living room floor and down the hallway. Sliding the bolt back, he unlocked his front door and slipped through its opening. He skulked past the naked light which illuminated his landing and down the old creaky staircase which still groaned with every step.

At the bottom of the staircase, he stopped abruptly in his tracks and pondered the possible consequences of his actions.

Acts of spontaneity were foreign to Duncan. He was of the opinion no good could come from them and, inevitably, they induced change. He was a creature of habit and, as such, he was as fond of change as he was of colonic irrigation: The thought of tubes stuck where the sun never shines sent a shudder through him; uncertainty and a lack of planning had the exact same effect.

His spontaneous plan wasn't the most sensible or logical action Duncan had ever proposed. Confronting this individual who stood loitering outside was one thing, but his plan didn't so far extend to what he would do if he, at least he thought it looked like a he, confirmed he had been following him. Of course, it was also possible the individual would say he hadn't been following him but, as he happened to be in the neighbourhood, it would be a crime not to relieve him of his wallet.

Perhaps it was tiredness which overruled his usual common sense or maybe it had been his overwhelming curiosity, but before he could second-guess his decision, he grasped the door handle and pulled it open.

The night air greeted him with a piercing cold slap, penetrating his tartan dressing gown and snaking its way over every part of his body. It raced up the bottom of his pyjama legs and chilled his nether regions then climbed up further.

He cringed as he stepped onto the footpath. Slurred jarring tones assailed his ears, as soothing as nails dragged down a chalkboard, 'Maybe, you're spinning me… I'm falling… Can't you saveeeee meeeee… I'm falling….'

'Hello… Hello… Excuse me? Could you please keep it down? It's late.' He waved his arm above his head, directing the figure's attention towards him.

Thankfully, the voice responsible for the appalling singing fell silent and turned to face him. The figure tottered and slumped backwards, landing with a sickening crash against the iron bars of the cemetery fence. Duncan winced at the sound. The man's head lolled from side to side and his eyes squinted, presumably in an attempt to focus. Duncan stepped forward then froze and recoiled in disgust at the sight of the man's undone zip with appendage hanging out. Realisation then hit him, the man was drunk and had obviously decided to relieve himself when he was rudely interrupted.

'Well, I'll be a dead man. We meet again,' came another voice.

Duncan spun around. Anxiously he cast his eyes over his surrounds for the voice's owner. The wind, swirling through the street, hampered his attempt to establish the direction.

'Who said that?' shouted Duncan, his voice choking.

A man emerged from the shadows in the cemetery and hobbled towards Duncan. 'The cold weather plays havoc with my joints,' said the figure pointing to his rigid legs.

'Who are you?' demanded Duncan.

A cascade of iridescent moonlight bathed the scene and cast silvery hues over the lingering mist. The figure shambled towards him with an odd, yet purposeful walk.

Duncan's eyes went wide, and he instinctively stepped backwards. 'Not you again.'

'Who did you expect? Jesus Christ!' exclaimed Gilly.

'What are you doing here?' said Duncan. For a moment, he considered screaming like a banshee and running around like a headless chicken but, as it was two in the morning, he decided his neighbours wouldn't appreciate it.

'Nice evening, apart from the cold.' Gilly attempted small talk.

'What do you want?' asked Duncan, ignoring the attempt at small talk.

'I think someone could do with getting some more sleep. You living folk should appreciate sleep while you can. You won't get much once you're dead,' said Gilly wistfully.

'Please. Not this again. I don't have time for this. Seriously. I have a lot to do. My week is bad enough as it is.'

'You're having a bad week? You should try being dead! It's been a bad millennium for me. Look at this, my finger dropped off last week.' Gilly raised his hand and wiggled his fingers. Duncan's eyes almost popped out on stalks at the sight of the hollow stub where Gilly's ring finger had previously resided.

Duncan glanced over his shoulder to confirm his front door hadn't suddenly relocated itself and was still within easy reach.

'Look, Gilgamesh, isn't it?'

'Excellent memory. But let's not be formal, you may call me Gilly. As I told you, my friends call me Gilly.'

Duncan shook his head. 'Could you please leave me alone?'

'Why would you want that? You'll have plenty of time to be on your own when you're dead. We could always party a little, if you like.'

There was a scratching noise from the end of the street. Duncan surveyed the garbage bins and the strewn rubbish for the source of the din but whatever made the noise remained hidden.

'*Probably a fox,*' thought Duncan.

'I'm not happy I'm here either. Given a choice I would rather hang out in Limbo than hang out with a deadest, but I don't have a choice in the matter. So, you may as well listen to what I have to say. It's not like I have anything better to do. Being dead has a way of limiting your options.'

'I wish you would stop saying that,' despaired Duncan.

'What? That I'm dead?'

'It is very tiring,' sighed Duncan.

'Fine then, I'm living impaired. Happy now?' said Gilly as if he had somehow been offended.

'No. I… Please… Just leave me alone?' Duncan snapped.

Gilly scratched at his right ear. 'I wish I could, but I can't. I need to talk to you. I think your life depends on it.'

Duncan nursed his head and glanced guardedly at Gilly. His face shrouded in the shadow cast by his hat. A few strands of wispy white hair escaped from beneath its brim and his skin strangely translucent. His cheeks were visibly sunken, and the protruding veins around his neck looked like a detailed inner-city road map.

Gilly repeatedly picked at his ear, his fingers burrowing deeper and deeper, twisting and pulling. He tugged and tugged until… POP! His hand jerked free.

'Hardly hygienic, I know, but it's been irritating me all week.' Gilly held his hand out in a pincer grip. A fat white maggot wiggled between his finger and thumb. He gave it a scornful look before flicking it to one side.

'What the…' bellowed Duncan. He floundered backwards, his face contorted with horror and revulsion. He began to sweat.

'What's wrong? I'm dead. What do you expect? These things happen. I'm walking worm food these days,' bristled Gilly.

'That… maggot was in your ear!'

'I know, they're everywhere these days. You should have seen where I picked one from the other day. A right nuisance.' Gilly paused then waggled his finger defiantly. 'When I agreed to this job nobody told me I would spend my days fishing maggots from my body. They conveniently left that detail out.' Gilly tilted his head skywards and started on one of his infamous rants, which eventually lead to him going off on a tangent about how the living continually persecuted him without cause, all because they happened to be alive.

'Sorry?'

'When I was alive, it was fun. It's no fun being alive anymore.'

'What are you talking about?' Duncan waved his arm in a histrionic gesture and scowled.

'Think about it. You can't smoke. You can't even drink! These days, if you have more than a couple of drinks, they say you're binging or have "alcohol dependence issues". People are wrapped in cotton wool but that isn't life. You can't even wrestle a bull without animal protection complaining. Imagine it: "Your body might hurt the bull's horns when it impales you". It's ridiculous.'

'No,' Duncan said as he rubbed his bleary eyes and shook his head. 'It's this which is ridiculous.'

'Don't get me wrong, I'm not saying being dead is more fun than being alive! Life would have to get pretty desperate for me to ever claim that. But the living have nothing to brag about.'

'Enough. Please. No more,' pleaded Duncan.

'I'd love to, but I can't. You know, bureaucracy being bureaucracy, there are a few things I need to tell you or when I am next in the office, I'll have to complete form ND20080305C and I can't begin to tell you how much I hate forms. You have to complete them in triplicate, in capitals and you have to use black ink. Triplicate! They are the bane of my life.' Gilly shook his head. 'Sorry, the bane of my death. You'd think I'd have gotten used to that by now.'

'What are you talking about?' As the words escaped Duncan's mouth, he immediately regretted asking the question.

'Well, you see, I did try to talk to you the other day, but you wouldn't listen. You see, that woman who well, exploded, she wasn't technically what you'd call a "she". Not even a "he", actually.'

'Please. I don't have time for this.'

'She— Well, she was actually an it, a Succubus to be precise.' Gilly waited for a reaction, but none came. Duncan simply stood with his mouth open. 'You do know what a Succubus is, right?'

Duncan shook his head.

'What? Everyone knows what a Succubus is. A demon which takes the form of a female to seduce men, leads them to eternal damnation, that sort of stuff. They're not friendly.'

Duncan stared incredulously.

'Hmm. You see, every twenty years or so one of them pops up and attacks a living person,' explained Gilly deadpan.

'You're saying I was attacked by a demon?' Duncan asked as he continued to impersonate a goldfish wrenched from water.

'Exactly!' Gilly adjusted his hat. 'Now, it could be that you were unlucky, and this is one big coincidence, but I don't think so. You see, I've been dead for well over five thousand years, and in that time, I've never heard of a Succubus spontaneously combusting before. Actually, come to think of it, I've never heard of somebody surviving an attack before either. You're the first, and no offence, but you hardly have the physique to resist an attack.'

'Wait.' Duncan raised a hand. 'What do you mean this could be a coincidence?' asked Duncan, as he slowly digested the conversation.

'Ah. Yes. That. Err, well. This is a little delicate. Where do I start? You see, this private equity group has launched a hostile takeover of the company I work for. If they're successful, they'll probably strip the company of its assets and sell them off. Nasty bunch of people, they're right demons. Anyway, I think they may have learned of our plans and have taken matters into their own hands.'

'I don't understand. What does this have to do with me?'

'Well, you see, my employer, Purgatory has asked me—'

'Purgatory!' exclaimed Duncan in a falsetto voice.

'Yes, Purgatory. It's the Operations department for the company I work for. Anyway, Purgatory is where all the boring stuff happens; you know, the processing of the deceased, supporting the company, maintaining the share registry, responding to shareholder correspondence, marketing, sales, that sort of stuff.'

Duncan immediately inched back towards his building. His hands held out front warning Gilly to stay back. 'Please leave me alone. This isn't funny. I'm calling the police.'

Gilly sighed as Duncan rushed inside and slammed the door shut. 'This really isn't going well,' he muttered. He shrugged his shoulders and hobbled through the rusted old gate, which hung open loosely by its bottom hinge, and made his way into the cemetery. His legs barely bent, forcing him to almost swing them like a bowlegged cowboy with each and every step.

Abruptly, he stopped and turned. His head swept from left to right as he scrutinised the surrounding shadows. Then with a flourish of his long coat, he disappeared into the cemetery, the darkness of the night consuming him.

A few houses from the entrance to Duncan's house, a pair of eyes blazed red, penetrating the inky blackness of the darkened doorway. A voice behind the eyes hissed, 'Duncannnn… Play with me!'

16

The next morning Duncan awoke blearily as if hungover, which he wouldn't have minded if he had actually consumed alcohol. He stirred stiffly and groaned. His eyes crept half open and floundered left to right. Without rising, he deduced that as his head was resting uncomfortably on a wooden surface, he had fallen asleep at the kitchen table.

He propped up his throbbing head with his palm and contemplated his surroundings while deciding on his next action.

Eventually, the acute pain in his head decided the next course of action for him, and he staggered from his kitchen, across the hallway and into the bathroom.

Duncan rummaged through the cabinet, a hypochondriac's dream, shifting various vials, potions, jars and lotions. The loud crashing noise, as they clattered across the floor made him wince. He felt terrible. Hardly the start to the day he would have hoped for.

Duncan sought solace from the darkened living room, sitting quietly on the deflated looking sofa; his eyes stared at the bland wallpapered walls. The gentle throbbing of his head punctuated his meditations. Eventually he rose to his feet, looked at his watch, and hobbled into his bedroom to get dressed in a haphazard manner. He staggered his way to the kitchen where he collected the scattered papers from the table. Shuffling them under his arm and left for work, leaving at his usual time of 6.25 a.m.

He stumbled down the stairs and faltered in his footsteps when he reached the footpath.

In the gloom of dawn, the cemetery loomed eerily. His gaze, at once apprehensive and suspicious, regarded each tombstone individually. Once satisfied the cemetery was empty of shabbily attired people claiming to be dead, he hurriedly made his way to the train station.

***

At 7.32 a.m. Duncan exited Green Park tube station, crossed the road, and immediately scanned his surroundings to get his bearings. Ahead on the left he could see the old-fashioned Ritz Hotel signage. He retired to the nearest wall and watched the hands on his watch languidly turn.

He deliberately arrived early, partly out of concern that he might be late but predominantly due to his revulsion of public transport. If he had left home any later, he would have found himself squeezed onto a train where he would be forced to endure a concoction of stale air infused with a multitude of perfumes, reminiscent of a bucket of prawns left in the sun. He failed to find anything redeemable about public transport in London; the stony, miserable faces of each passenger, which if you were forced to stare at for longer than a few minutes, would lead you to the conclusion that death was arguably a better option. And to think, people paid for the privilege.

It was now 7.53 a.m.; his breakfast meeting was about to start. He sauntered to the road and stuck out his arm. A black cab pulled up beside him. Duncan hopped into the rear of the cab and muttered his destination to the driver.

'Sorry, mate. I must have misheard you. I thought you said the Ritz,' the driver said between chuckles.

'Um, I did.'

'But it's just there,' said the cabbie pointing across the road.

'Um, I know.'

Duncan felt embarrassed catching a cab for such a short distance, but he had decided it was absolutely necessary on the off-chance he happened upon the Sheol Trading executive team in the lobby; he didn't want them to think he was cheap. He had read how it was all about image when it came to dealing with these high-flying city types.

Less than a hundred metres later, the cab pulled into the Ritz. Duncan pushed a few coins through the small hole in the window of the driver's cage, and quickly alighted the cab, careful to avoid the cabbie's glare. The hotel's porter doffed his hat in greeting. Duncan smiled and ploughed through a large set of swing doors. His jaw plunged as his eyes consumed the extravagant décor before him. He glanced down at his shoes, shuffled them together and tugged on his trousers to lower the cuffs as much as possible. It would have been obvious to every member of staff, visitor and guest milling around this was not his usual environment.

Duncan moved through the lobby.

The maître d' guarding the restaurant entrance, secure behind a podium, regarded Duncan with belligerent despondency as he approached. Duncan cleared his throat, introduced himself and announced he was expected. The maître d' referred to a list that rested on top of the podium, her index finger inexorably running down the many lines of names, once, twice and a third time, before stopping half way down. She flicked a brief smile on and off, and then beckoned Duncan to follow him.

The restaurant had that restful quiet usually associated with libraries and funeral parlours; in an odd way it reminded him of his home, except for the lavish fixtures and fittings. The crowd in the restaurant, clearly affluent and professional, ignored Duncan as he clumsily weaved his way through the tables, unlike the maître d' who elegantly glided.

For a moment, Duncan found himself engrossed in the décor of the restaurant: The stiff linen tablecloths which all hung an equal distance from the floor; the Victorian cutlery; the lack of crumbs on the expensive carpets. He looked twice, three times, but no matter how hard he searched he couldn't spy any food morsels; there were none to be seen on the tables, none on the lush red carpet. He began to question if the restaurant even served food.

The only restaurants Duncan visited had no shortage of crumbs, dirt and the occasional rat. This distinct lack of all these things pleased him, and he wondered what it would be like to live in such splendour on a day-to-day basis.

Ahead he spied Lucy seated at a table, her head immersed in a newspaper.

The maître d' slid the chair out and waited impatiently for Duncan to sit down. Then, with a whip of her hand, she scooped the napkin from where it sat neatly presented on the table and positioned it across Duncan's lap. Duncan mumbled a thank you.

'Good morning, Ms Smith,' said Duncan cheerily. 'Are we waiting on the others?'

There was a delay before Lucy registered his greeting. 'Call me Lucy, darling.' She folded the newspaper and placed it on the table. 'I thought for this morning's meeting it should be more personal. Just the two of us.'

At Lucy's beckoning, the waiter deferentially took their orders. Once he had done as bid, he silently departed.

'Have you seen the newspaper this morning? Shocking,' said Lucy in a dismissive manner. In a deft move, she tossed it in Duncan's direction. It flew through the air, unfolding as it did, and fell on the plate in front of him, waiting to be read.

Duncan looked down at the open newspaper. The main story on the page was headlined 'Sheol Traders Celebrate our Misery'. Duncan read the article while Lucy finished her cup of coffee and, with a discreet wave of her hand, ordered another. By the time he finished the article, she was onto her third cup.

The article focused on how the traders at Sheol Trading were photographed the previous night celebrating in grand style at one of the most exclusive restaurants in London. An anonymous source had provided details of their meals, including the final bill being in excess of fifty thousand pounds. The source went on to describe their behaviour as *'inappropriate, given these economically challenging times'*. The traders had smoked cigars, defying the smoking ban, and toward the end of the evening when they were barely coherent, they stood on the tables and placed thousand-pound bets on the outcome of a coin toss — with the loser of the toss whooping and hollering in celebration of their loss. The article concluded by recapping the chequered past of Sheol Trading; including the recent death of Gordon McBride, their CFO, and the unfortunate demise of their head trader over a year ago when, on Guy Fawkes' night, a firework veered off course and exploded in his face.

'I can understand why you're not happy,' said Duncan.

'Happy? I'm not, I'm ecstatic. This is excellent news.'

'This is good?' he asked disbelieving.

'Who do you think released this story? Our PR department! You can't buy publicity like this. I guarantee you, by the end of the day our share price will have gone up and we will have received another thousand CV's from victims, eager to be part of our family.'

'Victims?' Duncan's eyebrow rose.

'Very apt don't you think?' Lucy was pleased with herself. 'What else do you call people who would want to work for a company which encourages such irresponsible behaviour by its employees?'

The table fell silent, with only the tinkle of Lucy's cup as she placed it on its saucer.

'I don't understand,' Duncan said at last.

'What don't you understand, darling?' asked Lucy, her tone sounded almost condescending.

'Doesn't this article give Sheol Trading a bad name?'

'I most certainly hope so,' said Lucy in an authoritative tone. 'The victims, the prospective employees, they want to work for a company which will make them rich. The stock market, our investors, everybody, they want to know we will make them rich. Coverage like this, tells people exactly that. If we weren't making money, would our victims be splashing money around like this?' Lucy allowed herself a special moment of giddy, smug delight.

'I see. But isn't it,' Duncan checked himself. 'Irresponsible?'

'Irresponsible? Duncan, you disappoint me.' She feigned dismay at his remark. 'Consider for a moment the video game developers who claim it isn't their fault if a sixteen-year-old butchers people after playing their game. Are they irresponsible?'

'I really don't understand the relevance. Sorry.'

Lucy giggled. 'Of course, you don't, darling. My point is, we don't hide or distort what we are about. We are open and honest. I think that is being responsible. Yes,' she beamed at Duncan who slowly nodded his agreement.

'But… you said the article was trash.'

'No, darling, I said the article was shocking. Did you not read it? There is no mention of our share price, our quarterly results, and their use of grammar is simply appalling. What hope is there for the youth of today when the tabloids can't even get the basics right?' Lucy sipped her coffee.

Breakfast arrived at the table, putting an end to their conversation. Lucy's meal consisted of fruit and yoghurt drizzled with chocolate sauce, while Duncan ordered a traditional English breakfast with an extra sausage on the side. They discussed everything from the weather to football.

After they finished their breakfasts, the conversation shifted to business. The company's forecasted growth, its current revenue, the share price, latest acquisitions, and anything finance-related. From here they moved swiftly onto Duncan and his future with

Wollenwal & Wollenwal, and his relationship with Sheol Trading. Duncan's heart was warm with excitement and pride with Lucy's revelation that she had 'big plans' for him.

As Lucy finished her sixth cup of coffee, all trace of her smile disappeared. She reached over the side of her chair and collected another newspaper. Duncan spied the well-known tabloid masthead as Lucy handed him the newspaper.

'Is there something you need to tell me, Duncan?' she asked.

'Um, no. I don't think so,' he replied hesitantly, as he moved his plate to one side and laid the newspaper down.

He immediately noticed tomorrow's date heading the newspaper. His brow creased. His gaze moved down to the headline. Duncan swallowed audibly. Thick black font screamed: *"Kinky accountant explodes sex worker"*. The subheading generated a groan from him, it was a classic example of witticism by the editorial team: *"Accountant has a blow job"*.

Lucy ordered another cup of coffee. 'Must have been quite a night, darling?'

'No. No.' Duncan said hurriedly, his tone defensive. 'This is wrong. I didn't do this.'

Lucy convulsed with laughter. Stunned heads within the restaurant turned in their direction. 'It doesn't bother me, Duncan. I have a liberal approach to life, but your firm might not be so open-minded. This type of news is scandalous, Duncan; career-breaking.' She allowed her words to sink in as she sipped her hot, black drink. 'It was lucky for you that one of my many informants tipped me off to this. Fortunately for you, this story will never see the light of day. I have arranged for it to disappear.'

'You can do that?' he asked in a small, shocked voice.

'What can I say, Duncan? I like you. You are now part of the Sheol Trading family and, as family, we take care of each other.' She leaned across the table and gently patted his hand. His skin tingled.

'I don't know what to say.'

'You don't have to say anything. What's the point of me having all of this so-called power if I can't exercise it and do tiny favours for my friends every now and then?' She sipped again and smiled sweetly.

The waiter reappeared, seemingly from nowhere, to clear the

plates and cutlery. As quickly as he appeared, he disappeared.

'You need to be a little more careful next time. That's all I'll say on the matter. There is a reason why these types of activities happen behind closed doors.'

'No. I didn't—'

'Anyway, darling, back to work. I have made the necessary arrangements for you to be based at our head office. I need you to familiarise yourself with our operations. You are going to be a very busy man. I have big plans for you, darling.' She replaced her cup on the saucer.

Duncan, flattered by her instructions, assured Lucy he wouldn't let her down.

'You had better get a move on, darling. They are expecting you in the office at ten.'

Duncan peeked at his watch; it was nearly ten already. He drew himself upright and instinctively proffered his hand. It hung above the table for a second before he remembered her disdain for shaking hands and promptly removed it. Lucy, without looking up, gave a curt goodbye wave.

'Oh, Duncan. I nearly forgot.'

Duncan froze mid-stride.

'I have arranged for a welcome gift for you. Call it a signing-on bonus. You'll find it out front.' She smiled, raising her coffee cup to him in congratulations.

'Out front?' repeated Duncan gently.

'That is what I said.' She retrieved yet another newspaper from beneath her chair.

'Thank you.' Duncan hesitated before leaving Lucy to her editorials.

He stumbled from the restaurant, apologising profusely to those he bumped on the way. Once outside, like an excited child on Christmas morning, he quickly cast his eyes about but nothing unusual stood out. He turned and asked the hotel's porter if they were holding anything for him. The porter smiled, confirmed his name and pointed to the roadside where a man lounged against a metallic blue BMW roadster, its roof retracted.

Duncan stepped from under the cover of the canopy and approached the man.

'Mr Bottomley?' the man enquired.

'Yes, I'm Duncan Bottomley.'

The man vigorously shook Duncan's hand. 'My name is Sam; I am Ms Smith's chauffeur.' He turned and patted the bonnet of the car and then launched into a discourse of praise for the car, detailing its fuel consumption, horsepower and the many features.

Duncan glanced at his watch and impatiently moved from foot to foot. 'I'm sorry but I need to be in the office. Ms Smith said there was something here for me.'

'Yes, Mr Bottomley.' Sam patted the roadster again.

'Um, could I please have it. I need to get to the office?'

Sam tapped the roadster. 'Yes, Mr Bottomley. It's a lovely car.'

Duncan glanced at the car and back at Sam. 'Yes, it's lovely, but I do really need to get a move on. I'm very late.'

'Mr Bottomley,' Sam looked quizzical, 'the car is your signing-on bonus.'

Duncan stood stunned, almost as if he hadn't heard Sam's words, and then his jaw fell open before closing and then opening again.

'The car… is mine?' stammered Duncan.

'In all but name, Mr Bottomley. It belongs to the company but has been reserved for your exclusive use.' Sam dug his hand into his pocket, withdrew a set of keys, and deferentially handed them to him.

Duncan accepted the keys in stunned silence. He reached for the door handle and expected Sam to reach out and slap his hand. Sam stepped backwards and gestured for him to continue. Duncan opened the door and slid into the driver's seat. His hands caressed the steering wheel and absorbed the feel of the leather. Sam turned on his heels and strolled into the hotel.

The car roared to life. Duncan listened to the engine purr, shifted the gears and moved his feet. The motor gurgled, grumbled and popped, then promptly stalled: An impressive feat when you consider the car was an automatic. He tried again and, accompanied by a cacophony of horns and not so subtle verbal abuse, crawled into the flow of traffic.

His journey to Sheol Trading's office continued at a snail's pace. And, while others raged at the traffic, Duncan never stopped smiling.

17

'So,' Ballsy fixed Gilly with an icy stare. 'Three visits in less than a week. Is this a sign you are warming to us? I do hope not.'

Gilly sighed, and fell backwards into the no thrills swivel chair, built for practical purposes and not comfort. The chair rolled backwards several feet. He shuffled his feet to bring the chair back to its original position.

'Do I look happy to be here?' asked Gilly.

'How would I know? Perhaps if you removed your absurd hat, I might see your face.'

'You don't like it? That is a shame, Ballsy.'

'Balthasar. My name is Balthasar.'

'Yes, yes. Can we discuss business?' asked Gilly, his voice frustrated.

By way of reply, Ballsy simply smiled.

'I think we've made a mistake with Mr Bottomley. He is highly strung. Every time I try to speak to him, he has a panic attack,' said Gilly. 'Honestly, it is beginning to get a bit tiresome.'

'I don't think that is an unreasonable reaction considering your appearance,' Ballsy inhaled deeply. 'And there is your rather pungent body odour. Perhaps a bath every now and again would help? I am certain that is something we would all appreciate, not just Mr Bottomley.'

'I suppose it's my fault my body is decaying?'

'That's not what I'm saying, Gilgamesh. I am merely stating that if you perhaps started to make an effort to take better care of yourself, then you wouldn't have so many invertebrates residing inside you.' Ballsy screwed up his nose and stabbed a finger in the direction of Gilly's head. 'Just look at your hair. How can you live with those lice?'

'I'm a walking corpse, Ballsy,' said Gilly, his face absent of emotion. 'It's physically impossible for me to look flawless!'

'My name is Balthasar. And perfection is hardly what I'd expect from you.' Ballsy sighed deeply. 'What do you want Gilgamesh? You are keeping me from business, and not for the first time.'

Gilly inched forward in his chair. 'I have approached Mr

Bottomley twice and there are certain areas of concern we cannot continue to ignore.'

'Such as?'

'Well, for a start, he clearly has issues with dead people. He's like a walking panic alarm. Every time I broach the topic of his prospective death, I barely get two words out before he is threatening to call the police and running away.'

'As I said, perhaps a bath might allay some of his fears.'

Gilly fixed Ballsy with a baleful stare. 'I think, in light of the Succubus attack, coupled with Mr Bottomley's lack of suitability, we should reconsider our decision, before it is too late.'

'How many times are we going to discuss this? We adhere to the SAINT2[*] methodology here and accordingly all decisions must be meticulously planned and documented. These decisions take centuries to be made; you cannot simply change them on a whim. Constantly whining and whinging about it serves little purpose. In the meantime, you have your instructions so please follow them.'

Gilly wrapped his hands around the edge of the chair's seat and thrust himself forward. He tried to steady himself.

'When will you listen?' Gilly cried in exasperation. 'We don't have time for your princely methodology! We have to act, Ballsy, before it's too late.'

'It's Balthasar!'

'Fine. Have it your way.' Gilly shot a sharp look at Ballsy. Ballsy's head had dipped as he watched his fingers dance across the surface of the table, typing in commands. Gilly sighed and hobbled from the room. The audacity and pomposity of Ballsy knew no bounds.

At the bottom of the stairs he gazed at the sign marked 'exit'

---

[*] Authors Note: SAINT2 stands for Souls and Afterlife IN a Totalitarian environment; the two refers to the second major version of this method. SAINT2 is a structured approach to managing the afterlife and provides a clearly defined framework. It is considered one of the main drivers in converting Purgatory from a swift moving entity into the bureaucratic and process obsessed shambles of today.

which pointed to the left. His eyes followed the direction of the sign and, at the end of the short corridor, he could see Ms Fairchild at her desk. He turned right and shambled through numerous long well-lit corridors until arriving at a plain wooden door. The sign on the door read, 'After Death Services'. He paused, his shoulders slumped, and then, with a determined push, he flung the door open to reveal a room of extraordinary size; a room which was nothing like he remembered from his last visit.

In a dazed and confused state, he shuffled into the room and cast his eyes about the room, consuming the chaotic scene before him.

There was a constant juddering commotion which was suddenly punctuated by a thunderous crash, causing Gilly to hop backwards. A wall collapsed, causing the recently settled particles to swirl upwards and linger in the air like a low-level cumulus cloud.

The bored looking albino was seated behind a table that had been pushed into a corner. Surprisingly, and in stark contrast to Gilly's previous departure, the albino looked far more depressed now.

The room, which had once been no bigger than a cloakroom, was now a cathedral sized room, wallpapered with scaffolding. Men dressed in bright orange jackets and hardhats swung sledgehammers and carted wheelbarrows of rubble.

Huddled at the far side of the newly formed hall was a group of about twenty suit-clad people. At the front of this mass, scrawling on a whiteboard, was Gordon McBride.

Gilly, his jaw ajar, hobbled towards the albino. 'What is going on here?'

The albino tried to bury his head into the desk.

'Hello. Remember me?' said Gilly, his hand swaying from side to side in front of the albino's face.

Slowly the albino stirred. The blank expression transformed into one of recognition. 'Oh, it's you, Sir! I'm sorry. I wasn't expecting you. I thought you were part of the work detail. Um, actually, Sir, I'm not allowed to speak to you. I have orders to notify Deceased Resources if you show up.'

'In that case, it's probably best we keep my being here our little secret. Yes?' Gilly nodded his head and waited for the albino to reciprocate. 'So, what is going on?' asked Gilly.

'The recently deceased you met with has started a law firm, Sir.'

'Yes, I heard that, but what is all this?'

'It caught everybody by surprise, but there's no such thing as a law firm here. He claimed the lack of legal resources infringed his deceased rights and demanded they provide him with the necessary resources to help him prepare his appeal. They refused his request at first but then he gave an interview to 'The Soul' newspaper saying he was being discriminated against because of his religion. I guess they didn't want to make things worse, so they gave in and said he could do whatever he wanted to do as long as he didn't leave this office.'

Gilly shook his head. 'And all this?'

'Well, he then hired all these construction workers to make the office larger.'

Gilly stared incredulously at the scene. 'This is insane. Deceased rights? This is Purgatory. He's dead!'

'They are aware of that, Sir, but they think it would be politically incorrect to deny him his rights solely on the basis of him being dead.'

'But he has no rights!'

'DR is hopping mad, Sir. They don't know what to do with him.' The albino paused. 'And between you and I, Sir, I don't think they like you. I did as you asked, and requested they transfer me, but they denied my request, Sir.'

'That doesn't mean they don't like me,' said Gilly in a defensive tone.

'When I told them, it was a favour for you, they said they would rather spend eternity with diarrhoea than do you a favour.'

'I can see how that looks.' Gilly focused on a distant point, then shook his head and flashed a wan, impish smile. 'Clearly they're not familiar with the concept of employee engagement. I will sort this out, I'm sure it's a minor misunderstanding.'

Gilly tapped the desk with his gloved fingers, looked across at the congregation of suits and distractedly waved goodbye to the albino, before shuffling across the cavernous room.

Gordon stood at the front of the audience, his hands held high as if in papal benediction, sermonising the audience on the need for diligence in the tasks that lay ahead, because if they were successful, they would establish a precedent and the floodgates would open wide and millions, if not billions of deceased aggrieved by their deaths would be seeking justice.

As Gordon wrapped up his sermon, he noticed Gilly at the rear of the room. He raised his hands, and, like the Red Sea in response to Moses, the crowd parted. He shook hands and thanked his colleagues for their time as he made his way through the newly formed corridor.

'Impressive isn't it?' said Gordon as he stood to one side of Gilly.

'What are you doing?' asked Gilly, his voice at once incredulous and despairing.

'Doing? It's quite simple really. I am creating the offices of McBride & McBride, Purgatory's first ever law firm.'

'McBride & McBride?' said Gilly with an eyebrow raised.'

'It's standard practise for law firms to have multiple names. Besides I don't think "McBride" has the required gravitas. "McBride & McBride", is insurmountably better. You see my point?'

'Yes,' said Gilly, his eyes wandering around the recently created vaulted ceiling.

'So, have they sent you to make a settlement offer?' asked Gordon, rubbing his hands with glee.

'No. They told me not to talk to you.'

'Oh.' Gordon's face fell.

'You started your own law firm?'

'Yes. Are you impressed? You should be. You were quite correct in your assertion that there are no law firms in Purgatory. No law firms, no florists and, surprisingly, no betting shops, yet they are everywhere amongst the living, how do you explain that? Do you know there are now more betting shops on the high streets than pubs? A shocking turn of events.'

'And your point is?' asked Gilly.

'No point, just an observation. Pubs are a place where people can socialise and betting shops, well, they're a place where people don't socialise. Actually, come to think of it, there are no pubs here either.' Gordon turned to his flock of acolytes and in a commanding voice said, 'We forgot pubs. Can one of you add that to the list?'

'What are you doing?' asked Gilly exasperated.

'Quite simple. Once I learned there were no law firms available to represent me, I decided to start my own. I intend to extricate myself from this predicament that I find myself in now and return to my rightful place amongst the living. You see I was — sorry, I meant to say I am — a stratospherically important person. Until my unscheduled death, which was both extremely inconvenient and a violation of the contract I signed, I was, sorry, I am the Chief Financial Officer for Sheol Trading, the world's most powerful company.'

'And again, your point is?'

'My point is, I shouldn't be dead. There are plenty of less important people who can die.'

'That might be true, but they didn't sign the contract with Hell, Mr McBride. You did.'

'True. But you tell me where in the contract did it state that a consequence of my actions would be the premature termination of my life? Purgatory were negligent in not advising me as such.' Gordon folded his arms and pushed out his chest as if he was a human exclamation mark for his own uttered words.

'Yes. I know. Poor you. We already covered that. Now who are these people?' said Gilly with a shake of his head and a wave of his arm towards the other suited people.

'Recently deceased lawyers, mostly. Oh, and a couple of paralegals. They jumped at the chance to join me. Understandably, of course. When they were alive, they thought they were miserable in their lives and, at times they wished they were dead. Then, one day, they died and found themselves in Purgatory. Now they truly know what being miserable is.'

Gilly shrugged his shoulders and nodded. He couldn't disagree with that. 'I don't suppose you would stop all this and just accept you are dead?'

'By God man, why would I do that?' Gordon spat.

'Maybe because we are busy trying to fend off a hostile takeover and don't have time for your idiotic antics?'

'I see. So now you are saying I am an idiot as well as being deluded. I hope you realise that is libellous. You are making this far too easy for me.'

Gilly glared at Gordon. He gritted his teeth to prevent further words from escaping, then swung his leg round and shambled towards the exit. Abruptly, he stopped mid-stride and looked over his shoulder at Gordon.

'Far be it from me to correct you, Mr McBride. You being the lawyer and all,' Gilly said calmly. 'But libel is when somebody defames you in writing. Slander is when somebody verbally says something like "You are a self-deluded, idiotic, pompous fool".' He turned towards the exit and as he passed the albino, he gave a curt wave and muttered something indecipherable before leaving the room with a flourish of his long coat.

Gordon shrugged his shoulders and sauntered back to the group. With a wipe of his sleeve he removed the previous contents of the whiteboard. Then scrawled across it, 'TAKEOVER — WHO, WHY AND HOW?' The gathered lawyers, as one, jotted it down on their respective pads of paper.

18

Duncan stood at the base of Sheol Trading's building; his back arched as his eyes traced the building's length. It was one of the tallest, most magnificent buildings in London, and next to the surrounding buildings it stood out like the proverbial sore thumb.

Sheol Trading occupied the top ten floors of the 'Towering Innuendo', as the press had dubbed it. It was unique in its design, for despite dominating the skyline, pedestrians were oblivious to its existence until they were directly underneath it. Passers-by would walk along, humming a tune or chatting on their mobile phones, then suddenly stop as they became aware of the shadow across their existence. Gazing skywards exclamations were often made along the lines of: 'Where did that giant penis come from?'

Duncan herded his stray thoughts into line and remembered the time before he scampered into the building. With his mouth ajar and his eyes jiggling in their sockets, he tried to combine walking quickly while trying to take everything in.

The reception area was plastered with digital displays and large plasma televisions which constantly highlighted the health of the company, and standing in the middle was a man who, at the risk of stating the obvious, was plain and seemingly two-dimensional. He appeared to be in his mid-twenties and was so skinny he looked as if he'd give you a paper cut if you touched him. A clipboard was tucked under his arm and a device with a pulsating blue light protruded from his ear. He hurried to Duncan's side and introduced himself as Wesley, Lucy's personal assistant, and he had been tasked with the responsibility to greet and escort Duncan to his office.

Duncan nodded, and followed the under-nourished man, only pausing to look at a sculpture by an artist whose abilities might have been questionable but there could be no doubting his taxidermist skills.

The abundance of company information was a common theme throughout the building. In the elevator a red LED display ran along the top of all four sides providing the company's real time share price; it always indicated the price had gone up. By the time Duncan reached his new office on the twenty-fifth floor, his head throbbed from the bombardment of company information. It had been a visual and verbal assault which left his brain reeling with statistics and outrageous claims. He sought solace in the toilet, but the barrage continued with LCD displays mounted on the back of the cubicle doors and above the sinks, which all constantly ran 'Sheol News', their company's own in-house news broadcasting channel, which aimed to 'bring you, the employee, the very latest on Sheol Trading'.

Duncan found the experience of sitting on a toilet and staring at a beaming face disconcerting.

Over the coming days, he found the entire toilet experience more and more discomfiting. For a start, the toilets were unisex; he was embarrassed by the thought a woman might be using the stall next to him, especially considering the sounds which quite often emanated from his bottom when nature called. But what he found most disturbing was the blatant drug taking. Groups of staff regularly congregated at the bathroom sinks to snort lines of cocaine. It appeared to be a running joke within the office; people would hop up from their desks, wink and exclaim loudly they were off for their 'coke break'. Management appeared oblivious to it all — either that or they were happy to allow it. Either way, for Duncan, it had proven to be unnerving.

Duncan had been provided with an office the size of a small flat, with floor-to-ceiling windows which provided him with a spectacular view of the city. The first time he entered the office he was struck by the view, which at once filled him with awe and dread. Unfortunately for Duncan, he did not like heights, hence his repositioning of the furniture, to allow him to sit with his back to the window and as far away as physically possible.

Soon after settling in, Wesley reappeared and suggested, although it felt more like a command, that Duncan follow him; it was time for the grand tour of the company.

Wesley reverently introduced Duncan to countless numbers of people, most of whom were standing by a water cooler. Others sat at their grand desks surfing the Internet, while some were in the middle of important meetings where the ultimate objective was to arrange even more important meetings. There were also a few who delighted in throwing an American football between cubicles, Duncan quickly realised it was important to stoop when crossing the office in order to avoid these low-flying balls. Interestingly enough, and what was most strange to Duncan, was despite the countless members of staff he had been introduced to, not a single one appeared to be in the act of doing anything constructive. It seemed all anybody did was talk about how busy they were, without actually working.

The floor below was the trading floor, and it was a sight to behold, hosting a frenetic whirlwind of activity. Row after row of polished red tables, anodized aluminium seats and understated modern sculptures, and the walls were lined with flat screen televisions. Traders ran backwards and forwards, hurling abuse at one another and barking orders at squawk boxes, accompanied by the constant shrill of ringing telephones. Mute televisions were everywhere, displaying a mixture of business news and sports. Despite the charged atmosphere, it did, however, appear to be a controlled chaos.

Duncan hesitated at the threshold of the floor, not wanting to wander around, eyeing the activity. Wesley grabbed him by the elbow and together they ploughed into the heaving mass.

One thing was for sure, all the traders wanted to meet Duncan. No doubt about that.

Word of Duncan's arrival had spread instantaneously, and people dropped whatever they were doing and queued for the opportunity to shake his hand. He was treated like royalty, like a celebrity, or a man who had won the lottery. Duncan even entertained the thought some of the women — and even a couple of the men — had been flirting with him, but as he didn't exactly know what flirting entailed, he dismissed the thoughts. He made polite small talk and enquired as to what each person did, and all but a few answered: 'Make money. We're always making money'.

Two hours later, as his quick tour of the twenty-fifth and twenty-fourth floors wound up, the device in Wesley's ear pulsed red. His hand sprung to his ear. 'Good morning, Ms Smith,' he glanced at his watch. 'Sorry, I mean "good afternoon".'

He nodded his head in silent agreement, occasionally grunting. 'Yes… Fine… Ah ha… Yes… He is with me now… Of course… Ah ha… Yes, I will do that… Thank you… Yes… Goodbye, Ms Smith.'

Wesley turned to Duncan and corralled him towards the centre of the building and into a waiting elevator.

'Lucy has asked you to join her and Oliver for lunch. This way please,' said Wesley. He leaned across Duncan and pressed the button marked thirty-three then shuffled to the rear of the elevator. Instrumental music played softly, a familiar tune which Duncan found himself humming along to. Moments later, a friendly male voice resounded its canned welcome to the executive management floor, and then the lift doors opened with a ping. Duncan looked over at Wesley who gestured for Duncan to proceed. He entered into a naturally lit, Spartan lobby area.

Wesley pranced past Duncan, crossing to an elaborate wooden door on the left-hand wall. He lightly tapped on the door and waited a few moments before pushing it open. With a sweep of his arm he beckoned Duncan to enter.

Duncan hesitated before stepping through the doorway and into an office that was easily four times the size of his own. At one end of the room nearest him, black leather sofas had been positioned into a square seating area. In the middle of the room stood a dark wooded bar area, stocked with every drink Duncan could imagine; behind the bar a man in a white suit with black bow tie stood to attention. At the other end of the room a large, intricately carved desk with Lucy on the far side and Oliver seated to one side. They both smiled as Duncan entered the room.

Lucy thanked Wesley and waved for Duncan to join her. At the desk were three plates of sushi. Duncan's stomach somersaulted at the sight of the raw fish.

'One moment, Duncan,' said Lucy, motioning for Oliver to continue.

'Where was I? Ah, yes. The annual review process has concluded. Staff are anxious to hear if there will be any redundancies this year and, if so, how many?'

Lucy leaned back in her chair and turned to face Duncan. 'What do you think Duncan? What shall we do?'

Duncan glanced at both of them and stammered, 'Um, well, some people are saying we're in a recession, but your company is profitable...' His words trailed off as he struggled to think of what to say.

'Excellent, Duncan.' Lucy smiled as the fingers in her palm

curled outwards. 'You're absolutely right. No business can ignore these times of economic uncertainty and must prepare accordingly.'

Duncan's lips parted; he was about to point out that wasn't what he meant.

'Excellent.' Lucy turned to Oliver. 'You heard Duncan, Oliver. Times are tough. We have an obligation to our shareholders to take all steps to remain profitable during these difficult economic times. Let's make the bottom, say, twenty-five percent redundant. Effective immediately.'

Oliver scribbled out a quick calculation on his notepad. 'That's about four thousand employees then, give or take a few hundred.'

Duncan's jaw flapped about in quiet protest.

'What else is on the agenda?'

'Bonuses,' said Oliver.

'Morale is important during these times; wouldn't you agree Duncan?'

Duncan nodded.

'Increase bonuses by thirty percent from last year,' said Lucy.

'But… You just made people redundant,' said Duncan.

Lucy turned her head and frowned. 'And your point is, Duncan? Our employees are our greatest assets; we need to retain them and, in this worrying climate, the best way to do this is by appealing to their pockets. Or would you rather they joined our competition, darling?'

'Um, no. Sorry. You're absolutely right.'

'Now what else is there, Oliver?'

'We have received a request from the FSA to provide them with information concerning their Insider Trading investigation. How shall we respond?' Oliver ticked off a bullet point on a yellow pad of paper next to him.

'The usual. Ignore them, then invite them to our corporate box at whatever sport they fancy,' Lucy said with a wave of her hand. She looked down at her plate of sushi, caressed her lips with her tongue and beckoned Duncan to sit.

'That…'

'What is it, Duncan?' asked Lucy.

'I… don't think you can do that.' Duncan lowered himself into the chair. 'I think there are laws against hospitality… Bribes.'

Lucy tittered. 'Oh, Duncan, you really are a treasure. You have so much to learn. We can do whatever we like. There are ways around everything. The law is merely a guideline, a suggestion if you will.' Lucy dropped her chopsticks and fixed Duncan with a glittering smile. 'Lesson number one: We have hundreds of lawyers working for us whose sole purpose is to create red tape. It would literally cost the government hundreds of millions to pursue us legally, and when they lost, they would have to pay our highly inflated costs and explain to the taxpayers why they have to increase the cost of their beer to recoup their costs. And, even if they did manage to succeed, which is impossible, we would simply keep the action tied-up in the courts until a new government is appointed in and then, after a few well-placed donations, the problem would simply disappear.' Lucy swallowed a salmon nigiri in one gulp 'During the financial crisis, did any banker go to jail? Of course not, the government knows it has to play nicely with us. You'll soon understand, Duncan.'

'Bloody Mary's all round?' asked Oliver, raising his hand to attract the attention of the bartender.

'Excellent,' tittered Lucy.

'It's actually a little early for me,' said Duncan, in what he realised was quite a pathetic voice.

'Don't be silly, darling. There's always time for a drink.'

The bartender was a flurry of activity; his hands blurred, bottles flew, and glasses clinked as cubes of ice were deposited in them. In what felt like seconds, the bartender presented the drinks to the table. With a deft move of his hands, he shifted the glasses from the tray to the table, spun them across the table in each person's direction, before bowing and backing away to the bar, where he stood to attention awaiting the next instruction.

'Military training. Wonderful, isn't it?' said Lucy, tilting her head towards the bartender. 'Thank you for joining us, Duncan. How is everything going?' Lucy sipped her cocktail.

'Oh. It's… It's interesting, Ms Smith.'

'Lucy, darling.'

'Sorry, Lucy. There is so much going on. It's all a bit overwhelming.' Duncan considered raising the issue of drugs but, after a few seconds of contemplation, with the words hanging on his lips, he decided it wasn't his place to speak — the last thing he wanted to do was jeopardise the new account on his first day.

'I appreciate some things may seem a little — how to say? — untoward, but we do like to do things differently here, Duncan. It's important for us to encourage individuality amongst our employees. What we do can be very stressful, and it's important for our employees to have fun as well.'

Duncan nodded.

'It also makes good business sense,' said Oliver, his voice interrupting Duncan's thought. 'A recent survey amongst the staff showed productivity was thirty percent higher as a result of our initiatives.'

Lucy dunked her chopsticks with some tentacles gripped between them into a pot of soya sauce. Duncan watched as she sucked in the final tentacle like a piece of al-dente spaghetti. His stomach twisted and turned.

'And how do you like your office, Duncan? You may not be aware but it's the third largest in the building, after Oliver's and mine, of course,' said Lucy.

'It is much more than I expected. Thank you. The view is…'

'Breath taking,' said Oliver, not knowing Duncan had another, less kind, word in mind.

'And the car?' asked Lucy as she drained her cocktail.

The pitch of Duncan's voice quavered. 'It's stunning. I've never actually owned a car before.'

'It is the first of many wonderful things to come your way. You'll see. Do you remember what I told you at breakfast, Duncan? We're family here, and family take care of each other.' Lucy collected a manila folder containing a set of spreadsheets from her in-tray and handed them to Duncan.

'Would you be a dear and have a look at this for me. I can't make heads or tails of them, all those misapplied amounts. Be a dear and get rid of them? I don't care how.'

Duncan opened the folder. His eyes darted left and right across the sheet, before he retrieved a green pen from his pocket and started scribbling notes across the first sheet.

'Not now, Duncan. Later,' said Lucy, her voice and expression tired.

'Sorry.' Duncan slid the papers back into the folder and placed it on his lap.

Lucy and Oliver's attention turned to their plates of sushi. Duncan frowned at the gobbets of fish; he wasn't a fan. It wasn't that he found the taste offensive, but the aroma turned his stomach. The odour of raw fish conjured images in his mind of nasty, unhygienic bacteria using his stomach as a nest to plant their eggs, where they would grow into mutant creatures and explode forth in the manner made popular by the Alien movies. Despite believing this would happen, armed with a fork, Duncan stabbed at a piece of what he hoped would be cooked fish. He studied it and sniffed it tentatively.

'Duncan,' said Lucy, her tone serious. 'We have an important matter to discuss with you.'

He quickly lowered his fork to the table, relieved to be given time to procrastinate with the sushi. 'Yes, of course.'

'You may not be aware of this, Duncan, but last week our Chief Financial Officer died in a most unfortunate accident. His death has left a gaping hole in our board.' Lucy waited for Duncan to signal his understanding. 'I know it may seem to be a touch insensitive but we, as a business, have limited time to grieve for such a loss, you understand? It is our priority to always move our business forward, and we can only do this by identifying and appointing his replacement.' The corner of her lips curled upwards. 'Can you see where I am going with this, Duncan?'

Duncan sat considering her words for a moment. Thoughts of inadequacy entered his head: Had he dozed briefly and missed a snippet of conversation, or was it a case of him not being the brightest star in the sky?

'No. I'm sorry, Ms Smith, I can't.'

Lucy flashed her award-winning smile. Her teeth immaculately white. 'Lucy, Duncan; please call me Lucy.' She cast a quick look at Oliver before turning back to Duncan. 'We have decided you should be Sheol Trading's new CFO.'

The words hung in the air for an interminable time, almost as if Duncan could have reached out and taken hold of them. Lucy and Oliver exchanged smiles. Duncan sat there, unmoved, his jaw slightly ajar.

'Duncan?' Oliver said.

'Me?' he muttered at last.

'Yes,' said Oliver. 'We have been waiting for a candidate of your calibre for quite some time. Congratulations!'

'But I can't. I... I work for Wollenwal & Wollenwal.'

'Is it a case of money?' asked Lucy.

'No. No. Just that... it would be a conflict of interest?'

Lucy ignored Duncan's concern. 'What does a partner of a top professional firm earn these days, Oliver?'

'Depends on whether they were a salaried partner or an equity partner,' said Oliver. Lucy's glare scolded him. 'Well, I believe an equity partner would earn in the vicinity of six hundred thousand to one, two million pounds,' said Oliver.

'Not bad,' said Lucy, her lips pursed. 'Well, I believe a man of your considerable ability would be worth at least twice that much. Your talent is wasted at Wollenwal & Wollenwal. I am prepared to offer you a salary of four million pounds, plus 100% bonus, and the usual executive perks of course.'

'Four million?' choked Duncan.

Lucy feigned affront. 'Not enough? I told you Oliver he would be tough at negotiating.' She studied him intently across the table. 'Very well. Five million pounds then.'

Duncan's jaw quivered then fell open in a cartoonish manner; all that was needed to complete the scene was for his tongue to unfurl like the red carpet at a movie premiere.

There was a long silence, broken only by the sound of Oliver's clumsy use of chopsticks.

'Duncan?' asked Lucy.

'I... I don't know what to say.' Duncan gulped down his Bloody Mary, his face contorted.

'Is that a yes,' said Lucy.

'Yes. But I... I... don't know. I am flattered. You have no idea how much. But... I don't know.'

'Do you appreciate what we are offering you, Duncan? You will be one of the most important men in the city of London. You will receive invites from the Prime Minister to join her for tea at Downing Street. You will live the life only a few can ever hope to experience.'

'I appreciate that. I do but... I'm not sure I'm not even a partner at Wollenwal & Wollenwal.'

'Gordon, our last CFO, was a regional accountant for a small retail bank when we hired him. We look for people with...

potential. And you, dear Duncan, have unlimited potential.'

Duncan's cheeks turned a vibrant red tinge. His head lolled for a moment. 'I really need to think about this. I will need to speak with the partners, legally they may have a problem with this.'

'I doubt that very much.' Lucy patted the table top. 'You take your time. Think about it, speak to whoever you need to, and when you are ready, let us know.' Her tone was friendly and warm, as it had always been, but, despite this, Duncan knew lunch had come to an end and he had to leave.

Duncan collected the papers from his lap, thanked Lucy and Oliver for their kind offer and for their time, and in a limp, child-like fashion, waved goodbye. He stepped away from the desk, turned and padded to the door.

'Oh, Duncan,' said Lucy. His head swivelled in Lucy's direction. 'You really need to do something about your attire. A man of your importance should dress the part. Wait one moment.' She pressed a button on her phone and almost immediately the door to the room sprung open and her assistant, Wesley, charged in.

'Wesley, be a dear, will you, and speak to Jonathan at Baker, Bygrave and Palomar. Tell them, I am sending Duncan to see them this afternoon to be fitted for some suits and shirts. Have them put it on our account.'

Wesley jotted down her instructions, bowed and left the room. The door closed quietly behind him.

'Lovely. I know their name sounds like a law firm, but they are master tailors on Saville Row. I recommend them to all my friends. They do some wonderful work, especially with Egyptian cotton.'

Oliver's head bobbed in agreement.

A flood of gratitude was about to cascade from Duncan's mouth, but Lucy silenced him with a wave of her hand and a curt flick of her wrist. He knew he was dismissed.

<h1 style="text-align:center">19</h1>

Duncan spent the afternoon doing his best impersonation of a scarecrow at the shop of Baker, Bygrave and Palomar on Saville Row; not what he would normally consider to be a constructive use of his time, but today was different.

The store was resplendent in its old-world charm. Mahogany leather club chairs dotted the room, interspersed with suit clad mannequins and fabric books. A small counter stood off to one side of the room and by the old-fashioned register, which occupied half of this desk, was a sign that read: 'Credit and Debit cards politely refused'. The walls were lined with dark wood, and the distinct smell of cigar smoke hung in the air.

His cheeks ached from grimacing non-stop during the two-hour fitting session. He was unaccustomed to the fuss being made over him — his usual experience with shop assistants left him feeling like a leper with particularly bad body odour.

He found the whole experience surreal, yet strangely comforting.

One of the tailors had hovered around him the entire time, measuring and scratching chalk lines over the sheets of fabric which hung loosely from his body. The scissors in the tailor's hand clipped and snipped, their blades glinting under the room's fluorescent light. Then at the end, when the tailor stepped back and nodded, Duncan peeked in the mirror and was pleasantly surprised to see the draped cloth now bore the semblance of a suit.

The tailor, content with his work, thrust two bags upon Duncan and bade him farewell.

***

Despite his best efforts to resist, Duncan found the old-world charm of the tailors intoxicating and, as he stood in the comfort of his sitting room, he looked forward to emptying the bags which rested on the collapsed soufflé that people occasionally mistook for a sofa.

Like a giddy schoolchild he spilled the bags. There were several pairs of 'Bel y Cia' boxers, long black socks and crisp cotton shirts. He fingered the material, rubbing it between his fingers, and almost swooning at the quality.

Under normal circumstances, Duncan had neither the time nor the inclination to purchase new clothes, but he found himself surprisingly willing to reconsider his stance, especially when faced with the lavish attention money bought from these shops.

After considering it for the briefest of moments, Duncan drew the curtains at the bay window, and found himself modelling his new acquisitions for an audience of one — himself. The shirt felt soft against his skin; the boxers were fitted but not too tight, preventing anything from swinging free; and the socks ended below his kneecap, long enough to prevent any downward slippage.

A monotone sound, reminiscent of a mosquito, startled him. He glared at his mobile phone pulsating on the coffee table.

'Hello?' whispered Duncan.

'Hello. May I speak to Duncan Bottomley?'

'Yes. Speaking.'

'Ah, Duncan. It's Harold Wilson here. I'm sorry to bother you, I just wanted to see how your first day went?'

Already Duncan found the voice on the other end of the phone grating. 'Hi Harold. No… No problem at all. I meant to call you but got… distracted. Um. It's been an incredible day, really.'

'Really?' said Harold, his tone one of surprise and curiosity. 'What happened?'

'It started with breakfast at the Ritz. Then Lucy, sorry, Ms Smith, gave me use of one their company's convertibles to drive around in.' Duncan's mouth was an out-of-control car, racing to get the words out. 'I was shown around the office, and they do things very differently to what I expected. I had lunch with Lucy and Oliver, sushi, in the boardroom. And then, and I want to assure you I haven't said yes, but they offered me the role of Chief Financial Officer. I told them I need to speak with the partnership first, I'm not sure if it's legal even.'

Harold made a choking noise. There was a long silence before Harold spoke. 'Really?'

Duncan detected a hint of concern in Harold's voice, but his mouth was on a roll and wasn't about to stop, what with so much to say and so little time. 'Um, yes. Then this afternoon they sent me to these tailors on Saville Row to get fitted for suits and shirts. They've been incredibly generous. The boxers, they're so comfortable and, get this, they have two mother-of-pearl buttons on the waistband.'

'Really?'

'Yes!' said Duncan. 'Can you believe it?'

There was a long pause. 'Duncan, please don't take this the wrong way, but I am a little concerned?' Harold chose his words carefully. 'We have just been appointed their auditing firm and… frankly, none of this makes sense. For the time being, you need to remember that you are responsible for auditing them and, you do need to remain impartial. The fact they are lavishing you with these gifts could be seen as exerting some type of influence over you. I need to look into this—'

The doorbell in Duncan's flat sounded out its poor excuse of a ring, consisting of a series of limp, flaccid and impotent toots and beeps.

'I'm sorry, Harold. Somebody is at the door. Can you wait one minute?'

'Yes, that's fine, Duncan. We can talk tomorrow. Don't worry about this. I am sure it's nothing to be concerned with. Just me looking for conspiracies.' Harold's tone instantly lightened and his voice no longer jarred Duncan's ears; it even began to border on normal sounding.

Duncan stabbed a button on his phone's screen, cursing the small buttons. He dropped the phone onto the sofa and ran for his front door, bounding down the stairs three at a time, panting heavily and bent at the waist he flung the door open.

'Hello! Fancy meeting you here,' said Gilly as he flicked a long white worm to one side then banged his palm against his ear.

'You again?' Duncan shook his head in disbelief. 'You're like a bad smell. Actually, you do smell bad.'

Gilly's head tilted up and down but remained shrouded in the shadows of the hat's brim. 'No need to get personal,' Gilly said, and then noticed Duncan's attire. 'Do you have a thing for only wearing underwear?' asked Gilly pointing at Duncan's semi-nude frame.

'What?' said Duncan, whipping his hands out in front of him in the hope they would provide some measure of protection. For the briefest of moments, he once again admired the quality of the shirt and the comfort provided by the boxers.

Gilly chuckled and inhaled loudly. 'Seriously, we need to talk.'

'I've got nothing to say. Leave me alone… please. I'll call the police.'

'I'm dead, not a serial killer. Look, we have to talk. I'm just going to keep asking, it's not like I have anything better to do.'

'No offence, but you're crazy.' Duncan waved his arms in a histrionic gesture and scowled.

'You're such a deadest. What is your problem? Do you think having a dead person in your house devalue it? I've got news for you, living opposite a cemetery won't help the price.'

'Duncannnn,' a voice hissed.

Duncan's stared over Gilly's left shoulder in the direction of the voice. The hedge separating his property from the road blocked his view. He turned and regarded Gilly with furrowed brows. 'Is this some kind of joke?'

Gilly shrugged his shoulders. 'This has nothing to do with me.'

'Duncannnn… Play with me.'

Duncan's eyes narrowed. 'I'm calling the police.'

'Are you going to call your Mummy too?' joked Gilly.

They both took two steps and leaned forward until their bodies hung out over the footpath. The final rays of sunshine bathed the street in an orange glow, while shadows from the tombstones snaked across the road. The street was empty.

Duncan straightened his body and stepped out onto the path. From the end of the street came a scratching noise. Duncan turned to survey the garbage bins. Nothing… And then…

From the midst of the strewn rubbish emerged a small tan coloured dog, of comparable size to a large rat or ferret, with a feather duster for a tail, and a thick pink collar dotted with spikes around its neck.

'It's a Chihuahua,' said Duncan smiling.

Gilly's gloved hand grabbed Duncan's elbow and pulled it towards him. He whispered: 'That's a killer.'

Duncan glared at Gilly and wrenched his arm free from Gilly's grip. 'What is your problem?'

'Apart from being dead?' said Gilly. 'That's not a Chihuahua.'

The dog yelped and pranced towards them; its tail rocked from side to side in time to each step.

'Personally, I don't think a Chihuahua is a dog. Listen to its bark. They're more like a giant rat if you ask me, but technically speaking it is a dog.'

The dog stopped in its tracks and curled its lips.

'Oh. No. Now you've done it. You've upset it.'

'What are you talking about? What? You're afraid of that,' scoffed Duncan.

Thunder rumbled loudly, and oddly enough it sounded like it had come from the dog. Duncan shook his head; he must have been mistaken. He looked again at the dog, then at Gilly, his expression conveying one big question mark.

In a quiet voice, Gilly continued. 'Listen to me. That's not a Chihuahua. That is Cerberus.'

'Sorry?' said Duncan.

'Cerberus. You know, the guard dog of Hell.' Gilly kept his eyes on the dog. 'You know Hell, the company who is trying to take over the company I work for? You know, the bad guys! The really, really bad guys.'

'Wait. You think, that dog, is the guard dog for hell? You're crazier than I thought!' Duncan's voice was fast approaching a glass shattering pitch.

'Oh, sorry. When was the last time you visited Hell?'

'This is madness. You need help?'

Gilly sighed. 'Now is not the time, Duncan.' He gestured towards the dog with his head as if greeting it.

The dog, with a proud, pompous walk, moved towards them. Its tail wagged with increasing intensity, and then it stopped a few metres from them.

'This is ridiculous,' said Duncan.

The Chihuahua smiled with what appeared to be a human smile. Duncan bent at the waist for a closer look. No, he had been mistaken, it wasn't a smile, more a smirk, and an evil one at that.

Duncan swallowed. He had a bad feeling about this.

The fading sunlight glinted from a drop of drool which delicately but disgustingly hung from one of the dog's canine teeth. A shiver sprang to life at the base of Duncan's spine and ricocheted up to his skull.

'Don't make any sudden moves,' said Gilly from the corner of his mouth. 'Slowly walk backwards, keep your eyes on the dog and when I say run, you run like your life depends on it. And by the way, it does.'

Duncan nodded and started to inch his way towards his building. 'Yeah, okay, it's probably for the best. You know, rabies and all.'

The dog panted, wagged his tail and hopped forward.

'But it does look harmless.' Duncan as he paused in his tracks.

'What are you doing? Don't stop,' said Gilly in a loud whisper.

Duncan smiled. 'Look, this is ridiculous. It's a small, annoying dog. Some would say it's cute.'

'Why did you say the C word?' Gilly's shoulders slumped.

'Huh?' said Duncan.

'Time to play,' said the Chihuahua, its voice deep and guttural.

Duncan stared at the dog, stunned by what he thought he had heard. If time had allowed, he would have been captivated by the sight of its eyes glowing bright red

'What a great party trick'

The dog drew back, a tuft of hair on its neck stood on end, and then it lunged forward. Its claws churned up the road causing a shower of gravel to trail behind it. Duncan screeched, spun on his heels and sprinted for his door, glancing behind as he ran. Each time he looked back the dog had grown in size. First it doubled in size, then it tripled, and it continued to get bigger. Previously unseen muscles popped out and smoke leaked from its nostrils.

In the doorway ahead he could see Gilly waiting, gesturing for him to run faster.

From behind, Duncan felt hot breath bathing his back, and the distinct odour of a barbeque tickled his nostrils. As Duncan dived through the door, Gilly slammed it shut. A mere moment later the door splintered and cracked, again and again. Its hinges buckled but held fast as splinters of wood sprayed through the hallway.

Then there was silence.

Duncan, splayed on the floor, brought himself up to a seated position and noticed a plume of smoke behind him followed by a distinct heat. He tore at his shirt. Buttons popped as he ripped it from his body and let it fall to the ground. He spun around in time to see his shirt engulfed in flames and then devolve into a primordial blob of goo.

Duncan spun on his heel and futilely craned his neck for a view of his back. 'Is my back burned?' he asked finally.

'Nothing permanent, just some blistering.'

'That shirt was expensive,' moaned Duncan.

'I don't like your chances of getting a refund for it,' deadpanned Gilly.

Duncan glared at Gilly. 'What the hell is going on?'

'Oh, so now you want to talk?' Gilly took an exasperated breath. 'It is all rather straightforward. Cerberus wanted to play, but let me tell you, its version of playing might not be yours; it's not friendly. Personally, I don't think he gets out enough, all that guarding the gates of Hell and all. But what were you thinking, using the C word around Cerberus? Do you have a death wish? Let me tell you, being dead isn't fun.'

'What C word?'

'Cute. Cerberus hates being told it's cute. Very sensitive. And fair enough too, "cute" is pretty patronising when you think about it.'

'I've had enough.' Duncan slouched up the stairs, followed closely behind by Gilly. 'Where do you think you're going?'

'I'm coming in.'

'No, you're not,' said Duncan Intently.

'You can't be serious. What do you want me to do? Go out and play with Cerberus? You're the one who upset it, you go out there! Once you've calmed it down, I'll go.'

'This is ridiculous.'

'Are you so prejudiced against dead people you would willingly send me to my death?' Gilly glared at Duncan.

'Will you stop saying that? I'm not prejudiced.'

'You're a deadist.'

'I am not!' said Duncan indignantly.

'Look. I'm only going to stay until Cerberus is gone, which is only reasonable, if you think about it. I did save your life, and don't forget, I did try to warn you. That must count for something?'

There were a few moments of silence.

'Fine.' Duncan glowered.

Duncan flung his flat's door open and waited to one side for

Gilly as he shambled up the stairs.

'You walk very strangely,' said Duncan.

'What, you mean one foot in front of the other?'

'Never mind,' mumbled Duncan.

Once inside, Gilly fell onto the sofa, his stiff body resembling an ironing board as he lay there propped against the sofa. Duncan appeared a minute later; the palm of his hand wrapped across his nose with a can of air freshener in his other hand. Without hesitation, he sprayed above and around Gilly.

'Is that really necessary?' asked Gilly.

'If you are going to be in my flat, then yes. You smell really, really bad.'

The stench emanating from Gilly may have been barely tolerable in a well-ventilated area, such as outside, but inside the confines of Duncan's living room was a totally different matter.

'Nice place you have here,' muttered Gilly, in search of words that might start a conversation.

'Do you want a cup of tea or coffee?' asked Duncan.

'Do you have any tar?' asked Gilly.

'Tar?' repeated Duncan.

'You know, stuff they use to fix the road.'

Duncan shook his head, his mouth gaping.

'Never mind,' sighed Gilly.

They exchanged a few pleasantries. Duncan prowled his living room, occasionally venturing to the bay window to scan the road below; he was convinced he could see a shadow amongst the bins at the end of the road, but he didn't want to say anything for fear it would prolong Gilly's stay. Eventually, he resigned himself to the knowledge Gilly would not be leaving anytime soon. He flung himself into the armchair opposite Gilly.

There was a long silence.

'So how did you… um… die?' asked Duncan.

Gilly smiled to himself. 'Now, that is quite a story I haven't thought about it for a long time.' He nestled into the sofa; his body creaked as he did. Unbeknownst to Duncan, beneath the huge brim of his hat, Gilly's eyes misted over as he stared through the window.

20

Approximately five thousand years ago in a large city, in what is now southern Iraq, a man clad in soiled rags with pitiful footwear lay motionless on the banks of the Euphrates River, clutching a reed bucket of sweet wine to his chest. If somebody happened to wander past, they would have paid him scant attention, dismissing him as 'just another drunk'. However, under different circumstances, the owner of such an opinion would have found themselves buried to their neck in sand and left as fodder for the scorpions in the surrounding desert.

You wouldn't have guessed it by his attire, but this was no ordinary vagabond. He was the equivalent of a modern-day pop idol, complete with groupies, palaces and fast chariots.

In the twenty-first century, people crave celebrity status the quick and easy way — just add water as if it was a packet of two-minute noodles. But five thousand years, before the age of television, to be famous you had to regularly risked your life wrestling bulls and fighting hordes of barbarians in order to garner a modicum of fame.

This vagabond performed such deeds, and many more. In testament to his legendary status, his name has survived through to modern day in folklore. However, if you took the time to ask for his opinion on the matter, he would tell you he got a raw deal and the story passed down from generation to generation had scant attachment to the actual truth.

'Why let the truth get in the way of a good story,' he would mutter if asked.

This vagabond's name is Gilgamesh — also known as the warrior King, son of Lugalbanda, the fifth King of the first dynasty of Uruk, or simply, Gilly to his friends.

A week before he found himself lying in the muddy river, his life was of a pampered King but, upon the unexpected death of his friend Enkidu, he experienced a sensation he did not recognise. Previously, he had only encountered death on the battlefield where his raging testosterone prevented him from mourning the multitude of scattered bodies on the grasslands. However, his friend's death rocker his world. He reeled in shock

141

and had no idea how he should react. He felt a gnawing at the pit of his stomach, a sensation which bore no relation to hunger. Irrational, frustrated and angry, he unchained his fury against those in close proximity, until an uncomfortable calm descended on him.

Grief-stricken, he turned to the only thing he knew for certain would alleviate the pain; he embarked on the 'bender to end all benders'.

Seven days of debauchery and treating his body as a derelict temple inhabited by alcoholics, took its toll.

One night he staggered through the city's tangled web of narrow alleys and lanes, desperate to find a secure location to sleep off his drunken stupor. It wasn't until the next day's sun bore down on his prone body and the tide gently lapped against his parched face, that he regained consciousness and realised he had unceremoniously passed out on the banks of the Euphrates River.

Gilly stirred.

He spat alluvial soil from his mouth and propped himself up on one elbow. His head pounded like a bass speaker beating in time to a song only it knew. He collapsed to the ground, allowing his head to sink into the silt. The cool sensation of the mud provided much needed relief.

At that moment, a shadow moved across him. Gilly looked up and squinted into the sun and was startled to see an elderly man, with a grey beard that reached down to his waist, standing before him.

'Good afternoon, Gilgamesh,' said the old man.

Gilly pushed himself upright and shook his head slowly. 'I'm not signing autographs today.'

'Is it your intention to lie here all day?'

Gilly grabbed the bucket beside him and sloshed down a gulp of the sweet wine instead of replying. It did little to quench his thirst.

The old man extended his hand and left it out there.

Gilly hesitated, studying the hand, before allowing himself to be hauled to his feet. He belched sweet wine as his stomach somersaulted.

'I need food,' muttered Gilly.

'Sweet wine at night is sour by day.' The old man said sagely. 'Come. I know a venue that serves slices of pig leg and duck eggs; the perfect cure for such ills.'

Gilly gingerly followed the old man up the riverbank, nursing his aches and pains. His stomach grumbled and his mouth watered at the thought of pork and eggs. Suddenly, he stopped in his tracks as he remembered his bucket of sweet wine.

'I wouldn't worry about that; you won't need it,' said the old man.

Gilly looked at the bucket, then at the old man: Back at the bucket, the old man, bucket, old man. He gave a small burp and swallowed a distasteful substance that had popped up through his epiglottis.

'Good idea, old man,' he croaked.

The city was a cacophony of alleyways which all led to its centre, where a magnificent palace with sweeping courtyards was situated. On either side of the narrow dirt lanes were dusty market stalls hawking their wares. The fevered haggling generated a din that echoed through the streets. Gilly's head reverberated as he and the old man weaved their way through the crowds.

'Two pieces of silver for this bag of dates?' said a shopkeeper disbelieving to one of his customers. 'These aren't ordinary dates, they're organic! Look how fresh they are. It only took the mules a week to transport them here from the Babylonian Mountains.'

They rounded a corner into a lane, identical to the last, and arrived at a stall. A canopy jutted out from the wall. A sign hanging above in mottled paint read: 'Greasy Fingers'. Underneath the canopy were three stools beside a granite boulder which lay on a bed of hot coals. The cook slapped a few tubes of unidentifiable meat onto the surface of the rock. Instantly, they began to sizzle.

'Whadda ya want?' asked the cook.

'Two Sumerian breakfasts please,' replied the old man as he and Gilly sat themselves down on two of the stools.

The cook cracked four large, pale blue eggs onto the granite surface, then delicately placed thin slices of pig leg.

'Whenever I am in town, I make an effort to drop by here. Simple food of divine nature,' said the old man.

Gilly grunted and took several glugs of water from a leather bladder, hanging from the wall behind them. There were a few minutes of silence as they both pondered the sizzling food.

'I understand you are on a quest for immortality,' said the old man.

'So, the press tells me,' muttered Gilly.

Gilly glanced sideways and briefly considered the old man. Based on his appearance, Gilly presumed he was from the palace, no doubt a priest sent to find out when he intended to resume his royal duties. After Enkidu's death, Gilly informed his circle of advisers he was 'taking a break' and would spend as long as humanly and kingly possible to drown his sorrows. His decision had been greeted with solemn silence. He failed to appreciate that, as he was the King, if he wanted to remain popular then it was essential for him to remain in the public eye. The public would take a dim view of him if the gossip columnists reported tales of his boozing and whoring.

Immediately after this announcement, the machinations of the PR department[*] rolled into action. Ever diligent to put a positive spin on Gilly's behaviour, they promptly released a press release headlined: 'Gilgamesh embarks on quest for immortality'. The release went on to explain that, in honour of his deceased friend, King Gilgamesh had agreed to undertake a hazardous quest. If he were victorious in this quest, then the realm would be blessed with seven years of prosperity and bountiful crops.

And so, while Gilly busied himself with the arduous task of drowning his sorrows, the PR department fed the public on a diet of tales from his supposed latest quest. Yesterday's news story told how he had been engaged in fierce combat with an ogre. In his drunken stupor, he thought this story 'quite odd' as the only combat he could recall engaging in recently was with his liver, and that was only after it decided to go on strike.

'I'm not ready to go back yet,' said Gilly.

'Go where?' asked the old man.

'The palace… You are from the palace?'

---

[*] Authors note: Contrary to popular belief, Public Relations is not a new concept. An example of its early use was when Cleopatra instructed her PR team to convince everybody that she was beautiful — a legend that persists through to today.

'No. No. No.' The old man laughed.

The cook handed them their Sumerian breakfasts wrapped in palm fronds. Gilly shovelled the food into his mouth as if his life depended on it, while the old man picked at his.

'If you're not from the palace, then who are you?' asked Gilly between mouthfuls, in an inquisitive, almost demanding voice.

'Well, that depends. I am many things and many people. I am an old man, a young man, a father, a son, the truth and the light, but most of the time, I am the Chairperson of a particularly large company.'

'That must keep you busy,' muttered Gilly.

The conversation was interrupted. 'Extra… Extra… Read all about it… Get your Sumerian Times here,' bellowed a boy dragging a large bundle of clay tablets behind him. Gilly glanced at one of the tablets as the boy walked past. The headline blared 'Gilgamesh's next stop on his quest: The Scorpion people'. He let out a long, deep sigh.

'Is immortality something that interests you?' said the old man.

Gilly shrugged his shoulders and gave the old man a cursory glance before returning his attention to the food.

Once finished, he dropped the frond on a heap by the cook, belched and held up his hand in way of an apology. The old man grinned and handed his uneaten meal to Gilly.

'I thought you said you liked the food here?' asked Gilly.

The old man smiled. 'I do. I'm not particularly hungry.'

Without hesitation Gilly accepted the frond and began to devour the food.

'Would you like to be immortal?' asked the old man.

'Who wouldn't?' Gilly paused, then continued. 'Nobody should have to go through the pain of death. The heartache. The loss. Enkidu was a good friend… It wasn't his time to die.'

Gilly focused on a distant point. The old man, after what he considered a respectable amount of time, cleared his throat to interrupt Gilly's meditations. He hopped sprightly from his stool, his white gown unfurling as he did.

'If you were to work for my company, you need never face what Enkidu did,' said the old man.

Gilly spluttered. Bright orange yolk dripped from his lips.

'Company? Eh. Work? I can understand why you might not have noticed this, but I am a King. King of all this. I appreciate you're obviously not from around these parts so this may be a new concept for you, but Kings don't work!'

The old man chuckled and patted Gilly on the shoulder. 'Perhaps some clarification is required. A company is like a kingdom, and my company is far larger than your realm. I am offering you the opportunity of getting in at the beginning of my company, at the ground level so to speak. There is also a very generous and attractive compensation package.'

Gilly looked around to ensure nobody was paying undue attention, not that anybody would have believed that this soiled man clad in rags with pitiful footwear was actually their King looking worse for wear — who, incidentally, was meant to be off slaying ogres and not his brain cells.

'I didn't realise this was going to be a job interview. I doubt there is anything you can offer me that I don't already have.'

The old man paused. 'How about immortality?'

'You need to get out more,' riposted Gilly.

The old man smiled. 'Well, for the sake of argument, let's say I can. Would you be interested in working for my company then?'

A few minutes passed. Gilly nodded slowly.

They left the stall and, over the next few hours, they wandered through the maze of alleyways, ignoring the noise and activity around them.

'Imagine you created and nurtured your kingdom, built it from the ground up. This is what I have done with my company. But one day, as you stare out from a parapet in your palace, you spy on the horizon a hostile army preparing to invade your kingdom, to take it over. You need to take immediate action to save your kingdom.'

Gilly nodded.

'Excellent! You see, my company is under threat from a private equity group, they are remarkably similar to a nasty marauding horde of barbarians. And they will stop at nothing to take over my company. Unfortunately, I am detained for the foreseeable future as I am also in the process of establishing my next company, another kingdom, and I don't have the time to fight a takeover battle. My board of directors, my advisors if you will, do not share my fears.'

'They are in cahoots with the barbarians?' asked Gilly, though it sounded more like a statement.

'Perhaps. But I have a plan. After a great deal of thought, I have decided I need to appoint somebody to represent my interests, to fight the battle on my behalf.'

'You need a general,' bellowed Gilly.

'Exactly! And, I have decided you shall be my proxy, my general.'

The old man quickly moved onto explaining the role in more detail, including the responsibilities. There would be considerable travel to various parts of the world (the concept of the 'world' was lost on Gilly, but the old man wisely decided it was not the time to attempt to explain how the world was round, not flat, and much, much larger than Mesopotamia).

The role, the old man advised, would also involve liaising with third party suppliers, the management of board level relationships and the development of strategies. Ultimately, the role would report directly to him, but day-to-day oversight would be by the company's board of directors and the operations department.

The brown brick walls of the palace loomed as they discussed the vaunted compensation package, which included a competitive salary, a generous healthcare plan, free accommodation, travel, on-the-job training and, of course, immortality.

The soldiers standing guard by the palace doors regarded them suspiciously.

'So, if I am interested in being immortal… in this job… then what do I need to do?' asked Gilly.

The old man promptly produced a clay tablet from under his gown.

'What is that?' asked Gilly.

'This is what we call a contract. If you want to accept the position, as my general, then you simply need to sign your name at the bottom of the tablet, and I'll send somebody to collect you to begin your training. But… And, this is very important, do not sign the contract until you are ready to leave your current life behind. For once you have signed the contract, you will never be able to return.'

Gilly accepted the clay tablet. He mumbled he would think

about everything, and then regally strolled towards the guards, cutting their protestations short with a flick of his wrist. He stopped, as if jerked to a standstill by a rope, and turned back. The old man had vanished.

***

Ten years later, as Gilly lay on his bed of straw dying from a spear wound, he reflected on the day when the old man found him lying on the banks of the river of his country's lifeblood. He smiled as he recalled his chance meeting with the mysterious old man and the contract he left him with. He wondered.

'Why not?' he murmured, spraying blood as he did.

He reached into the cupboard beside his bed and retrieved a dusty clay tablet. Then, using one of his long fingernails, he etched his signature at the bottom.

It had been his final act before he died.

Shortly after his body had been ceremoniously deposited in the Euphrates River, he found himself conscious and gasping in lungs of water.

He was suddenly aware he was lying on the riverbed wrapped in a white sheet. The surrounding water weighed down on him. Panic-stricken, he clawed at the tangled layer and eventually wrestled himself free. It was at this point he realised it had taken about thirty minutes to extricate himself from the sheet and, during that time, he had been gulping in water. Yet, despite this minor detail, he had not suffered any discomfort, nor had he drowned. He opened and closed his mouth and watched the water swirl before his flapping jaw. Calmly he stood erect, oblivious to the fish encircling his head, and sauntered to the edge of the river and exited.

As he emerged from the water, a tall man dressed in a dark suit and bowler hat approached him.

'Welcome to Tellus Limited, Sir,' said the man.

Gilly stood, his mouth agape. Water dripped from his sodden clothes and pooled at his feet before seeping into the desert floor.

'I appreciate it may be a shock but now is not the time to dawdle, Sir. We wouldn't want anybody to spot us. If you don't mind, Sir, please follow me. I have instructions to escort you to

Purgatory.'

'Purgatory?' sputtered Gilly.

'Yes, Sir; Tellus Limited's operations department.'

Gilly swallowed hard. 'Am I… dead?'

'Oh yes, Sir. Most certainly,' said the man. 'But not in the conventional sense you might understand.' The man gestured for Gilly to accompany him.

Together, they strode into the depths of the desert. Their figures blurred and melted into the shimmering mirage.

21

Duncan awoke with a start the next morning.

His body vaulted upright and, for an instant, his eyes went wide, before he slumped back into the chair. Gilgamesh was gone.

He wandered to his bay window and surveyed the surroundings. Apart from his Roadster — *God, do I really have a Roadster?* — the street and cemetery were empty and bathed in a murky grey shadow. He glanced at the sky and grimaced at the overcast weather and the drizzling rain. It was typical London, the type of day where venturing outside was as welcome as scorpions in your underpants.

Duncan gazed at his watch and exhaled loudly; for the first time in his career he would be late for work.

This time last week, Duncan's life had been ordered and structured. If back then somebody asked him where he was going to be the following week, he would have answered without hesitation: At his desk, eating an egg mayonnaise sandwich on wholemeal bread for lunch as he did every work day, and occasionally at weekends. He would have scoffed at any suggestion he would be at home in his dressing gown — the likelihood of such a scenario the same as him being out with a woman who spontaneously combusts.

Regardless of the fluctuations in the space-time continuum, Duncan was indeed at home in his dressing gown staring at his watch, wearing a shocked expression.

He swore profusely several times in a loud voice and then haphazardly set about his morning routine, except it was now lunchtime. His watch struck 1.00 p.m. as he left his flat. His unshaven and bedraggled form fell into the roadster. The car started with a squeal and screeched as it careened around the corner on its way to the office of Sheol Trading.

Despite his journey being only five miles, it still took over an hour for him to arrive at his destination. The usual lunchtime congestion combined with the speed humps, traffic cameras and traffic lights all conspired against Duncan and his hopes of a swift trip.

The brakes on the roadster screamed their complaint as the car stopped abruptly across two spaces in the car park beneath the building. He fell through his car door, scrambled to his feet and lurched towards the elevator. He stopped abruptly in his tracks. Slowly, his head turned, and he stared at the brass plaque fixed above the parking space where he had parked, a plaque which had not been there yesterday. He glanced at his watch, cursed his misfortune, and stamped over to it. The brass sign was engraved with black, Times Roman font and read, 'Reserved. Duncan Bottomley. Chief Financial Officer, Sheol Trading'.

His eyes went wide, and his mouth opened and closed like a malfunctioning drawbridge.

'Mr Bottomley?' cried a high-pitched voice.

Duncan turned to the elevator. 'Um, hello…' He struggled to recall the name of Lucy's personal assistant. It might have been the onset of old age, or perhaps the assistant's name was easily forgotten, but whatever the reason, Duncan always managed to forget the assistant's name.

'It's Wesley. I've been looking everywhere for you, Sir. You are required in the boardroom,' said Wesley, gesturing for Duncan to move to the lift.

Duncan pointed at the plaque.

'There is no time to waste, Sir. You are late and Ms Smith hates to be kept waiting,' said Wesley.

'Sorry,' said Duncan. He glanced once more over his shoulder, and then padded over to the elevator. As he entered the confines of the metal box, Wesley smiled and stepped backwards. The button marked thirty-three was already illuminated.

'*The girl from Ipanema*' serenaded his thoughts as he stared at the mirrored door before him. Wesley stood at the rear, his head moving up and down in time to the song.

A friendly male voice welcomed those in the elevator to the executive management floor. The ping of the door sliding open prompted Wesley into action. He stepped forward and quickly walked to a set of oak panelled double doors on the right-hand side, opposite the door to Lucy's office, and pushed them open to reveal a small auditorium. Lining the sides were tables of canapés, and waiters attired in black suits and pressed white shirts strolled around dispensing glasses of champagne. At the far end of the room, on a small stage was a microphone stand, and standing behind it was Lucy, Oliver and the managing partner of Wollenwal & Wollenwal, Mr Wollenwall. Milling at the foot of the stage were members of his firm's partner committee and others he didn't recognise but presumed were senior management from Sheol Trading. And, hovering at the rear of the room, sharing a joke with Lucy's chauffer Sam, was Richard. Duncan did a double-take, mentally confirming it was, indeed, Richard. He was surprised to see Richard here, especially after the way Lucy dismissed him during their first meeting.

He continued to scan the room. Off to one side, discreetly eating a *vol-au-vent*, Duncan noticed Harold, and he was surprised to notice the relief he felt at seeing a friendly face. A waiter handed him a glass of champagne.

'Harold. Hi. How are you? What's going on?' asked Duncan.

'I'm not sure,' Harold warmly shook Duncan's hand. 'Our managing partner called the meeting this morning. To make an exciting announcement.'

Duncan scratched his ear. 'Have you spoken to anybody yet about our discussion yesterday? You know…'

'No, not yet. Don't worry, Duncan, you haven't done anything wrong.' Harold tentatively patted Duncan's shoulder; he was clearly unaccustomed to gestures of reassurance.

There was a loud sound, like an amplified heartbeat. The heads of those gathered turned as one to face the stage. Lucy stood at the front, smiling expansively and tapping on the microphone with her left hand while her right hand gestured for silence.

'Welcome, all. Some of you may not have noticed our guest of honour sneak in. Could everybody please put their hands together for Duncan Bottomley.'

There was polite, if not muted, applause. Duncan glanced around the room and nodded his gratitude. Richard glared in Duncan's direction and raised a glass of champagne in a mock toast.

'*If eyes could shoot daggers, I would be a dead man.*' Realising his own thoughts, he mentally scolded himself for thinking of dead people; a topic he had considered far too much recently.

Lucy launched into a monologue, waxing lyrically about Sheol Trading and its future. She skipped through the financial figures and provided some impressive-sounding statistics on the usage of their products and services. With each comment made, those gathered laughed obsequiously. Then, to the accompaniment of rapturous applause, she reminded everybody that Sheol Trading was going from strength to strength and despite some recent bad press their share prices had continued to rise. She grinned knowingly at Duncan as she revealed her final applause-inducing statistic.

'This meeting heralds a new dawn for Sheol Trading. A new age which promises untold wealth for our shareholders and for the world as a whole.' The crowd were in a fevered state. Lucy stretched her arms out wide and tilted her head back to absorb the ovation.

As the crowd's applause began to die down, she continued her rousing oratory.

The crowd were awe-struck and by the time she finished, twenty minutes later, their hands stung from excessive clapping.

'Which brings me to Duncan,' she paused before introducing and praising him to the assembled. Duncan blushed. His weight shifted from side to side as he closely examined his shoes.

'We are extremely pleased with our original decision to approach Wollenwal & Wollenwal. In a short space of time, Duncan has made an incredible difference to this firm.' She smiled and raised her finger as if a thought had entered her mind. 'Why just the other day, we were in a quandary over the current economic climate and its effects on Sheol Trading. Without hesitation, Duncan immediately cut to the core of the problem and suggested we strengthen our bottom line by reducing our head count.' The applause even more muted this time. A few people glared at Duncan, including Harold. Duncan shook his head in denial. 'He brings to our company a wide breadth of knowledge and dedication. A man of his calibre is an incredible asset for us.' The crowd returned to their feverish pitch.

'I have some very exciting news to announce. After some intense overnight negotiations, I am proud to say Sheol Trading arranged for the payment of a fifty-million-pound retainer to be made to the Wollenwal's bank account' There was an audible gasp from the audience, predominantly from the partners of Wollenwal & Wollenwal.

Mr Wollenwal, his face alight with happiness and a tear in the corner of his eye, advanced and proffered his hand to Lucy. She glared at it with disdain. He promptly removed it and shuffled backwards.

'As you all know, since the tragic car accident of our former Chief Financial Officer, Gordon McBride, we have been searching for his replacement. This is a vitally important role to the company, and we cannot afford to delay in filling this vital position. Therefore, we have taken the bold decision to appoint Duncan Bottomley as our new CFO. To reassure everybody, we have maintained our agreement with the Wollenwals to continue with them as our auditors.'

Almost on cue, the senior management from Sheol Trading applauded loudly. The partners from Wollenwal & Wollenwal almost fainted as they calculated the additional fees this would generate for their firm before demonstrating their appreciation.

Harold looked quizzically at Duncan. Duncan's eyes pleaded ignorance. He shrugged his shoulders and raised his hands as if surrendering.

'Honest. I… I knew nothing about this, Harold,' whispered Duncan.

'This is all highly irregular.' Harold scratched his bald scalp.

The applause died down and the heads of the audience moved left and right, as if watching a tennis game, flicking between Duncan and Lucy.

There was a long silence, which was eventually broken by a discreet cough. Harold stepped forward and raised his hand as if seeking permission to speak, which he was. He jerked his hand back to his side once conscious he had raised it. He coughed again and then, in an unusually loud, but still monotone voice, he spoke up: 'I am sorry, but this is wrong. There is a clear conflict of interest here. How can we audit Sheol Trading's accounts and yet have an unbiased view of the company with Duncan as their CFO? Surely it makes sense for Duncan to take a minimum of six months gardening leave before starting in this position. The whole point of being an independent auditor is that we are *independent*. How can we be truly independent in this situation?'

The auditorium reverberated with constant chatter as both sides heatedly debated Harold's concerns. The meeting appeared to be degenerating out of control when a loud voice from the rear quelled the crowd. Heads spun.

'Excuse me,' the voice bellowed above the din of the crowd. 'Excuse me!'

Richard pushed his way through the crowd. His face plastered with his usual smarmy smile. 'My esteemed colleague has made an excellent point. Indeed, this is a serious matter that should have been put to the partners before making any agreement.'

The managing partner tried his best to shrink into the shadows on the stage in order to avoid the glares from the audience.

'I say we should put this to a partner vote now. Let us settle this once and for all,' continued Richard. 'If the majority believe we can manage this impartially and without bias, then we must support it. But, if this isn't the case, then so be it.' Richard sounded conciliatory.

Harold was relieved, for once, Richard had opened his mouth. He wasn't accustomed to raising objections and preferred to avoid confrontation. For someone else to voice his concerns, and in a far more concise way than he would have managed, was fine by him.

'Some of you will know my depth of knowledge and experience was shunted to one side on this account. My reputation publicly sullied,' said Richard with as much bitterness in his voice as there is sand in the Sahara. 'I am big enough to admit, initially I was embittered by my treatment. However, even I am prepared to admit I was wrong. I believe this is a great opportunity for our firm, and I will be voting in favour of this proposal. This is a great day for our two firms.'

Immediately the fears and reservations of Richard's fellow partners evaporated. Any doubts they may have held melted away, for they all knew of Richard's massive ego and how affronted he had been when dismissed from the account. Common sense therefore dictated if he was willing to support this arrangement then their concerns must be unfounded — they all know his ego would never have allowed him to support this deal unless, of course, it was prosperous for him and the firm.

The final vote was unanimous except for one: Harold's.

While the champagne flowed in celebration, Harold quietly approached Duncan and congratulated him on his new role. He explained in a soft monotone voice how his outburst was not intended to be personal, but he firmly believed it will have serious repercussions for the firm. As a partner is was his duty to put the firm's best interests first and above his wallet.

'But the other partners?' asked Duncan in a voice of some concern.

'It appears they have their noses deep in the Sheol Trading trough,' said Harold.

'Can we talk about this? I mean… it's a great opportunity for me. Very flattering. But I don't want to do anything wrong.'

Harold reassured him that there would be plenty of time to talk, but it was essential he understood there was nothing personal in his stance. Besides, even if he wanted to talk more, he couldn't as his wife was at home waiting for him.

From the stage, Lucy watched Harold dawdle from the room. She glanced towards Sam, who stood in the shadows by the exit, and tilted her head in a tiny, precise movement. Sam nodded in an understood salutation, then turned and disappeared through the door behind him.

<h1 style="text-align:center">22</h1>

The glow from the cigarette illuminated Harold's sombre face. He crossed his arms and rested them on the railing of the small balcony. The street below was mostly empty with, only a few stragglers from the restaurants; if it had been the weekend, it would have been reamed with bustling, intoxicated people stumbling from bar to bar, laughing and enjoying their lives.

Harold had been a smoker for most of his fifty-four years. His wife had asked him to stop on countless occasions but, despite his best efforts, he couldn't, although he did manage to cut it down to one a day. The second to last thing he would do each night, second only to brushing his teeth, was smoke that lone cigarette. It was a moment he looked forward to and one he savoured.

He inhaled deeply and the glowing ember cast a red hue over his nose. With each drag his anxieties drifted away, like the smoke escaping his mouth.

'*I hope heaven allows smoking,*' he jested to himself, his face creased by a smile. It was an odd thought to have sail through his mind at that particular moment, but he continued in his contemplation. While Harold was not a religious man, he quietly hoped there was something more out there — Heaven; something for after the end. Harold didn't know the answers. He didn't even have an inclination. He might not have known at that point in time, but he would soon know the answer to that eternal question.

He leaned backwards and craned his neck for a better view of the living room. His body hung there for a moment as he listened to the mild, rhythmic snoring of his wife emanating from the bedroom. He smiled, still loving her so much after so many years. In the distance he heard a whistling noise, followed by a sharp bang and a crackling noise. Another, then another. He smiled.

'*A little early for Guy Fawkes' night.*'

He turned his attention back to the road and he scanned the night sky for the fireworks.

Seconds later a large orange flash of light exploded inches before his nose.

The sunlight streaming through the bedroom window woke Mrs Wilson. She stretched her arms high above her head and grunted contentedly. Slowly her arm trickled down the bed and patted around for her husband, but the bed was empty.

She propped herself up on her elbow and cast her eyes about the room. Harold wasn't doing his morning sit-ups, and upon closer examination, his side of the bed hadn't been slept in. She listened for sounds from the en-suite but there were none of the usual toilet sounds, and no trickling of the shower.

The woman swept out of bed, grabbed her satin dressing gown and threaded it over her shoulders. She moved through the doorway and stopped, raised her head and sniffed the air. There was a distinct, inoffensive smell, a sulphurous and charcoal-like odour lingered.

She dismissed it as something odd she would investigate later if it persisted. But for now, she wanted to confront her husband; he knew she hated it when he fell asleep on the sofa. She walked into the living room and froze mid-stride. Her eyes studied the burn marks around the balcony doorframe. She shook her head and made a tutting sound with her tongue. Mentally, she prepared herself for the tongue-lashing she would deliver to Harold when she found him.

'*I've told him before about smoking in the house.*'

She took another step forward and gasped. Her heart felt as if it had stopped. Her jaw sunk like the Titanic, and her eyes catapulted from their sockets.

The occupants of the other flats in the building, if not already awake, were now. The blood-curdling scream made sure of it. A few of the occupants, fearful somebody was being attacked or worst, phoned the police.

Mrs Wilson, soon after delivering the finger-tingling scream, fainted at the horrifying and sickening sight before her.

Harold Wilson, her beloved husband of twenty-seven years, laid in a crumpled heap in a pool of his own blood, his clothes scorched, his face noticeably absent.

Next to his charred hand laid an unfinished cigarette.

<h1 style="text-align:center">23</h1>

Detective Superintendent Malloy entered the room and moved to one side to allow the infamous trolley with its long, black PVC bag on top to glide past. The trolley rattled like a shopping cart as it rolled over a hump at the bottom of the doorframe.

'Wait a moment,' commanded Malloy.

Malloy gripped the zip which ran down the length of the bag and unzipped it until it gaped slightly at the top. He peered inside and quickly backed away; rubbing his nose in the hope it would remove the noxious smell permeating his nostrils. One of the attendants zipped the bag up before pushing it out the door.

To an outsider, the scene before Malloy would have appeared chaotic but it was, in some form, an organised chaos. Forensic scientists, attired in their white overalls, crawled over the balcony and doorframe like spiders. Outside on the balcony, a white outline in the shape of a sprawled body. Malloy turned his head towards the sounds of soft sobbing. An elderly woman sat on a sofa against the wall, who Malloy rightly assumed was the victim's spouse; a female police constable sat next to her offering comfort and support.

Malloy took a deep breath and approached the widow. With a curt nod he dismissed the female PC and took her place next to Mrs Wilson.

He started by expressing his condolences and asking her if she needed anything. She shook her head, sniffed, and wiped her eyes with a handkerchief.

Malloy contemplated his next words. He found these occasions difficult and, despite being in these situations more times than he cared to remember, it didn't seem to be any easier. At last, he explained how he understood if she was not ready to answer questions, but it would assist them in their investigation. He explained time was of the essence in these situations, but she should not feel rushed.

Mrs Wilson lifted her head, she shuddered as she breathed in deep. She nodded her head in reluctant agreement. Malloy removed a notepad from his shirt pocket and jotted a few notes.

'I understand this happened while you were asleep,' said

Malloy.

Mrs Wilson nodded.

'Did you hear anything? Anything at all?'

She sobbed. 'No. No. Harold always complained that not even an earthquake could wake me,' she sobbed again and dabbed her eye with the handkerchief.

'Did the vict… I mean… your husband have any enemies, or anybody who might have had a grudge against him?'

'No. He was well-respected. A lovely man. Dedicated to his work. Why do you ask? Do you think this was deliberate?'

'These are routine questions, Mrs Wilson, and nothing to be concerned with. We need to gather as much information as possible. Now, can you tell me what Mr Wilson did? His employer? His role?'

'An accountant. He is… was,' she sobbed, 'a partner with Wollenwal & Wollenwal.'

Malloy arrested himself from asking another question. Something about what she said stuck in his mind, lighting up like a light bulb. He flicked through the pages in his note pad and paused at a particular page. Moments later, he raised his head and gazed quizzically at Mrs Wilson. 'Did your husband know a Duncan Bottomley? I think he works for the same company?'

'Well, yes,' she answered, surprised by the question.

'How did your husband know Mr Bottomley?'

'They have been working on an account together, the biggest in their firm. He said it was a very important account. Before he came home last night he had been at a function for this client. I don't think he enjoyed himself, though. He was a bit quiet afterwards and even talked about retirement. He only ever talks about retirement when he is unhappy with work,' reminisced Mrs Wilson through sobs.

'Do you know the name of this… account?' enquired Malloy.

'Oh. I don't think so. It was one of those banks with an odd, trendy name. Quite a big company from what Harold told me.'

'Sheol Trading? Was that the name?'

'That might have been it. Possibly. Actually, I think it was. I remember thinking it a strange name for a company. Whatever happened to companies having simple names like General Electric? Now they are misspelled, missing letters, I don't understand.'

Malloy continued on his questioning until satisfied. Malloy beckoned the female PC to return to her post and thanked Mrs Wilson for her time. As he went to leave, he placed his non-descript business card on the coffee table in front of her. He mentioned, in passing, if she did think of anything else then she should give him a call. His office would stay in regular contact in case she happened to think of anything and to keep her updated on the progress of their investigation. He informed her, at this stage, it did look like a terrible accident.

Mrs Wilson nodded her head while wiping her eyes and blowing hard into a tissue.

Malloy retreated and walked across to the balcony. He turned to the nearby police constable, 'Have they identified the body as Harold Wilson's?'

'The coroner will confirm it, Sir, but they have made an initial identification based on possessions found on the body and the general description given by Mrs Wilson. If his face had remained intact it would have made the ID process a lot easier.'

'No doubt,' said Malloy sarcastically.

24

Duncan's drive into work that morning had been the usual stop-start affair. The traffic lights which dotted the road at hundred-metre intervals would turn red as soon as the lights before turned green. Then there were the speed humps to contend with, designed to ensure drivers maintained the thirty-mile per hour speed limit but, in reality, only succeeded in damaging vehicle suspension and wheel alignment while slowing traffic to marginally faster than a snail.

Despite the obvious reasons for the proliferation of road rage in London, Duncan remained in good spirits. Smiling, he bathed in the realisation that he, plain old Duncan Bottomley, had been appointed CFO of the world's largest, most feared hedge fund and, perhaps more importantly to his immediate thoughts, he had enjoyed a good night's sleep for the first time in days; a night free of dead people, rabid dogs and exploding temptresses.

'Good morning, Mr Bottomley,' the attendant beamed as Duncan pulled into the car park.

Duncan waved his thanks and drove down the spiral driveway, crawling through the valleys of cars. He drove past car after car, all neatly aligned, and parked in what would now be his usual spot, three parking spaces away from the lifts. The first two were occupied with cars he recognised belonging to Lucy and Oliver.

As he hopped out of the roadster, he spied the brass plaque. The line of his mouth stretched outwards, curling upwards; he was the proud owner of his own personal parking spot, a rarity in London.

His smile knew no bounds. His spirits bounced.

As further proof of his good fortune that day, the elevator waited for him with the door promptly opening as he stepped into the lobby area; it was as if it had been instructed to wait there.

Duncan stepped in and lightly ran his finger down the panel of buttons, and pressed the button marked thirty-three. The lift jerked and hummed to life. The usual instrumental music played softly in the background and, within seconds, he found himself humming along as if part of his new routine. He adjusted his tie and straightened his lank hair in the mirrored doors.

162

A friendly male voice resounded its canned welcome to the executive management floor, before the lift doors opened with a cheery ping. Duncan entered the bright lobby area and, standing in the middle of the room, was Lucy's personal assistant to welcome him, the man whose name he could never remember.

'Good morning,' mumbled Duncan, his cheeks turning pink.

'Wesley, Sir. Welcome. Ms Smith is expecting you.' He whispered into the blue pulsating earpiece, nodded his head and then beckoned Duncan to follow him.

'Ah. Thanks…'

'Wesley, Sir. Have a nice day.'

'Good morning, Duncan,' said Lucy, her gaze both welcoming and suspicious.

Oliver entered from a side door, a plate of pastries in his hand. He strolled over to Duncan. 'Good morning, Duncan. Croissant?' He held the plate out. Duncan shook his head. Oliver bit into a croissant sending shards of pastry flying in all directions. He moved to the desk, placed the tray in the middle, and sat at the end, adjacent to Lucy.

Lucy gestured for Duncan to sit in the vacant chair between her and Oliver. Duncan shuffled forward.

'Have you been working out Duncan?' asked Lucy with raised eyebrows.

'Um, no.' Duncan felt his face flush. He lowered himself into the chair and wedged his hands between his legs.

Lucy grabbed Duncan's biceps in a pincer grip and squeezed tightly. 'Are you sure you haven't been? Don't you think he is looking more muscular, Oliver?'

'Absolutely,' said Oliver, crumbs scattering from his lips.

'Yes, indeed. Very impressive, Duncan.'

Duncan subconsciously flexed his muscles and stammered his gratitude.

'Unfortunately, Duncan, I am a little concerned. The clothes. I thought we discussed this. Did you not see Jonathan?'

'Well, yes I did. I found it very enjoyable. He said the suits would be ready next week. He also fitted me for a new pair of shoes, some shirts and underwear. I think he was probably trying to tell me something,' laughed Duncan, though stilted.

'I doubt that?' Lucy frowned. 'Then why are you wearing that nylon rag?'

Duncan glanced at his shirt. 'They only had one shirt in my size for me to take, they were ordering the others in.'

'And why are you not wearing that shirt?'

'Um… Funny story actually. I was trying out the shirt they gave me, but a… dog… ate it. Destroyed it. I can't wear it.'

'You don't need to make excuses, Duncan. We're family now.'

'I'm not,' said Duncan meekly.

Lucy smiled darkly, shifting in her chair, before shifting her attention to the television on the side cupboard opposite her desk. She held up her hand for silence. A hush enveloped the room.

The news headlines rolled across the bottom of the screen. She grabbed the remote control and steadily increased the volume. The orange bar moving across the bottom of the screen moved to the right, in correlation to the newsreader's voice getting louder.

'… it appears to have been a tragic accident. The police have released the victim's name, Mr Harold Wilson. According to early reports, he was killed in a freak firework accident. Anti-pyrotechnic bodies have used this opportunity to remind people of the dangers posed by fireworks. We are now crossing to our reporter, Diane Fallon, who is on the scene.'

Duncan's jaw dropped and he popped forward in his chair. His eyes fixed on the screen. Lucy relaxed back in her chair and exchanged glances with Oliver.

'Thank you, Stephanie. I am outside the building where this dreadful incident occurred in the early hours this morning. Looking up you can see the balcony where the alleged firework exploded.' The camera moved slowly up the spine of the building and then zoomed in on a scorched balcony. 'Police are urging any individuals who were in the Fulham High Street area between midnight and 4.00 a.m. last night to identify themselves to police.' The camera refocused on the reporter, and a grey-haired man who had the appearance of a soldier. 'We are joined by Detective Superintendent Malloy, the investigating officer.'

'Do the police have any idea how this incident occurred?' asked the reporter.

'A firework exploded in the face of the victim and killed them?' said Malloy drily.

'Yes. I see. Is it unusual for firework injuries at this time of year?'

'We are talking about a death here, not an injury. A man died.' Malloy evidently had little patience for reporters and their inane questions. As far as Malloy was concerned, the television reporter was the modern-day ventriloquist dummy.

'Yes. We understand the victim's partner was in the house at the time. How is she feeling?'

Malloy remained silent and gave the reporter what could only be described as the evil eye.

'Right. Yes. Are you able to tell us whether the police are treating this as an accident or a homicide?'

Malloy turned to face the camera and fixed it with a steely glare. 'It is too early to say but we have identified a few leads which we are currently investigating.'

If Duncan didn't know any better, he would have sworn Malloy was staring at him. He dismissed the notion, knowing there would be hundreds upon thousands of people watching the same interview and feeling the same way.

Lucy pressed a button on the remote control and the television volume subsided. She carefully selected a croissant while holding a small saucer aloft to catch any stray crumbs; she needn't had bothered as her delicate nibbling didn't generate any crumbs.

The colour in Duncan's faced drained. He crumpled into his seat and threw his head back; his hands supported his head. His head lolled from side to side and he silently tried to speak but no sounds came. In the distance, he could hear the faint cacophony of a vacuum cleaner at work.

Finally, he spoke: 'Harold is dead.'

'Did you know the chap? I'm so sorry, Duncan. Terrible news,' said Lucy as she continued to daintily eat her croissant.

'Yes. I was talking to him at the announcement last night. He was the person who objected… We all saw him last night… I… I must have been one of the last people to speak to him.' Duncan buried his head into his lap.

There was a long silence, interrupted by delicate pastry crunching sounds.

'Croissant?' asked Oliver, offering the plate around the table.

'Do you remember that newspaper article you showed me at

the Ritz?' Duncan lifted his head at last.

Lucy shook her head; it was a brief movement.

'The article mentioned how your former head trader died in a firework accident.'

'Really. Are you certain? Oh dear, what a tragic coincidence.' Lucy glared at Oliver. 'I appreciate this is unfortunate news. It is indeed very distressing. However, life inevitably must go on and money waits for nobody. I know this sounds callous, but we have a business to run,' she paused. 'I wanted to see you today, Duncan, because I have some wonderful news for you.'

Duncan nodded but his eyes remained fixed on the television as a lump rose in his throat.

She flicked a button on the remote control and changed the station to the stock market channel. The screen was divided into four equal sections: In one corner of the screen were various graphs; in another, news headlines; in the third a reporter stood discussing trends; while the final quarter detailed the latest share prices which flashed across the screen. Eventually, Sheol Trading's ticker, SHT, filled the screen, accompanied by the news that the share price was up eight percent on the news of Duncan Bottomley's appointment as CFO, which brought bright prospects and filled a void within the company.

'Excellent. As expected, a very positive response from the markets. This is wonderful news.' Lucy placed the saucer on the table and rubbed her fingers over it before dabbing her full lips with a linen napkin.

Duncan's disposition brightened considerably as he absorbed the news, and he forced a brief smile. His eyes scanned the headlines accompanying the story.

'But that is not the news I wanted to share with you. We have received a request from the "Business before Lunch" television show, requesting an interview with our newly appointed Chief Financial Officer.' Lucy paused, waiting for a response from Duncan which was far from forthcoming. 'That is you, Duncan. Our PR department thinks it would be an excellent idea, and I must confess we do too. It will provide the world with the opportunity to get to know you, learn about you, like you, and I am sure our share prices will reflect that. You are an important man now, Duncan, you will need to get used to this.'

'They want to interview me on television?' asked Duncan in a soft voice.

'Indeed. Scheduled for Monday. Their studio is located on Threadneedle Street, just down the road. They are expecting you at 11.00 a.m. sharp for makeup and so on. It's a live broadcast to be aired at eleven thirty, so make sure you aren't late. Oliver and I will be looking forward to watching it. Have you cleared your schedule Oliver?'

Oliver's head flopped up and down between bites of the croissant.

Duncan's jaw dropped then closed and dropped again in silent protest.

'You are the CFO of Sheol Trading, a celebrity in your own right. You're famous now, Duncan. There will be plenty of interviews for you to look forward to over the coming months and years. Why, I imagine it won't be long before you are on the cover of CFO magazine and Forbes. After all, you are a master of the universe now, Duncan.'

'But… What will I talk about?' stammered Duncan.

Lucy tossed her hand into the air. 'The usual things. Our financial stability, future projections, new products, routine questions a man of your intellect could answer in your sleep.'

'Um, okay. Monday at eleven. Threadneedle Street. Okay.'

'Duncan, it has to be said you are looking decidedly pale this morning. I'm sure the news of your colleague's death has come as a shock to you. Why don't you take the day off? Go home and rest? It's only Thursday, go home and come back in tomorrow feeling refreshed.'

Duncan stood erect, mumbled his thanks, and drearily walked to the door.

'Duncan,' called Lucy. He turned to face her. 'You do know, if you ever need to talk my door is always open? If you are ever in trouble or if strange and unusual things are happening, then you can always talk to me. We are family. Yes?' she said with a smile drenched with concern and caring.

'Thank you. Yes. I will. I'll be fine tomorrow.' Duncan closed the door behind him. His day had taken a horrible turn for the worst.

'Indeed,' said Lucy.

Lucy selected another croissant. Oliver moved to the chair vacated by Duncan. Wesley's voice squelched from the telephone on her desk. 'He has left the floor, Ms Smith.'

'Thank you, Wesley,' said Lucy, holding down a button on the telephone.

She rubbed her fingers together over the saucer, picked it up and dropped it into the bin. It shattered as it hit the base.

'I find croissants so tiresome. Could we try something with freshly whipped Jersey cream next time?'

'Of course,' responded Oliver.

'I think everything is progressing rather nicely, wouldn't you agree, Oliver?'

'It is most certainly happening as you planned,' he replied unctuously.

'Of course, it is. Things always go to plan. But I do think it is time we moved to the next phase with Duncan. Be a dear and arrange for Berith to visit him tonight,' said Lucy.

'I don't understand, Lucy. Why would you do that? It's too soon,' said Oliver with raised eyebrows and alarm in his voice. 'You always want to stick to the plan.'

Lucy narrowed her eyes at Oliver. He immediately knew he shouldn't have questioned her instructions. 'The plan is as it has always been, Oliver. He will need our help soon enough.' Lucy grinned.

Oliver inclined his head, stood up and backed out of the room.

'Oh, Oliver.' He froze mid-stride and raised his head. 'Please tell Sam to stop using fireworks. Is it too much to ask for some originality around here?'

Oliver nodded, turned and exited the room.

'Wesley,' Lucy's finger pressed down a button on her phone.

'Yes, Ms Smith?' squelched Wesley.

'Could you please summon Richard Steel to my office immediately?'

25

The twenty-fifth floor was its usual hubbub of frivolity. Duncan weaved his way through the cubicles; his body hunkered down low to avoid flying footballs. A few of his colleagues slapped his back to offer their congratulations, each subsequent slap felt harder than the last. He reciprocated their slap with a few mumbled words.

He staggered through his office door and fell into the huge chair.

Placed overtly in the middle of his desk were a bundle of papers, which upon closer inspection turned out to be financial accounts. A yellow note rested on top of the pile. Scribbled in Lucy's handwriting were instructions, the accounts were a matter of urgency and needed to be signed off by tomorrow morning.

He sighed, tucked the papers under his arm and headed home.

***

Duncan leaned forward. In his hand he delicately balanced a document, as if the words were about to fall off the page. His eyes squinted as he read the document for the tenth time.

The light in his living room had darkened considerably. He absently grabbed the mug that sat midst a plethora of scattered papers and took a slurp of the tea that had long gone cold. He shifted some of the papers to one side and replaced the cup on the coffee table.

His deliberations were disturbed by the moribund sound of his doorbell, which had started chirpily before forgetting what tune it had been playing and finishing with random beeps and toots.

Duncan despaired as he prised himself from the sofa, papers falling to the ground in an unorganised, unforeseen shambles. He made his way downstairs to the building's front door. Presuming it would be a polite man with an American accent, wearing a short-sleeved white shirt and a black name badge asking for some of his time in order to preach the Lord's word, he was reluctant to answer the door. Had he known Richard Steel was behind it, he probably would have abandoned the idea altogether.

Duncan opened the door.

'Oh… Hi. I wasn't expecting you,' said Duncan.

Richard straightened his tie. 'Yes, sorry about dropping by unannounced like this.' He craned his neck for a better view of the graveyard behind him. 'Pleasant area you live in. Must be quiet.'

'Um, yeah. It is.'

'The partnership thought, in light of the tragic news, it would be prudent for me to drop by to check in on you. Naturally, we are all shocked by this news, but Sheol Trading is very important to our firm and we need to make sure everybody is operating at full capacity. We don't want to appear callous; you understand?' said Richard.

'No… It's fine. I understand. Please come in.' He stood to one side and beckoned for Richard to enter.

They ascended the stairs. Richard stopped at the doorway to Duncan's flat and sneered. Duncan hurried into the living room and swept aside the few papers which remained scattered on the pothole-ridden sofa and motioned for Richard to sit down.

Richard obliged, crossed his legs and stretched his arm along the top of the sofa. 'How are you feeling, Duncan?'

'I guess I'm fine. Shocked. I spoke with Harold last night, you know. I might have been the last person to speak to him,' lamented Duncan.

'It will be a difficult few days for all of us, and it is important we are there for one another, to help each other through this terrible period. But you should know Harold would not have wanted this to interfere with our work. Work was always the priority with Harold.'

'I know. It's just such a shock. He seemed like a good man.'

'Yes, indeed. Nevertheless, I have some news for you that will no doubt please you. The firm has discussed this with Sheol Trading, and in light of this tragedy, it has been agreed I should avail myself to you in Harold's stead. So, if you have any questions or concerns then I am here to help. You only have to ask.' Richard set his lips in a slight smile.

Duncan raised his eyebrow. 'I didn't think Ms Smith wanted you on this account?'

Richard tittered. 'It was a simple misunderstanding, Duncan.

A funny one, but it was actually her suggestion I take Harold's place.'

'Uh huh.'

'So… What are you doing now?' Richard sneered as he eyed the documents strewn across the coffee table.

'Ms Smith asked me to review their accounts urgently. It's all fairly straight forward, except there are some off-balance sheet partnerships which I can't follow. I don't understand their purpose.'

'Really?' said Richard. 'Do you mind if I have a look?'

'Not at all. I'd appreciate your opinion.' Duncan sat on the bedraggled sofa next to Richard and sifted through the documents on the table, periodically passing him a few sheets followed by a few more.

The room fell silent. The regular droning of planes flying overhead on their way to Heathrow airport and the shuffling of papers the only sounds to permeate the air. Duncan hadn't got around to having the windows in his flat double-glazed, so he had grown accustomed to the sound of the planes flying overhead, to everybody else it was almost deafening.

Richard smiled his own brand of a forced smile. 'Ah. I understand the confusion. Duncan, this is common practise amongst many large firms. It suits their share price. It is only natural for companies to push their accounts to the edge and exploit available loopholes. Large companies can get away with so much these days.' Richard lowered the pages to the table, leaned forward and pointed at one of the pages. 'Did you know last year a quarter of Britain's largest seven hundred companies didn't pay any corporation tax? Large companies have a duty to their shareholders to pay as little tax as possible. It's the little people like you and I who get screwed in the process. The taxman will harass and harangue small companies, bankrupt them, put people out of work to get their money, but large companies who make billions of profits pay less tax than the average person.' Richard rose and rested his open palm on Duncan's shoulder. 'Your new position entails a great deal of responsibility. The last thing you need is to add unnecessary worries and stresses on your shoulders. Perhaps you should take a holiday before you start this new role?'

'No. I'm fine. Really. I… It's just been manic this week, and I guess what with Harold's death added to it—'

'Whenever you have concerns, you should feel comfortable raising them with me.' Richard cleared his throat and asked if he could use the bathroom. Duncan nodded and pointed to the hallway.

Duncan bent at the waist and signed several pages of the accounts. He then stacked them together and patted down each side of the stack before pushing them to one side.

A few minutes later, Richard emerged from the hallway, waggling his hands dry and smiling indulgently.

'I will see you tomorrow at Sheol Trading's office,' said Richard.

'Yeah, sure. Thanks for your help. I'll be fine tomorrow.' Duncan's spirits improved noticeably and, while it could have been down to Richard's kind words, Duncan preferred to put it down to the fact, Richard had left.

Duncan waved goodbye from the top of the stairs and closed his flat door. Like a sixth sense, Duncan had a bad gut feeling, something nagged at the back of his mind. He wasn't sure exactly what, but it had something to do with Richard's behaviour when he emerged from the toilet, he could have sworn Richard looked sheepish? Despite dismissing his fears as paranoia, Duncan decided to investigate anyway.

There was nothing unusual about the disinfectant smell in the toilet. He rummaged through his medicine cabinet, noting again how there was nothing unusual or out of place. He inspected the sink, his hairbrush, his toothbrush, and rifled through the assorted items on the ledge above the sink. Everything appeared to be where it should have been. Duncan shrugged his shoulders; it must have been nothing. After everything that had happened to him over the past few days, it wasn't surprising that his imagination was overactive.

He returned to the comfort of his sofa. It never failed to amaze him how the sofa, with all of its cosmetic imperfections, was so comfortable. He sighed in contentment.

***

Later that day, the doorbell again interrupted Duncan with its depressing tune. He sighed and lowered his glass of whisky to the table surface.

It was an unusual event for him to drink whisky at home and, even more peculiar, was that his doorbell had rung twice in one day. He moved to the curtains, the floorboards creaked under his weight, to gaze outside. The street was dark apart from the circles of light emitted by the streetlights, though the front door's light was on. It only came on when it detected motion, but from his position he couldn't see anybody at the front door.

He closed the curtain and returned to the sorry-looking sofa. As he sat down, the doorbell limped to life again.

The view from the window remained the same.

'*Kids having a laugh*,' thought Duncan.

He slouched down the stairs. Fumbling with the lock, he opened the front door so that his right eye could peer outside. Nobody was there.

Emboldened, he opened the door wider and leaned outside. He tilted his head and listened closely but, apart from the whistle of the chill wind, it was silent.

'Hello,' he called out, his voice faltering.

He tentatively inched out onto the footpath, closing his gate behind him, and looked both ways. The street was empty apart from the parked cars. His Roadster remained parked on an angle just as he had left it in his rush to get inside that afternoon, though he noticed a yellow bag with black stripes wedged under the left wiper blade. Duncan groaned at the sight of the parking ticket.

He glanced at the cemetery long enough to satisfy himself it posed no threat. Out of the corner of his eye, in the darkened entranceway to the house next door, he noticed a shadow move. He froze and swivelled on his legs, staring into the darkness with fear beginning to rise in his throat, his eyes willing the gloom to part. Something moved again.

From the shadows a man, at least seven foot tall, emerged. What immediately struck Duncan was the tight-fitting scarlet military uniform with its gold buttons lining the tunic, which sparkled in the streetlights. On the top of his head sat a simple gold crown.

The man stopped, braced his legs apart, and placed his hands on his hips and regarded Duncan with cold loathing.

'Did you ring my doorbell?' Duncan's voice quivered.

'I am Berith,' the man said in a loud voice.

Duncan thought he could feel the ground shake. Before he could say anything, a red blur tore past him. Berith's slipstream scooped him into the air and flung him to the ground like a rag doll. Duncan rose to his knees and looked around. Berith was standing at the other end of the road, laughing wholeheartedly.

'What the—'

Berith charged, his fists pumping the air before him, and he careered into Duncan, sending him spinning backwards through the air. His arms flailed about like a crash test dummy hurtling from a car. Duncan landed on top of a hedgerow bordering the front of his neighbour's property. He rolled off the hedge and landed on the ground with a dull thud, bruised and cut. In a moment of genius, Duncan decided to retreat to the safety of his flat while he could.

He scrambled to his feet and sprinted for the front door. A maelstrom of wind surrounded him, pummelling him to the ground. Duncan sprawled across the pavement, gulped in the air like a half-spent fish. His chest ached. He patted his upper body to confirm his ribs were intact.

Duncan groaned. 'You have to stop this. I'm calling the police.'

In a blur, Berith assailed him from all sides. The punches were frenetic. He desperately tried to block the blows with his arms, but he could only see a haze around his arms, followed by a sickening crackle of bones.

'Berith!' a voice roared from the cemetery.

The hammering ceased, providing Duncan with the opportunity to curl into the foetal position. His spine throbbed and his brain sloshed around in his skull. Everything went white.

Berith whirled round, his fists clenched. 'Who dares interfere with Berith?' he raged.

Gilgamesh waved his fingers in greeting. 'Just little old me.'

'Gilgamesh!' exclaimed Berith, the timbre of his voice instantly jovial.

'In the dried and shrivelled flesh. What do you think you're doing?'

'I should ask you the same thing, old friend.'

'Oh, come now, Berith. Friend? That is pushing it. I might be dead, but I am hardly desperate or stupid,' he said with a sly grin.

Berith cocked his eyebrow. The line of his mouth curled into an evil lopsided smirk. He glanced over his shoulder to see Duncan unmoved on the ground. 'Come, old friend. What business is this of yours? Leave before I am forced to hurt you.'

'As much as I'd love to, Berith, I can't. You see, I need him in one piece, and alive. You're not known for your delicate touch.'

Berith stomped forward; his body grew in stature. Then, in a blur, he hurtled toward Gilly.

Gilly held his arms aloft by his sides, with the faintest hint of a smile on his lips. He raised his right foot and paused. Then, when Berith was upon him, he lurched to his left, as if he had lost his balance. It had only been a fleeting moment but sufficient for Berith to miss Gilly and career past. Gilly returned his foot to the ground to prevent his fall and spun on his heel in time to see Berith collide into the cemetery fence with a resounding clatter.

Berith howled and violently shook the fence; the iron bars from the fence fell like surrendering skittles. Seething, he bolted upright and faced Gilly. Steam escaped his flared nostrils, his face flushed with rage. He lunged at Gilly. His fingers flexed as they clamoured for their target.

Over the centuries Gilly had encountered Berith on numerous occasions. They would exchange a few words and then engage in a bout of roughhousing which usually ended with Berith in need of medication, and quietly pondering how he could have lost to a walking corpse. It wasn't because Gilly was an expert in martial arts or renowned for his combat skills, but simply because he used his powers of observation. Added to this, it was generally accepted Berith was hardly the brightest star in the sky. For instance, he knew Berith's next move would be to leap at him. He made the same move every time; routine and no surprise. First, he would charge, then spin, and finish with a lunge. You could use a lot of words to describe Berith, but never original or intelligent. You would most certainly never describe him as a forward thinker, a planner, nor sensible. Why would someone who persistently lost continue battling?

Gilly waited until the splayed body of Berith loomed and, in one sprightly move, hopped backwards. Berith frowned as his body arced downwards and, a millisecond later, his head ploughed into the road. His body acted as a trowel, digging a trench the length of the road, coming to a stop at Gilly's feet.

Gilly hobbled over the semi-buried body on his way to assist Duncan.

'Owwwww,' squealed Duncan, struggling to his feet. Blood stained his white shirt with an ugly, undesirable shade of red. His hand tentatively rubbed his side, and his face contorted in pain.

'Are you okay?' asked Gilly.

'Not really,' said Duncan feebly, accompanied by an audible groan from his neck.

Duncan studied the scene of carnage: The dismantled fence, the churned bitumen, strewn debris, and the sprawled figure. 'Why did he attack me?'

'I don't think he gets out much. Last time I saw him I suggested anger counselling, but he never listens. Personally, I think it would work wonders for him.'

Duncan cradled his chest. 'I think I've popped a rib.' He grimaced. 'Is he… dead?'

'Probably not. It's actually very difficult to kill a demon, and trust me, you don't want to do that. It would take you a century to complete the paperwork, in triplicate, capitals and black ink,' said Gilly.

'Demon?' said Duncan, his voice incredulous.

'Is it not obvious?' Gilly asked from beneath his hat.

'I… Why is this happening to me? And… and why is it that whenever I am in trouble you are there?'

'You could be a little more grateful,' said Gilly. 'I did just save your life.'

'You did not.'

'I did so.'

'This is stupid!' exclaimed Duncan.

'Look, you've only got yourself to blame. I've been trying to warn you. I did say you were in mortal danger.' Gilly waxed indignantly.

'I… I'm sorry. You're right. I've had a rough day.'

'That's okay. I've got an idea. I know how you can make it up to me. Why don't you come with me to my office?'

'To Purgatory?' asked Duncan.

'It'll only take fifteen minutes. Besides, it's the least you can do after I saved your life for the second time.'

Duncan hesitated as he studied Gilly. 'Fine. But, after this, you have to leave me alone.'

Gilly mumbled something along the lines of Duncan being an ungrateful sod before hobbling to the cemetery. Duncan hesitated at the edge of the pavement, where the fence once stood providing some form of protection.

'Where are you taking me?' asked Duncan, his voice suspicious.

'I thought we'd established that. My office,' said Gilly.

'No, I mean, why are we going into a cemetery?'

'You don't expect us to walk? We have to catch the Tomb to get to Purgatory.'

'The Tomb?' Duncan spat the words.

'Come on.' Gilly gestured for Duncan to follow him. Duncan crossed the threshold of the cemetery and picked his way between the graves.

Gilly leaned against the mausoleum and shoved hard on its thick steel door. At first it didn't move but, after a few more thrusts, it opened with a groan. Gilly stepped forward and melted into the darkness. Duncan gulped audibly and reluctantly entered the darkened mausoleum, his arms outstretched in front of him, feeling his way. Behind him, the door quietly slid closed.

26

Instantly, the room lit up. There was a jolt, followed by a shudder and then a gentle humming noise. A gentle, bland instrumental arrangement emanated from above their heads. Duncan inclined his head and noticed the speaker in the corner. It was '*The girl from Ipanema*'.

'That song is everywhere,' said Duncan.

Gilly cringed in response. 'I know. It's worse than having your ears stuffed with maggots.'

'Are we in an elevator?' asked Duncan, sounding surprised.

'This is the Tomb. Purgatory's transport system. Similar to your subway, but much less crowded, obviously. In fact, outside of Purgatory I'm the only person who uses it.'

'We're in an elevator going to Purgatory?'

'You have to get to Purgatory somehow' replied Gilly nonchalantly.

'You do know, there is no such place as Purgatory?'

'We're catching the Tomb to Purgatory, and you think there is no such place? You better be wrong, or we're going to be in here for a while.' Gilly smiled.

'This is insane. We're not going to Purgatory. We're not even in an elevator. We're standing in a mausoleum.'

'Kind of, but you can't exactly leave an elevator in the middle of a road. People would start using it as a toilet or something.'

'So, you're telling me, that opposite my flat is a Tomb stop that leads to Purgatory?'

'Yes. You know, if you think about it, it does make sense, it's not like your street has any other reason to be there. The Tomb stop gives your street purpose. Actually, most cemeteries have a Tomb station. You just have to know where to look.' They both stared forward. 'Legally, Purgatory has to cater to the disabled and, as you can imagine, my decayed condition makes it difficult for me to get around these days, so they need all the Tomb stops. I used to have to use conventional travel like trains and flying, but that's a nightmare. Have you ever tried to obtain a passport when you are dead? Let me tell you, it's impossible. Besides, a flight to New York takes how long? Eight hours? Using the Tomb system,

I can travel between London and New York in ten minutes. Though I do miss watching the movies on the flights.'

'I see,' remarked Duncan perplexed. They remained silent until Duncan spoke again. 'You do know you smell. It isn't pleasant.'

Gilly mumbled obscenities under his breath.

The doors slid open. Gilly gently steered Duncan out into a large white reception room, glowing with warmth. The beaming face of Ms Fairchild greeted them from behind her desk.

'Welcome, Sir, and is this the famous Mr Bottomley I have heard so much about?'

Duncan stared, unable to speak.

'I thought I would give Mr Bottomley a quick guided tour, put us on the map, so to speak; for some reason, he is finding it difficult to believe Purgatory exists.'

'The Living are funny, Sir.' She smiled her own brand of forced smile.

A door suddenly appeared to one side, causing Duncan to fling himself backwards and grab his chest as if his heart had fibrillated. His expression of a stunned mullet.

'Have a good day, Sir,' she said chirpily. She turned to Duncan and the chill of her gaze belied the warmth of her voice. 'And do enjoy your visit, Mr Bottomley.'

Gilly hobbled over to the corridor and turned, beckoning Duncan to follow. Duncan lowered his head and raised his hand to shield his eyes from the light. They passed a glass staircase, with Gilly whispering behind a cupped hand that the stairs led to a real pain in the arse who was best avoided whenever possible. They passed through a double set of doors, which swung slowly behind them until closed.

Duncan froze in his tracks. Before him, stretching into the horizon, as far as he could see, was row after row of cubicles. The occasional head of an occupant could be seen bobbing above the walls. Five metres away, a large cabinet suddenly appeared without warning, causing Duncan to jump.

'Ah, yes. Best you don't stand still for too long. The last thing you want is for a VSF unit to appear where you are standing. It can be very messy,' said Gilly.

'A VSF unit?' enquired Duncan, as they walked on.

'Vanishing Storage Facilities. It's a long story. Best saved for another day. So, here we are, welcome to Purgatory!' Gilly said cheerfully. 'This is the hub of operations for Tellus Limited. From here, all support, recruitment, day-to-day operations and administration takes place. Basically, it's where anything boring happens.'

They sauntered past various departments and teams, signs hanging above the desks informing them of the section name.

Nobody paid them any attention.

'This is the Reconciliations department,' announced Gilly.

'What do they do?' asked Duncan, though with his mouth agape it sounded as if he said 'wa du ey du?'

'They reconcile deaths against births, against shares on issue, and so on and so on and so on. All quite boring,' said Gilly matter-of-fact.

Duncan nodded his fake understanding.

They rounded a corner and entered a cavernous room easily the size of the last six or seven departments put together. Millions of computer screens littered the desks, all manned by well-heeled individuals screaming and shouting at each other, though in a very polite and pleasant way as if they were watching a choir abusing their competition through song whilst respectful of the fact they were in church.

'Oh, please, if you have a moment, I would greatly appreciate your assistance with the placement of this trade. Only when you have a moment of course,' shouted one of the well-heeled individuals.

'These are the rocket scientists. The traders,' said Gilly.

'Traders?' mumbled Duncan. 'What are they trading?'

'Commodities mainly. You know, trees, minerals, water, souls—'

'Souls?' interjected Duncan.

'Absolutely. That desk there,' said Gilly, pointing to a table of about fifty people. 'They trade dolphin souls. And that desk over there, gorilla souls. And do you see that group in the middle?'

Duncan raised himself onto the tip of his toes for a better look, there were at least a thousand people in a frenzied huddle in the middle of the room.

'They trade the human souls, they're the best of the best.'

Duncan shook his head. 'I don't understand.'

'Understandably, you've only been alive for a few decades. You probably know it best as "reincarnation". In purgatory, we call it trading. You know how some people might believe in a past life they were a dolphin? Well, they probably were. That's what these traders do. They buy and sell souls, placing them where there are gaps in the market. Simple arbitraging, nothing complicated.'

'Sorry? They do what?' shrieked Duncan, loud enough for a few heads nearby to turn.

Gilly made a hushing sound and grabbed Duncan by the elbow, steering him away from the trading floor and safely out of earshot.

'What do you think you are doing? This is Purgatory; you have to watch how you behave. They take a dim view of visitors causing trouble. You're lucky they didn't send an ANGEL!'

'An Angel?'

'Oh yes, and you don't want to encounter one of them. Hate them. A stupid idea by Gabriel, he's the Chief Strategy Officer.' Gilly looked at Duncan who stared blankly in response. 'ANGEL. It's short for an Airborne North-star Guided Evangelical weapon Launcher. If you get hit by an ANGEL you're instantly incapacitated by a bout of religious guilt. Very nasty.'

Gilly ignored Duncan's flapping jaw and continued the tour.

'Over here is the Carbon Emissions team,' Gilly waved his hand towards the employees huddled underneath a large computer monitor with a rotating image of the Earth, covered in splotches of red, blue, orange and green.

'I'm going to hate myself for asking this, but what do they do?' Duncan asked feebly.

'They do the modelling. You know, running through various "what-if?" scenarios. At the moment, they are calculating the effect on carbon emissions if all of the cows were eliminated.'

'They want to kill the cows?' whispered Duncan.

'Well, theoretically they do. When you think about it, it's not a bad idea. Flatulent cows produce more CO_2 than cars. Something needs to be done to protect the planet and, if the living won't do anything, then Purgatory needs to. We considered removing the cars but dismissed that idea; the Americans would be in uproar if they had to start walking. Far more trouble than it's worth. However, on the other hand, nobody would question a disease suddenly wiping out all the cows? I wouldn't worry about it; you'll find Purgatory can be quite slow when it comes to making a decision. Maybe next century.'

'Why didn't Purgatory just stop them inventing cars in the first place?' said Duncan.

'Do you see any cars around here? No. They were a dividend from the competition. It took us all by surprise, had nothing to do with us.'

Duncan's upper lip quivered. 'I don't understand… Purgatory… It's a place for tormented souls.'

'Indeed. Have you tried working for a corporation? It doesn't get much more tormenting than that.' Gilly's smile grew until it almost met at the back. 'You see, Purgatory is where those who have not cast a vote in the shareholder meeting stay. Those who aren't ready to vote or those who prefer to abstain from voting for whatever reason. Everybody else passes through here on their way to whoever they have allocated their vote to.'

'Their vote?'

'And here is our custodial area. They are responsible for the management, issuance and allocation of shares.'

There was row after row of tables facing a wall-sized screen, dominated by charts. In the middle, dwarfing the neighbouring graphs, a large bar chart with only two bars. Blue and red bars, though the blue bar almost doubled the size of the red bar.

'Do you see that graph there?' asked Gilly, his lesion dotted finger pointing at the screen. 'That graph shows the shareholdings in Tellus Limited. Those voting for the Chairperson is the blue and the competition, that private equity group I mentioned, is the red bar.'

'Shares? Voting? None —'

'Of this makes sense?' interrupted Gilly. 'How did I know you would say that. Let's start at the beginning. The Chairperson founded Tellus Limited millennia ago. Hugely successful, but eventually, became too big for even him to manage. Subsequently, he took Tellus public, and the company went from strength to strength. Unfortunately, a former employee started a private equity group and immediately launched a hostile takeover bid for the company. And, since then, they have been buying shares in the company and steadily increasing their holding.'

'I don't… I'm confused. What shares? What company?'

'You do ask a lot of questions. Each soul on issue represents a share in Tellus Limited. There are different classes of shares, some have voting rights and others don't — those allocated to squirrels, for example. But basically, when somebody dies, they are required to cast their vote at the shareholders meeting.'

'This is ridiculous. You're saying I am a share in a company?'

'Sort of but, if you want to be precise, you're actually the shareholder. You can't think your time on Earth has no purpose, surely? Everybody has a purpose and that is to vote. It's the right of every person. The time you spend on Earth is intended to educate you so when you do die you will be able to make an educated and informed decision on who should be running the company. Your life is one giant prospectus.'

They weaved their way back to the reception. Gilly led the way with Duncan tramping behind vehemently shaking his head. Suddenly, as if jerked to a standstill by a rope, Duncan froze.

'Wait a minute. Tellus Limited is the Earth?'

'You are quick. Yes, and Purgatory is the operations centre for Tellus Limited, or Earth, if that makes you happy.'

'Then the Chairperson is God?' stammered Duncan.

'The Chairperson goes by many names. You could probably say "hey you", and he would answer but, God is one of the names he uses. Or one that has been assigned to him.'

'And when you say a person casts a vote? You mean they are choosing between good and evil?'

'A bit simplistic. Most votes aren't cast for good or evil but for the organisation considered to have been most helpful during the shareholders time in Tellus limited.' said Gilly.

Duncan remained po-faced.

'Unfortunately, the Chairperson doesn't want to get involved, the Chairperson's hands are full founding the new company. From what I've heard, it's quite cutting edge.'

'God, is creating a new planet?'

'A new company, yes. I believe it's called Gorf. You won't have heard of it. It's about 150 billion miles from Tellus limited,' he replied in a matter of fact tone, as if the building of a new planet was comparable to noticing fluff in your bellybutton.

'Anyway,' he continued, 'with the Chairperson absent, the competition exploited this and have been a continual thorn in our sides since. I told you how cars were a dividend to the shareholders from the competition, this private equity group. At the time, we didn't really think much of it. After all, they were ugly metal boxes on wheels? We had no idea how much the shareholders would come to rely on them. As a result, shareholders are dying too soon and making uninformed decisions when they cast their vote, but we can't take cars away now? Most shareholders wouldn't vote for the company that took their cars away. Now we have all sorts of problems, unexpected deaths, carbon emissions, some shareholders are becoming extinct because their natural habitat is being bulldozed over to make more roads. But, if we take the cars away, shareholders will revolt, and if that happens, the competition's takeover succeeds.'

'I don't get it. Why would God create Earth, this company, and allow people to vote for evil?'

'Hold on there one second. The Chairperson did no such thing. The Chairperson created an eco-friendly company. The company was good, without problems. It was the shareholders who were not happy with the company's direction.'

They continued to stroll through aisles of desks, Duncan's head doing its best impersonation of an oscillating fan.

'So, you're trying to tell me that God, the Chairperson, is an entrepreneur like *Richard Branson*?' said Duncan.

'I suppose that is one way you might think of it, if your mind was small with limited experience. And the Chairperson most definitely does not have a goatee.'

A gigantic room suddenly appeared beside them. 'The server room,' noted Gilly.

'I don't understand any of this.' whimpered Duncan.

'I really don't understand why any of this difficult for you?' Gilly sniped.

'Oh, I don't know. Maybe because everything you've told me, goes against everything I believe in. I'm walking through Purgatory, which is about as surreal as my dog talking to me,' bridled Duncan.

'You don't have a dog.'

'I know that. It was a figure of speech,' snapped Duncan.

'Oh. While I remember, when we see Ms Fairchild, can you please not mention any of this, especially not your confusion. Otherwise they will make me fill out form XP04082008 in triplicate, in capitals, black ink, blah blah blah. The level of bureaucracy here is astounding.'

'See. There you go again. That doesn't make sense, why would God create bureaucracy in Purgatory?'

'Now that is the first good question you've asked. And I'd love to know the answer. It baffles me. Personally, I put it down to the Chairperson hanging out in black holes too long, it can stuff up your head.'

Duncan stopped, yet again, to ingest what he had just heard. He quickened his pace to catch up with Gilly, for somebody who walked like an ironing board he could move like he was on rollerblades. Gilly moved to one side to allow Duncan through the double doors into the brightly lit corridor. A few paces later they entered the reception area. Gilly exchanged brief pleasantries with Ms Fairchild as they passed her desk. The lift doors promptly opened. They both entered and Duncan turned to stand facing forward, his jaw ajar. Dazed, he waved feebly at Ms Fairchild.

'Excuse me, Sir,' said Ms Fairchild. 'Mr Balthasar has urgently requested your presence.'

Gilly grimaced. 'Oh. Wonderful. You've made my decade. I'll escort Mr Bottomley home and be right back.'

The lift door closed. There was an uncomfortable pause, and the instrumental music started up. The lift shuddered and began to move. Duncan's gaze remained fixed on the door.

The Tomb door swung open and they stepped into the darkened cemetery. Cold night air wrapped itself around Duncan. He noted Berith had disappeared, though the trail of carnage remained.

Duncan folded at his waist, his head on his open palms. 'This is too much,' he wailed.

'I realise this might all be a bit of a shock,' said Gilly.

Duncan lifted his head and glared at Gilly.

Gilly coughed. 'I know I should probably wrap what I'm about to say in cotton wool, that's what Purgatory would want, but I think you can handle the unvarnished truth. Your life is in danger.'

Immediately, Duncan heaved, vomit flew from his lips, pooling by their feet. Gilly's expression scrunched.

'I guess you had carrots for lunch,' Gilly said with disdain.

Duncan pulled himself erect, his hands on his waist as he sucked in breath after breath. He exhaled loudly.

'Feeling better?' asked Gilly. Duncan nodded. 'Listen, this is for your own safety. You need to stay at home and keep your doors locked. Don't answer the door for anybody, apart from me, of course.'

'I can't do that. I have too much on at the moment. Why can't you leave me alone? I can't deal with this. I've just been appointed the CFO of Sheol Trading. I'm an important person now. I have work to do. I have an interview on Monday. People expect things of me now. The last thing I need is to be a target for the dead and demons of this world.' Duncan took a deep breath and stared up to the dark sky. 'What am I saying? Are you hearing what I am saying? I am officially insane.'

'Sorry. A small point,' said Gilly. 'Did you say Sheol Trading?'

'Yes. It's the world's largest hedge fund. I am now the CFO.'

'That is… fascinating,' Gilly paused. 'I have things to do. You do what you need to do, but I have warned you.'

The mausoleum door closed. If Duncan was paranoid, which he was, then it did so with an ominous sound.

27

Gilly stormed into Ballsy's office. His hand descended onto the desktop like a claw hammer, causing the few adornments to hop in place. Ballsy reclined in his chair, a huge smile sliced across his face.

'Was that really necessary?' asked Ballsy.

'Not really, but I enjoyed it,' Gilly said with a smirk. His tone of voice darkened as he continued, complaining about being unable to fulfil his role due to these constant interruptions. He saved his greatest tirade for last when he explained, in far from polite words, how outrageous it was for him to be made to wait nine hours on the grounds of not having an appointment, despite it being Ballsy who urgently requested his presence.

Ballsy apologised with a flutter of his wrist and motioned for Gilly to be seated. Gilly glanced around the room and frowned when his eyes set upon the small swivel chair. His shoulders slumped and he fell like a log into the chair.

'This is a particularly embarrassing and highly unusual situation,' mumbled Ballsy.

In that moment, Gilly cocked his eyebrow and leaned forward as much as his rigor mortis-ridden body would allow him. He might have been mistaken but it sounded like the beginnings of an apology.

'I have received the initial findings from our internal investigation into possible leaks within our organisation. I do stress this is only the initial findings and they could be wrong. However, based upon the information we have, it appears you might have been correct in your fears. I repeat this is by no means conclusive and we have not yet concluded our investigation, but I decided it would be prudent to advise you now rather than later. After all, Gilgamesh, we are all on the same side, and working towards a common goal.'

Gilly blinked, his eyes in shock. He was surprised to hear they had even begun the enquiry, never mind completed an initial review. The last time he had made such a request, it had taken them several centuries to appoint an investigator, and several more to complete an initial review. He had never heard of

187

anything happening so efficiently in all of his millennia of employment at Purgatory.

'What exactly have you learned so far?' asked Gilly, pleased he had waited the nine hours for the meeting.

A cabinet suddenly appeared to the left of Ballsy. He leaned behind him to retrieve a paper clip bound file, then carefully spread it out in front of him, making sure each side of paper touched the side of the sheet next to it.

'Right. It appears yesterday an individual from Deceased Resources was discovered smoking a cigar in Limbo. Naturally, this was suspicious as tobacco products are banned in the Afterlife, as you well know,' Ballsy looked at Gilly through the top of his eyelids. Gilly cleared his throat, shuffled uncomfortably in his chair at the recollection of a distant memory. 'The individual in question attempted to escape when confronted, and it was necessary to incapacitate them with an ANGEL. When interviewed later they confessed to receiving the cigars in exchange for providing information to the competition.'

Duncan knew that once the ANGEL had struck this individual, they would have confessed to everything; including any past and present sins. They would have collapsed under the torrent of religious guilt like a bubble to the touch.

'You have a confession then?' said Duncan surprised.

'It would appear so.'

'And what information did this informant pass on then?'

'Largely inconsequential information,' said Ballsy dismissively. 'Mr Bottomley's name, his location.'

'Inconsequential? If Hell knows about Duncan Bottomley and our plans for him, it would be disastrous. How is that inconsequential?'

'I will need to refer that question to our Product Strategy director, and I will revert once I have an answer,' said Ballsy, stroking his chin.

Gilly pushed back on the chair and planted his feet. The chair rolled away from beneath him, leaving him fighting to regain his balance. 'I told you and the Board something was wrong when he was attacked by the Succubus, but nobody would listen to me.' Gilly shambled up and down the room. 'Were you watching the Living television channel today? Do you know Berith attacked him? He was lucky I was there.'

Ballsy nodded distractedly.

'This doesn't make sense. They know who he is, so why did they attack him?' Gilly asked, largely for his own benefit. 'There's something missing. What are they up to? Why haven't they approached him?' Gilly abruptly halted his pacing and craned his neck to face Ballsy. 'Maybe they have. Ballsy, we—'

'My name is Balthasar. How many times do—' interjected Ballsy.

'Yes. Whatever! Listen!' Gilly turned to face Ballsy. 'The recently deceased with the complaint, Gordon McBride, is he still here?'

'Oh him. Yes. Unfortunately. Which reminds me, I instructed you to stay away from him? And you contacted him again. Do I need to have a restraining order issued against you?'

Gilly patted the air in front of him in a calming gesture. 'Let me assure you, Ballsy, now is not the time. I need to speak with him.'

'It's Balthasar!' said Ballsy with a slap of his hand on the table. 'And you will do no such thing. You have caused enough problems. Are you listening to me Gilgamesh? You are to stay away from him,' his words trailed off. It was a wasted protest as Gilly had already left the office and was halfway down the stairs. Ballsy crossed his arms and grumbled his indignation.

28

'Excuse me, Mr Bottomley. There is a Detective Malloy downstairs in the foyer to see you.' The voice from the phone blared, disturbing Duncan's five minutes of meditation, which had the strange appearance of snoozing.

'Um, right. Okay. I'll be right down.'

Duncan stretched his body and glanced at his LED watch. It read 11.00 a.m.; not even halfway through the day. His late-night wanderings in Purgatory, and the surreal dreams which subsequently followed, ensured he got little sleep last night, and he was paying the price today.

Reluctantly, he pulled himself out of his leather chair and slipped on his suit jacket. Tiny beads of sweat slipped down his brow at the memory of the last time he had seen the detective; Malloy had been cursing his misfortune at not being able to incarcerate Duncan in some grimy cell, where all Duncan would have had to look forward to would be a diet of expired sausages. He girded up his loins and took the elevator down.

The large open space of the foyer was spectacular; it needed to be to rival the view from the offices above. Corporations the world over considered it essential to make an indelible impression on their guests, and the desired impression was one of intimidation and superiority. Duncan strode across the polished marble floor.

Malloy stood like a duck out of water, shifting his weight from side to side as if he was in a lingerie shop waiting for his partner.

As Duncan approached, he wiped his palms on the front of his trousers, removing any excess sweat. Malloy ignored Duncan's outreached hand and instead removed a notebook from his top shirt pocket. He motioned for Duncan to take a seat on one of the numerous black leather sofas located in the foyer. Malloy perched himself on the edge of the sofa and apologised for disturbing him. Perhaps he sensed Duncan's anxiety, but he immediately reassured him the events of last Friday night were long forgotten, and instead he was focussing on a more urgent matter: The homicide of Harold Wilson.

'Homicide?' spluttered Duncan.

190

'Yes,' said Malloy, as he flicked through a few pages on his pad.

Duncan ran a hand through his lank hair, brushing it from his forehead. It was a little over seven hours since he had exited the graveyard, and his understanding of life and the world he knew had been turned upside down. No longer did Duncan simply work for a very large company; he worked for a very large company which was part of the balance sheet for an extremely gigantic company. He wondered if Earth's accountant, assuming it had one, had classified them as an off-balance sheet partnership.

'I was a little surprised when I learnt you worked here,' said Malloy.

'It's all happened rather suddenly. I only learned about it yesterday,' said Duncan, fiddling with his thumbs.

'Yes, I saw it on the news,' he said. 'I understand you knew the deceased.'

Duncan frowned. 'Yes, I do, I mean, I did. It's terrible.'

'Mr Wilson's widow, Mrs Wilson, mentioned you and the deceased were actually working together on the Sheol Trading account. And I understand, you and he had been out together the evening of the incident,' he paused. 'Mrs Wilson also said the deceased returned from the meeting out of sorts, as if there had been an argument. Did you and the deceased have a disagreement that evening?' He gave Duncan a cool measured stare.

'What? No, of course not,' responded Duncan, his tone filled with panic.

'I have witnesses who say they saw you and the deceased having a "serious" conversation before the deceased left that evening.'

'Yes, we were. But it wasn't a disagreement. It was... work stuff.'

'Why don't you tell me about it?' said Malloy.

Duncan related the events from the evening and his conversation with Harold. Soon Malloy grew tired of Duncan's meandering chat and interrupted.

'Let me get this straight. The deceased objects to your promotion, and dies in mysterious circumstances a few hours later?'

Duncan's eyes flickered to life as the innuendo of the

statement dawned on him. 'No. Not like that. We weren't disagreeing. I agreed with him. He had a valid point.'

Malloy chortled. 'The problem is, you see, recently there have been numerous coincidences, and the only two things common to all of these coincidences are you and Sheol Trading. Now, I think you're harmless, probably innocent, but if you're innocent then…' he allowed his words to trail off.

Duncan stared blankly, not picking up on the man's unspoken suggestion.

'Were you aware that a little over a week ago the previous Chief Financial Officer from Sheol Trading, a Mr Gordon McBride, also died in mysterious circumstances?' Malloy waited for Duncan to nod his acknowledgement. 'Do you know how he died?'

Duncan shook his head.

'He had stopped at a service station and his mobile phone somehow sparked, or exploded, igniting the fuel at the station. As if he, or his mobile phone, spontaneously combusted. Unfortunately for him, it did cause a rather large explosion.'

'That is… very odd,' mumbled Duncan.

'You could say that. Let's see.' Malloy flicked to the next page on his pad. 'Then you said a woman picked you up in a pub and… she exploded, spontaneously combusted, while trying to have sex with you.' Malloy looked up from his notepad. 'Do you know in my entire time on the force I have never heard of anything "spontaneously combusting" before? Yet now, in a short space of time there are two incidents.' His eyes returned to the pad. 'Where was I? Oh yes. Even stranger, the remains of this woman were later identified to belong to a goat. Now, to add to all this mystery, we discover that shortly after this incident, you are coincidentally appointed CFO for Sheol Trading, replacing the recently deceased Gordon McBride. But it doesn't end there. Harold Wilson publicly objects to your appointment and he too dies in highly bizarre circumstances. And, coincidentally, he wasn't the first employee of Sheol Trading to die by fireworks.'

Duncan shook his head. His expression vacuous, and then slowly his eyes widened, transforming his look into one of astonishment.

'I didn't realise,' mumbled Duncan.

Malloy furtively glanced around him, then continued in a whisper. 'This is not the time to talk in detail about this. If what I suspect is true, then we don't want to be seen talking for too long. It might attract unnecessary attention,' he motioned with his shoulder at the small black domes, concealing security cameras in the roof above them. 'Meet me at four this afternoon in the alleyway behind the Honey Pot. I assume you know where that is,' whispered Malloy with a smile on his lips. 'Oh, and if anybody asks you why I was here, tell them I had some routine questions about Harold Wilson's death, seeing as you were the last to speak with him apart from his wife.'

Duncan hesitated, then nodded glumly.

Malloy rose, extended his hand and, in a loud, rehearsed voice, thanked Duncan for his time.

Duncan watched Malloy stride out into the overcast and dreary day. A long, bendy bus stopped at the bus stop outside the front of the building, a sign on its side proudly bragged about its environmentally friendly credentials but, unsurprisingly, neglected to mention the congestion-generating side effect, which wasn't so good for the environment.

As the bus pulled away, a black cab pulled up in its wake. The rear door popped open and Richard Steel hopped out. He swept into the foyer like a ship at full sail, and with a flurry of his arms, he removed his long overcoat, draping it over his arm. Duncan reclined in the chair and reciprocated Richard's wave with a limp movement of his wrist.

'Good morning, or is it afternoon? Still morning, I think. Come, come, Duncan, you are looking decidedly pale. You should take a holiday. Get some sun.'

'Um, yes, I think you might be right. Could I start today?'

'Come, come, Duncan. Not at a time like this. Everybody is reliant upon you. What seems to be the problem?' Richard swooped into the chair recently vacated by Malloy.

Duncan stuttered as he gathered his thoughts. He wasn't sure where to start. Did he tell him about Gilly? About his visit to Purgatory? About Earth being one massive galactic corporation? About all the coincidences Malloy had discussed. Perhaps this was one big hallucination brought on by stress, or a nightmare that he had yet to wake up from? Either way, he didn't fancy the situation getting any worse, which it surely would if he gave cause for people to suspect he was insane. In prudent deference, he opted to regale Richard with the details of his encounter with Malloy, leaving out the incriminating details about him and exploding women. He also explained Malloy's suspicions.

'Malloy, you say. I've heard of him before. I must say, his behaviour is definitely odd. I mean, what's his point? Of course, it's all a coincidence, and a coincidence by its very nature is strange. This is most unusual.' Richard sat there furiously shaking his head.

'I don't think I should meet him this afternoon,' said Duncan.

'No, no. You must go. The last thing we need is for this situation to be twisted, and your lack of showing up to be confused with you refusing to assist the police. However, I think it is wise for you to be fitted for a wire; at least we will have a record of the conversation. Better to be safe than sorry.' Richard noticed Duncan's hesitation.

'I have work to do,' said Duncan.

'It is essential for you and the company to be seen to be co-operating. But if he is up to something then we will have evidence to protect you. It's common sense, old boy.'

'*It doesn't stop*,' thought Duncan, feeling sorry for himself.

They exited the building as a united team. Richard's palm rested on Duncan's shoulder. As they stepped into the rotating doorway, Richard looked backwards and smiled at the small black domes in the ceiling.

***

Later that afternoon, Duncan's footsteps echoed through the narrow laneways, clicking and clacking like horse hooves. With each step he exhaled, steam escaped from his mouth obscuring his view. Every few steps he would stop, cock his head and listen, in case somebody was following him. Every ten or so steps, he stopped, then ran backwards to the nearest corner and looked around to see if he could catch anybody following him.

He slinked past the Honey Pot, peeking in the window. The pub was near empty; still too early for the after-work crowd to have poured in. The bar staff would have enjoyed this respite from the bedlam which would undoubtedly soon follow, especially as it was a Friday night. He briefly considered popping in for a quick one himself but, as his watch reminded him it was already four, he knew he didn't have the time.

He turned the corner and gazed down the empty alleyway.

The time was 4.03 p.m., but there was no sign of Malloy? The waft of stale odours and rotting foods floated on the icy breeze. In the darkened corners at the far end of the alley, he could make out a collection of bins. He shivered beneath his coat and hunkered down to shield himself from the cold.

A light drizzle beaded on his coat. In the not too far distance, he heard the familiar sounds of congestion: Horns honking, brakes squealing and spluttering of engines.

Beneath his shirt his nipple irritated him or, to be precise, the electronic listening device stuck beneath his nipple by a wad of tape, itched considerably. He wriggled his chest in an attempt to subtly reposition the device. He succeeded in shifting the tape, which removed a large portion of the few chest hairs he had. He winced in pain.

Judging by the sounds coming from behind him, the Honey Pot was starting to get busy. It wouldn't be long before this alley became a thoroughfare for those on their way to the pub or those in need of a wall to urinate against. He heaved a sigh and shambled through the alley to the other end where it opened into a courtyard. He looked around but there was still no sign of Malloy. Duncan stamped his foot and cussed under his breath. His watch read 4.16 p.m. A trickle of water pooled in the bald spot at his crown before running down a lock of greasy hair, which acted as a drainpipe leading it beneath his collar. A silent obscenity frothed from his mouth as he headed back towards the warmth and dryness of the Honey Pot.

'*I need a pint of lager,*' he thought.

Duncan stopped involuntarily mid-way down the alleyway. Something caught his attention.

To his right, protruding from the garbage bags, appeared to be an arm. With great uncertainty, he crouched down and prodded at the arm with his index finger. It did not move. This time, he jabbed at the arm hard, and then harder, but it still elicited no response. He reached over and pulled on the nearest large black bag, which was more of a sack, and watched it's bright yellow drawstring roll in and out of view as it fell from the mound of refuse. Duncan, his lips pursed as he frowned, smeared his fingers on his jacket, hoping to remove any stray bacteria which might have made the leap from the bag to his hand. His gaze returned to the mound and Malloy's lifeless face stared back; beneath it, his neck yawned wide, amidst vast quantities of congealed blood.

It felt like an interminable time to Duncan, as if everything slowed down around him, life freezing as the sheer horror ascended on his consciousness. He recoiled.

His eyes filled with horror and revulsion, and he stumbled to the ground bottom first. His feet scratched against the cobblestones as he scuttled backwards until he hit the wall. He pulled his legs tight to his chest and waved his hand in front of his face to disperse the fog generated by his rapid breathing. His back crawled up the wall's surface until he was able to stand with the wall behind him.

From nearby he heard footsteps approach, their sound ricocheted across the cobblestones; stilted laughter accompanying them. Duncan glimpsed down at Malloy and his slit throat. His mind raced.

This was perhaps one coincidence too many. Who would believe him if he told them he had stumbled upon the body? How would it be perceived if he told the truth, that he had simply been there for a prearranged rendezvous which had abruptly ended with Malloy's death before he had ever arrived? Neither explanation looked good for him, let alone for Malloy, who had definitely seen better days.

Scared for his life and worried for his freedom, Duncan sprinted from the scene pursued by a trail of steam.

He stopped abruptly when he reached Corn Hill, not out of necessity but to avoid attracting unwarranted attention. A scream cut through the night air. A police patrol ran past him in the direction of the screeching. Voyeuristic passers-by followed close behind the police.

Duncan looked left and right, then crossed the road. His pace quickened to a fast walk and he descended down steps into Bank tube station.

29

Duncan exited Clapham Junction train station. Absent minded from paranoia, he stumbled home on autopilot, oblivious to his surroundings. He recalled the last time he had been this paranoid, and coincidentally, that had been exactly a week ago, when this nightmare first started, and his life had begun to spiral into an unrecognisable form.

If he didn't hate coincidences before, he did now.

The dampness of the footpath chilled his feet. It was one of those rare moments where he cursed his miserly behaviour. If he had spent an extra thirty pounds, he wouldn't have found himself, in the middle of winter, wearing cardboard for shoes.

After years of constant use, his last pair of shoes developed a cavity in one of its soles, an issue he remedied by wedging a beer coaster into the insole. Unfortunately, a misplaced step in a puddle necessitated the need for a new pair. He spent days deliberating over a pair of finely made Italian shoes, or the Chinese equivalent, but he found it impossible to ignore the difference in price. Besides, in the eye of a casual observer, the Chinese manufactured shoes appeared identical to the Italian shoes. Unfortunately for Duncan, he failed to realise it wasn't only the price that was half of the Italian shoes, but also the thickness of the leather and the quality.

Police sirens wailed in the distance and grew in volume. His head sunk into his shoulders as far as it could go. He pulled the collar on his jacket up around his neck. As the sirens approached, he turned to nonchalantly inspect the nearby wall. The flashing blue lights howled past, briefly irradiating him.

Police sirens were a routine occurrence in the area and normally he wouldn't have batted an eyelid at the sight of one, but his rampant paranoia ensured he thought they were looking for him. He watched the blue strobes fade from view.

Splash. His foot sunk into a puddle.

The slush and water reached his shin. He raised his dripping foot, slapped his forehead with his open palm and swore profusely. A few passers-by giggled at the sight of his misfortune. His soaked shoe slapped against the ground as he stomped home.

A short distance later, the sole from his drenched inexpensive Chinese shoe, peeled away from the upper part. He gazed behind at the flaccid piece of rubber on the footpath and loudly cursed before limping home. One foot felt cold, the other positively chilled to the bone.

He crossed Battersea Rise and entered his street. As he neared his doorway, he turned to face the cemetery. He stood there resolutely, for the first time unafraid of the cemetery, his head swivelled as he scanned the surrounds.

'Gilgamesh,' he bellowed.

He waited for a response but there was none. He strode purposefully over to the mausoleum and shoved on the door. It didn't budge.

'Gilgamesh!'

No response.

'Typical,' he said aloud. 'He stalks me for a week and when I need him, he isn't around.'

He kicked the fallen fence and ruminated on what he had done to warrant this. Was it all some sort of cosmic joke that he was not privy to? Had he erred so much in a past life that this was fate's way of getting the last laugh? He sighed and retreated to the comfort of his flat.

***

Duncan spent that weekend in a state of paralysis, unable to speak or move, and barely capable of performing basic tasks like feeding himself. The curtains of his bay window remained closed apart from a small gap in the side which he frequently used to peek at the road below. He remained in the darkened living room, dressed in his tired bathrobe and threadbare slippers, illuminated in a kaleidoscope of soft hues cast by the television. Despite his frugal approach to energy consumption, he left the television on but muted, only raising the volume when news broadcasts came on.

It didn't take long for news of Detective Superintendent Malloy's death to reach the air. At first, the name of the murdered officer was unreleased, with reports only detailing that the victim was a man, and his body had been found in an alleyway near the

Bank of England. But, as the weekend drew to a close, Detective Malloy's name and the cause of death had been well reported, decorating every local and national paper, dominating the news channels and radio stations.

The Metropolitan police commissioner convened a press conference at Sunday lunchtime to express his disgust, and to reveal the more intimate details of the case. He informed the gathered reporters that they had mobilised one of the largest taskforce's in the history of the Metropolitan police, and that they wouldn't rest until the killer was brought to justice. He advised the waiting reporters — who sat like praying vultures, waiting for the next newsworthy detail — that they already had several leads, and he was confident they were close to making an arrest. Duncan moved uncomfortably in his seat and tilted his head as he listened intently for any outside sounds, only to be greeted by silence.

Duncan's attention returned to the television in time to hear the police commissioner say that a white male, in his mid-thirties, was seen running from the scene. Duncan's complexion went deathly pale, and he sunk into the sofa as far as was physically possible.

***

Meanwhile, Gilgamesh, oblivious to the events unfolding amongst the living, spent the weekend 'researching' in Purgatory, at least, that was what he told staff in the department responsible for After-Life statistics.

He had no way of knowing, he might have been needed.

30

There was something different about the albino. For a start, he no longer appeared bored, and it would have been inaccurate to describe him as uninterested. In fact, the opposite appeared to be true. Gilly stood in the doorway, considering the change.

The albino sat, his back ram-rod straight, behind a small glass desk wearing a drooling, idiotic smile on his face, an intercom on one side and an in-tray on the other. For all intents, the albino appeared happy. It was this last detail that confused Gilly the most. Somebody happy in Purgatory? Unheard of.

As Gilly advanced, he idly cast his eyes about the room. No longer was it of cathedral size and filled with clouds of dust and bustling workmen. Instead, sedentary and pleasant. The desk occupied the far end of the room adjacent to a door, and plain wooden benches, all fully occupied, lined the shiny white walls on his left and right.

For an instant, Gilly's eyes sprung wide after spying the sign behind the albino's head, which read: 'McBride & McBride LLP'. Gilly's shoulders slumped and he exhaled loudly.

'Welcome to McBride & McBride, Purgatory's leading law firm. How may I help you today?' chirped the albino.

'What is going on?' asked Gilly, airily waving at the benches and the people waiting.

'Do you have an appointment?'

'Of course not. It's me, remember?'

'Oh yes, Sir. Sorry, Sir. I didn't recognise you. How are you? Would you like to make an appointment? We are quite busy, but we should be able to fit you in a month's time. You could have a seat while you are waiting if you like?' The albino gestured to the already crowded benches.

'No, I don't want an appointment. What is the meaning of this?'

'McBride & McBride is now open. I must say, it has been non-stop. Honestly. People from all over Purgatory have come through those doors. I had no idea there were so many people unhappy with being dead, Sir.'

'Go figure.' Gilly smiled without humour. 'What are you

200

doing here?'

The albino crouched his head down low to the desk and beckoned with his index finger for Gilly to lean closer. 'I'm moonlighting, Sir,' he whispered. 'Mr McBride noticed I wasn't particularly busy and made me an offer of employment as their receptionist. I didn't think anybody would mind. It is sort of a service to those who are already dead, and isn't that what After Death Services is all about?'

'Why would you accept the job?' said Gilly, his voice raised.

'They have an excellent pension scheme, Sir.'

'What do you need with a pension? You're dead!'

The albino's cheeks flushed a hue of pink. 'I didn't think about that, Sir.'

'Why are people failing to realise the obvious lately?' And, with a flourish of his long coat, he hobbled to the adjacent door.

'Wait— Sir—'

'What?' Gilly glared over his shoulder.

'You can't go in there, Sir. You need an appointment,' stammered the albino.

Gilly throttled the doorknob as if it were a snake and flung it open. It crunched against the freshly painted plasterboard wall leaving a depression.

'Ah. Wonderful. Gilgamesh, isn't it?' said Gordon in his expensive accent.

Gilly absorbed the scene.

A series of curtained meeting rooms next to one another with plush carpeting spread throughout and, directly in front of him, Gordon barrelled out of a glass fronted office with an extended hand ready to greet him.

'Let me guess,' said Gordon, eagerly shaking Gilly's hand, 'Your superiors sent you to settle this distasteful situation.'

'No.' Gilly shook his head.

'Oh.'

Gilly dropped his stiff arm on Gordon's shoulder and ushered him back into his office. 'You and I need to have a talk.'

Gordon responded with a blank expression. He slumped into his high-backed leather seat, rose to his feet, straightened his suit jacket and then, gently this time, sat back down. He inclined his head, languorously stroking his chin as he gazed up at Gilly, who leaned against the edge of the table.

'I need your help on another matter I am dealing with,' said Gilly.

'And why would I help you?' Gordon set his lips in a slight smile.

'It involves your replacement at Sheol Trading.'

Gordon's lips parted and his eyes narrowed. 'They have replaced me? Already?'

'Oh, yes. They recently appointed Duncan Bottomley as the Chief Financial Officer.'

Gordon's eyebrows raised, nostrils flared, and his lips quivered. 'Do you now appreciate what my death has done? Not only am I dead, I am now unemployed.'

'You tend to be unemployed when you die.'

'And you now expect me to help you and this Bottomley chap?'

'I know you will help me.' Gilly smiled and tapped his nose knowingly.

Gordon chuckled by way of reply and waved his hand airily in Gilly's direction. 'Oh, will I?'

'Yes. You see, you have people queuing up outside waiting to see you and all because you have Purgatory running scared. People think you have already won your case. I wonder what impact it would have on your business if you lost your case. What would happen if your case were thrown out of court? A court, I might add, which doesn't exist?'

'I'm not following you.'

'I'll make it easy for you.' Gilly delved into his coat pocket and energetically rummaged about. Finally, his spindly, lesion-dotted fingers appeared grasping a document folded in half lengthways. 'You'll find this interesting.' Slowly, he unfolded the document and, using the flat of his hand, he smoothed out the crease before clearing his throat.

Gordon craned his neck for a better view of the text. 'What is that?'

'I'm glad you asked. After a bit of searching through Purgatory's records, I managed to track down your girlfriend. Sorry, your ex-girlfriend.'

'Err, right. And how is Sarah?'

'She's adjusting to being dead,' said Gilly with a shrug of his shoulders. 'But you were right; she absolutely doesn't like you. We had a very long conversation and, as it turns out, she holds you completely responsible for her death. She even signed this affidavit,' Gilly waved the paper about, 'declaring you were wholly responsible for her death and your own. She also states if it hadn't been for your greed and self-serving interests, then the both of you would still be alive.' Gilly chuckled for a few moments. 'She really doesn't like you. She was even toying with the idea of suing you for her wrongful death but, after I informed her yours was the only law firm in Purgatory, she dismissed that idea.'

Gordon's eyes widened.

'But I digress. Where was I? Oh, yes. Based on this testimony, there is no way Purgatory could be held responsible for your death, or "illegal termination" as you have professionally called it. Hardly qualifies as gross negligence if it was your own actions which led to your demise,' said Gilly smugly as he folded the document. 'And, as there was only one witness, I think the case would be pretty much over before it began.'

'This is preposterous. It's inadmissible. It's—' spluttered Gordon.

'I'm not a lawyer, I don't know, but it sounds fairly damning to me. However, if you were to assist me, then in exchange for your assistance, I will conveniently file this affidavit in a VSF unit where it will no doubt be lost for eternity.'

'You would do that?'

'Yes. I couldn't care less about Purgatory. My concern is ensuring the company survives. Besides, it will give me no end of pleasure watching Ballsy get upset.'

'What do you need from me?' Gordon regarded Gilly through suspicious eyes.

'It's really very simple. Tell me who gave you the job as CFO at Sheol Trading?'

'That's a silly question. The Devil of course.'

'Not one of her representatives?'

'Of course not. I only deal with the executive level. I am important, after all.'

'Fine. And who is the Devil?'

'You know. Satan. Beelzebub. Old Nick. Prince of Darkness.'

'Yes. Yes. Lucifer and I go back a long way. What I meant was, what human form has the Devil taken this time?'

There was a long silence, interrupted only by Gordon repeatedly clicking his pen. 'I can't tell you,' Gordon said finally. 'I signed a non-disclosure agreement. The Devil would sue me.'

'You're dead! Lucifer killed you. I don't think you should be overly concerned about her suing you.'

Gordon made an exaggerated gesture of clamping his lips shut.

Gilly rocked forward onto his feet, moved to the other side of the desk, and leaned next to Gordon. 'I appreciate this is a dilemma for you. If you tell me, then yes you may breach your non-disclosure agreement. However, if you don't then this document will become public knowledge, no doubt destroying everything you have built here.' Gilly paused to pluck a maggot that had been nestling in his ear, before continuing. 'I am reminded of that old expression: What the Devil doesn't know, won't hurt you. So, what is it going to be?'

'Fine,' said Gordon in a quavering voice. 'But if Lucifer kills me, then—'

'Honestly! You're dead already!'

31

The winter weather drove Duncan to despair. He left for work in darkness and returned home in darkness. For six months of the year he was lucky to even catch a glimpse of the sun.

At this time of year Duncan dreamt of leaving England for a country with a more amiable climate. Somewhere like Australia would be ideal, apart from the fact they incessantly said 'no worries'. This concerned Duncan greatly; were the inhabitants of this sun-kissed country subscribing to anarchy?

Let's rob a bank today: No worries.

We're going to change things for the sake of change: No worries.

Let's spontaneously combust: No worries.

No, this was no place for Duncan, as he believed in the institution of troubles and concerns. In a strange way, worrying made him feel alive. After all, it was something he excelled at.

Nevertheless, despite his concerns, on this particular Monday morning he found himself yearning to be somewhere else; anywhere would have been preferable to London.

Furtively, he stepped out onto the street. A cold wind chilled him to the bone, penetrating his long, thick winter coat. To be fair, it wasn't the weather that made him hanker for being somewhere else, preferably on the other side of the world, but the recent events. In such a short space of time, his life had been completely dismantled, leaving it in splintered shards.

Last night, suffering from the accumulated effects of being in a permanent state of paranoia combined with sleep deprivation, he decided he was in over his head much like a drowning rat and needed help. Despite it being most likely detrimental to his career, he had no recourse; he made the decision to seek help.

Whilst Gilly had saved his life on a couple of occasions, he still couldn't bring himself to trust a dead person, and besides, he hadn't seen him since Thursday. The only other person he could think of was Lucy. She had used her contacts before to save him from an embarrassing situation; maybe she could use her contacts again. She would believe him when he said he had nothing to do with the inspector's murder. By now she would know he was not capable of doing such a thing. Besides, she often said they were family.

Duncan slid into his car, turned on the ignition, and flicked a variety of switches, buttons and knobs: Headlights, heated seats, satellite navigation, heating and the radio all buzzed into fast, efficient life.

The car slowly turned until it sat facing the opposite direction and then stuttered to the end of the road where it paused before banking to the right.

Moments after the whine of Duncan's car receded into the distance, a red Ferrari grumbled into the street. The car lurched and crunched against the bitumen as it bottomed out, traversing the newly laid ditch.

The car came to a halt beside the cemetery. The door swung open and Richard ungracefully extricated himself from the car. He bent over and squeezed his knees in an attempt to erase the twinges of pain. For a man of his age, his car far from practical. Under his breath he spat curses at the ditch then quickly ran his open palm over the front bumper. That was the extent of his mechanical skills: A loving, lingering stroke to reassure the car.

He gazed up and down the road then hurried to the front door of Duncan's building. After a few minutes of fumbling, the door creaked open. Richard glanced about one final time then slipped inside.

Seconds before, while Richard was caressing his car, the mausoleum door opened silently, and Gilly emerged. He shuffled forwards, remaining shrouded in the shadowy borders of the cemetery, in time to watch Richard sneak into the building. Gilly sidled up to the lone part of the cemetery fence which still stood after Berith's visit.

A few minutes later, Richard emerged from the building and tip toed to his car, furtively peeking around.

'And what do you think you're doing?' Gilly said loudly.

Richard froze, as if somebody had grabbed him by the scruff of his neck. His head spun in all directions. A figure with an odd stance hobbled towards him from the cemetery. The ridiculously large summer hat the man wore, in spite the depressingly dark, cold winter, immediately caught his attention.

'Who are you?' asked Richard, his tone dismissive.

'Nobody you would know. At least, nobody you would *want* to know, but I know you and, importantly, I know what you're up to,' retorted Gilly.

'What are you talking about? Who are you? What are you doing here?'

'The name is Gilgamesh. My friends call me Gilly, but you can call me Gilgamesh. As for what I am doing here, well, it is all rather simple but no doubt too complicated for you. You see, I am dead, living impaired, if you will, and I am here to stop Hell from taking over Tellus Limited. You, as it so happens, work for Hell or, to be more precise, you are employed by the Devil. Shame on you.'

Richard laughed nervously. 'Poppycock!'

'What don't you believe?' asked Gilly in a querulous tone.

'What you just said. It's poppycock. You can't be dead, that's impossible,' said Richard, his voice sounding less confident with every syllable.

'You work for the Devil, and you don't believe I'm dead. Unbelievable!' said Gilly indignantly.

'Clearly, you are insane and, based on your appearance, homeless. As much as I would enjoy tormenting your disturbed mind, I do not have time for this.' Richard rolled on to his toes, extending to his maximum height and pushing his shoulders back like some sort of jumped-up peacock.

'What do you think will happen to you once you have served your purpose? The Devil doesn't care whether you live or die.'

'I will be a very rich man. I know where the skeletons are buried, so to speak,' riposted Richard.

Gilly gave Richard a patronising grin. 'Which is exactly why the Devil will kill you once you have served your purpose.'

Richard checked himself from responding. Mentally, he digested Gilly's last statement.

'Where is Duncan?' enquired Gilly.

'Not here. He has left for the office,' answered Richard haughtily.

'So, you were breaking into his flat?'

Richard stammered. He ran to the side of his car and levered himself into the Ferrari, screeching it into reverse. As the car backed over the ditch it leapt into the air and landed with a crunch of metal. The front bumper hung loose, sparks flying from where it contacted the ground. It swung out into the main road and squealed off with a puff of smoke and sparks.

Gilly sighed and retreated into the darkness of the mausoleum.

Four minutes later, he reappeared in a graveyard belonging to the church of St Botolph on Aldersgate. It was a rather plain church with a Georgian exterior, centred in the middle of the City of London. Finding suitable graveyards in the city to locate Tomb stops for Purgatory had proven difficult, and even St Botolph's was not the most discreet. Most of the graveyards had been converted into a tranquil open-spaces covered in green grass and protected by canopies of tree branches.

Gilly stood erect and slapped his shoulders; cobwebs and dust flew into the air. It had been a long time since he had visited this Tomb stop. He heaved on the granite angular lid of the outdoor grave. It grated against the solid stone base as it shifted back into place.

He weaved his way through the cemetery as he made his way to the footpath, encountering only a few city workers this early in the morning.

In the distance he spied his destination, the 'Towering Innuendo'. It dominated the landscape. He meandered down Aldersgate Street into Cheapside in the direction of the grotesque building.

***

Richard sped through the near empty streets, stopping every few hundred metres for the red lights. He had long since lost his front bumper, so he no longer cared about the speed humps. At the last minute, after crossing London Bridge, his Ferrari swerved across the vacant lanes and whipped down a side street.

The Ferrari rumbled as if the harbinger of a storm. It skidded to a halt at a jaunty angle in front of the building containing the offices of Wollenwal & Wollenwal. He swiped his security card on the door and disappeared inside.

Five minutes later, Richard emerged, smiling.

The Ferrari did a fifteen-point turn and continued its original journey.

32

Duncan's journey to the office was surprisingly quick. He made a mental note to investigate a new schedule, which would allow him to leave earlier each morning.

Duncan's Roadster pulled into Sheol Trading's car park. He stopped at the barriers guarding the entrance. The on-duty guard leaned out of the gatehouse and asked for Duncan's identification in a commanding tone, the timbre only a security guard could muster when armed with a gun. Duncan smiled weakly and handed his identification to the guard.

The guard scrutinised the pass, in reality he had no idea what to look for, but he when given the job they told him to act like he knew what to do, even if he didn't. He handed Duncan's pass back.

'Good morning. It's a bit early for you, isn't it, Sir?'

'Yes.' Duncan smiled weakly. 'The early bird catches the worm and all that.'

The barrier raised and the Roadster lurched forward, descending the long twisting ramp. The engine idled as it cruised to the bottom and into the empty car park. Duncan ignored the grids of white lines, taking the quickest route to his designated parking spot — a straight line, only deviating his path to avoid concrete pillars. He screeched to a stop in his parking spot, beside the parked car of Lucy's Mercedes.

The lift doors closed behind him, and the elevator shuddered to life. The giant orange numbers which dominated the panel beside the door rapidly escalated until the number thirty-three filled the screen. The manufactured male voice bade its greeting.

The lift doors opened, and Duncan stepped into a vast space of emptiness. He coughed discreetly and waited for a response. The room remained silent. He glided across the room to the door of Lucy's office and, with care, perched his ear against the door, his fingertips braced against the wood for extra balance. He could make out muffled voices and, after considerable straining, understood the occasional word and the owner of each voice.

'I … Richard … Visit … … After … Left to … … Evidence,' said Oliver.

'… Duncan … … No choice … … Join … This …'

'Wonderful,' said Lucy, sounding a little more distant.

Duncan stepped back and straightened his shirt before knocking on the door gingerly. From the other side, he could hear a muted commotion, stifled voices and footfall.

'Enter!' commanded Lucy in a loud voice.

Duncan prised the door open. A slither of light extended from the ground, across the floor and up through his torso. Duncan swallowed audibly before pushing the door open the remainder of the way. He stepped through, his head and shoulders slumped, and closed the door behind him with barely a click. The room appeared larger than previously. His eyes darted left and right. Lucy sat at her desk in her leather chair, preened as if she had just stepped out of a salon despite the early hour. She wiggled her long fingers in greeting and flicked a lock of hair from the shoulder of her pressed white cashmere woollen suit. Standing in front of the bathroom door to one side of the desk with his arms crossed was Oliver, his belly hanging over his belt.

'Can we help you, Duncan?' asked Lucy benevolently.

'Um, I hope so. I was hoping we could talk,' Duncan dithered for a moment or two, unsure of what to do, then shuffled to the front of the desk. 'You said I could come to you if I ever needed help.'

Lucy sat up in her seat and fixed Duncan with a glittering smile. 'Of course, Duncan. Please. We're family.' She motioned for Duncan to sit.

Duncan looked at the empty chair. He hopped from foot to foot in obvious agitation. 'I think I would feel better if I stood.'

'Duncan, you look a deathly pale, dear. Is everything okay?'

'Yes… No… Well, you might have seen the news reports over the weekend about the police officer who was murdered on Friday.'

Lucy nodded. 'Oh yes. I did. A terrible tragedy. What has become of the world today? So violent.'

'I… I think the police might, possibly, think I was involved,' said Duncan his voice cracking.

Lucy cocked an eyebrow. 'Why would they think that, darling?'

'I think they might think I did it.'

Her eyebrow rose. 'And did you?'

'No!' his voice jumped an octave, before recovering and continuing in an even tone. 'Of course not. It's a long story. I went to meet the police officer that afternoon. Richard told me I had to and… Well… He was dead when I got there. They showed CCTV footage of a man running away, they'll know it was me. I ran, I didn't know what to do. I panicked.'

Lucy clicked her tongue. 'This is serious. I think we should speak with Richard before we go any further.'

There was a dull knock at the door.

'Perfect timing,' smiled Lucy. 'Enter!'

The door swung open to reveal Richard. He strutted in, wearing a white, linen single-breasted jacket, faded denim jeans which were fashionably ripped across the knees, and sandals without socks; clearly Richard had watched one too many repeats of Miami Vice.

Duncan exhaled loudly, his shoulders sagged, and the corners of his lips turned up at the sight of Richard. The relief evident.

'Sandals, Dick? Really,' said Lucy with a disappointed shake of her head.

Richard frowned and rammed his hands into his pockets, which resulted in the cuffs on his jeans dropping an inch and shrouding his footwear.

Duncan stepped forward and vigorously shook Richard's hand. 'Thank God you're here, Richard.'

'I wouldn't thank God if I was you!' Richard grinned.

'Dick,' said Lucy, interjecting before Duncan had time to digest his comment. 'Your timing is perfect. We require your assistance with a rather delicate situation. It appears the police might be of the opinion that Duncan murdered Detective Superintendent Malloy on Friday.'

The line of Richard's mouth curled itself into a lopsided smirk. 'I saw that on the news. Terrible. Which reminds me actually, wasn't he the police officer you told me you were meeting with on Friday?'

Duncan's eyebrows rose in the middle and his lips pursed. 'What do you mean? You told me I should go. I didn't want to go. You even made me wear a bug.'

'Pardon? Did you say a bug? As in, a listening device? Did you tape the meeting with this officer?' asked Lucy.

'Yes, well no, he was dead. There was no conversation,' said Duncan. 'Richard told me to.'

'Indeed, I did,' harrumphed Richard. 'Duncan was insistent about attending this meeting, despite my cautioning him against it. In light of the circumstances and the implications for both of our firms, I thought it prudent to take precautions. To protect ourselves, just in case.'

Duncan's mouth opened and closed like a fish out of water.

'Excellent,' said Oliver with a wry smile. 'And where is this recorder now?' All heads in the room turned to Duncan.

'It's at home,' said Duncan. 'I didn't record anything.'

Richard fished into his inside breast pocket and retrieved a USB stick, which he handed to Lucy. Duncan quizzically regarded the device; it had a striking resemblance to the one he intended to use to record his meeting with Malloy.

'I happened to be passing by Duncan's flat on my way here this morning and stopped to see if he wanted a lift. Well, as it happened, his door was open and when I peeked inside… I spied this on a table in his hallway,' said Richard in a smug tone. 'You really should lock your door, Duncan.'

Duncan's lips quivered and his mouth opened, but no sounds were forthcoming.

Lucy plugged the device into her laptop and clicked one of the keys on the keyboard. She leaned back into the chair, crossing her legs as she did.

Static filled the room. Duncan's voice, muddled with the sound of rustling fabric, babbled forth from the little black box. He could be heard cursing his bad fortune. Duncan found it surreal listening to his own voice. His first thought was, *'Is that really how I sound?'* His second thought, which followed the first very closely was: *'I didn't say that!'*

A few moments of silence.

'Malloy,' Duncan's voice reverberated from laptop's speaker.

'Where's the money?' came another voice, Duncan immediately recognised as belonging to the police officer.

'I won't pay you a penny, Malloy,' said Duncan's voice in a menacing and uncharacteristic voice.

'Don't make this harder than it needs to be,' said Malloy.

'You'll pay or I'll talk. You don't want people knowing you murdered Harold Wilson. It's in your best interests for me to keep my mouth shut.'

'And you will,' replied the voice of Duncan.

The sound of deep breathing, presumably Duncan's, followed by the sound of feet clip clopping across cobblestones. A pause and then a scuffling noise, followed by a series of grunts and groans. A loud thud startled those listening. Malloy spoke in a muffled, barely audible voice; his words drowned out by a gurgling noise, much like water babbling through a creek. A moment later, the sound of a sack falling to the ground, followed by the crumpling of plastic. The deep breathing continued until the sound of hurried footsteps echoed through the room.

A faint scream could be heard on the recording. Lucy clicked another key on the keyboard.

Figuratively speaking, Duncan's jaw plunged to the ground and continued straight through it, before emerging 'down under'.

Lucy tut-tutted. 'Duncan, Duncan, Duncan. How can we help you if you lie to us? I think it is clear to all you killed that poor detective and then fled the scene.'

'No. I… didn't kill him… I… I never said those things. That wasn't me.' Duncan could feel sweat bubbling to the surface of his skin. Bile spilled into his mouth.

'Duncan. Please. The recording says it all.' Richard made a grandiose wave of his hand.

Duncan's head spun. In turn, he studied everybody's bemused expressions. 'No. Wait. No. You did this. You're trying to frame me.' Duncan made a stabbing action with his finger at Richard.

'Preposterous!' riposted Richard. 'Why would I do such a thing?'

A loud scratching noise accompanied by what sounded like snorting momentarily distracted everybody from the topic at hand. Oliver, without turning around, used his heel to kick the door behind him. There was faint whimpering then silence. Oliver exaggerated his smile.

'Duncan, Duncan, Duncan. I believe you when you say somebody is trying to frame you but, honestly, Dick of all people? We would be fortunate to discover a brain cell in that grey mush he jovially refers to as a brain,' said Lucy.

'Just one moment!' Richard spat the words.

'I believe you, Duncan… But who else will? Consider the evidence. The CCTV of a person matching your description fleeing the scene, this recording of the murder, and then all that nasty DNA evidence at the scene of the crime.'

'What…' Duncan's brow furrowed. 'What DNA evidence?'

'Oh. Didn't I mention that? Silly me. I heard the police uncovered DNA evidence belonging to you. Once they have finished their tests, they will confirm they belong to you.' Lucy tittered. 'Hair and skin samples, those sorts of things.'

Duncan's face fell. He stared uncomprehendingly at Lucy, then Oliver and finally Richard. His gaze returned to Lucy. 'I… I don't understand.'

The scratching noise started again, louder than before.

'That's not possible. I didn't do it. Honestly.' Duncan paused, and then his eyes widened. 'If they haven't confirmed the DNA then how do you know they belong to me?'

'Quite simple darling, because I told Richard to place them there,' said Lucy as if in passing.

The noise from the door continued. Oliver kicked the door again and the scratching noise stopped, replaced by soft whimpering.

'Oh, I can't possibly stay mad at him. Oliver, be a dear and let him in.'

Duncan remained po-faced, he found it difficult to stand. His head spun.

Oliver turned on his heel and opened the door. A small tan coloured dog with a feather duster for a tail pranced through the door. It yelped at the sight of Lucy, leaping through the air and landing in her lap. A smile sliced across Lucy's face, as she cooed and stroked the dog. The dog clearly enjoyed the attention, rolling and squirming, until one of its eyes popped open as it spied Duncan. It gave a guttural growl.

'Now, precious. There's no need for that,' said Lucy, gently tapping the dog on its nose.

'That… It attacked me.' Duncan's head began to pound.

'I know. Such a naughty dog,' said Lucy, scratching behind the dog's ears.

'That… That's Cerberus,' said Duncan pointing at the dog.

Lucy's eyes narrowed. 'How do you know my dog's name, Duncan? Have you not been telling us everything?'

'That's your dog? But...'

'But what?' snapped Lucy.

'It's the gatekeeper for hell... I... I don't understand.' Sweat began to pour down Duncan's brow and travelled to the tip of his nose, where it hung precariously before dripping to the floor.

'What haven't you been telling us, Duncan?' Lucy's voice steeled.

'Nothing... I don't understand...,' said Duncan. He turned to face Richard. 'You... You planted evidence. Why?'

'No real reason. It seemed like a good idea,' began Richard. 'When I visited your house on Thursday, I visited your bathroom and, while I was there, I happened to help myself to some samples of your hair, saliva from your toothbrush, and there was no shortage of skin flakes surrounding the sink. You really should use moisturiser. Anyway, after I slashed Malloy's throat, I left the samples I collected from your bathroom behind.'

The colour in Duncan's face drained. 'You killed, Malloy?'

'Don't be naïve, Duncan,' said Lucy lightly. 'You are such a darling.'

'Because,' said Richard. 'Then I will be at the right-hand side of the Devil. I'll have direct access to untold wealth and power. Who wouldn't jump at the opportunity?'

'The Devil?' Duncan intended it to be a statement, but it sounded more like a question.

Lucy coughed discreetly. 'About that, Dick. I know that's what we agreed, but there is a slight problem with that. You see, I already have a right-hand man,' she motioned towards Oliver. 'And I can't take the chance you might tell somebody about your involvement and my plans. I guess you are the proverbial loose end that needs to be resolved.'

Richard turned to face Lucy; confusion rife.

Lucy smiled in reply and clicked her fingers.

Suddenly, the dog on her lap vaulted forward. Its jaw grew impossibly wide, its teeth sharpened. The artificial light in the room glistened from its drool. And then, blood vomited from Richard's body. Shards of bone exploded into the air. The dog ripped, tore and shredded, howling wildly.

Duncan vomited, again and again.

All trace of Richard's trademark cockiness was gone, only a mangled pile of flesh remained.

The dog wagged its feather duster tail, licked what presumably was all that remained of one of Richard's internal organs, then pranced back to Lucy.

'I didn't have to click my fingers, but it adds such a lovely dramatic effect.' Lucy smiled, a wicked smile. 'It lets the victim know something is about to happen. It is truly delicious watching their expression change from joy to silent bewilderment to glorious suffering.'

Duncan reeled from the sight. His mind subconsciously announced to him: '*Your inner resolve has left the building*'.

'But... You... Why... I...' stammered Duncan, after finding his voice, which had been hiding in the vicinity of his diaphragm.

'So many questions and so little time.' Lucy fluttered her long, delicate fingers. 'As you have hopefully surmised, I am the Devil. Surprise! I wouldn't lose sleep over Dick's termination; he wasn't a particularly pleasant person.'

'But... you can't do this.'

'I'm the Devil, Duncan. Who's going to stop me? You? The law? The FSA? I don't think so. I can do as I choose. And nothing, and nobody, can stop me. My word is the law.'

Duncan instinctively stepped backwards, his hand reaching for the door.

'I like you, Duncan. And I would hate for anything bad to happen to you. The police can find the evidence and send you to prison for a very, very long time. Where I suspect your life will be a living hell and, trust me, it will be; I'll personally see to it. Or, alternatively, you can live a very comfortable life surrounded by wealth and the trappings belonging to a man in your position.' She paused to allow her words to sink in. 'Come now, Duncan, be a dear. You've had fun working for me. This doesn't need to be unpleasant. Sheol Trading needs a man with your talent.'

'You're evil!'

Lucy giggled. 'No, I'm only a little bit bad.'

Duncan stared at the mound of powder. Slowly he raised his head and gawped at Lucy and Oliver. His eyes spoke volumes, emanating rage, profanities and unadulterated fear.

'Why me? Why have you done this?' He shuffled towards the door.

'Now that would be telling. Suffice to say, you are special, Duncan. I need you.' Lucy smiled sweetly.

'Where are you going, Duncan?' asked Oliver. He flashed Lucy a concerned look who responded with a raised hand.

'I… I need to go.' Without taking his eyes off Lucy, Duncan reached behind him and fumbled for the doorknob.

'Don't leave, we have so much to talk about, Duncan.' Lucy looked at her fingertips and made a mental note to arrange a manicure.

Duncan shook his head and tottered out of the room.

'Don't forget your television appearance this morning,' called Lucy facetiously after the receding figure.

'Shall we send somebody after him?' enquired Oliver.

'No. That won't be necessary. Duncan is a smart man. He really has no choice. I imagine the sudden realisation he is now my bitch will take a little while to adjust to.' She sunk back into her chair, resting her hands on the table top and grinning wickedly.

33

Duncan fell out of the lift, his shoes slapping across the concrete floor. He skulked past Lucy's large Mercedes, which presided regally over the car park and faltered in his footsteps. His knees felt like they were about to give way.

He stared at the sailing boat of a car. His expression hardened. You could easily imagine the light bulb above his head flickering on. He approached the vehicle's front door, shook his arms, and then lunged at the side mirror. His arms locked it in a vice-like grip. There was a flurry of activity. His arms twisted, pulled, pushed and pummelled at the defenceless mirror. His feet lifted from the ground and dangled mid-air as he placed his not inconsiderable weight on it. With a grunt, his body swirled up, round and down.

Crack.

The side mirror fell limp and hung loosely from its hinge.

Duncan flicked his lank hair from his forehead and grinned from ear to ear at the debris before him. '*That will show her*,' he thought before scurrying back to his car.

In the shadows of one of the many concrete pillars, Gilly leaned at a jaunty angle.

'*The man is a genius. Why didn't I think of that? If you want to get even with the Devil, break her wing mirror.*' He chuckled and shook his head whimsically.

Gilly remained hidden until Duncan's car disappeared up the exit ramp. He then hobbled to the waiting elevator, pushed the button for level thirty-three and moved his head up and down in time to the piped music.

He exited the lift and wandered around the vacuous reception room to the door on the left side of the room, attracted by the murmuring sounds from the other side.

He knocked politely and waited to be invited in. He opened the door and removed his hat in deference to a woman being present, even if she happened to be the Devil. His wispy white hair sprung free and took the semblance of tumbleweed. His pockmarked skin looked deathly pale under the light in the room.

Lucy smiled as Gilly approached and made no sign of surprise at his arrival. 'Well, well, well. My dear friend Gilgamesh. I must confess, I suspected your involvement when Duncan knew my dear Cerberus. What brings you here, darling?' She delicately teased the Chihuahua's ears.

'I don't know, I thought I would slum it for a while.' Gilly padded towards them.

He nodded curtly at Oliver, who had surreptitiously backed into the corner next to the toilet door. 'Baal,' he said.

'I prefer Oliver these days!' retorted Oliver.

'Nothing changes. As always, you have the charm of a prostate gland, Baal.'

'Age hasn't been kind to you, Gilgamesh. Such a shame. I remember when you were a strapping young man,' commented Lucy. 'Enough to even seduce me. But now look at you... I've seen corpses with less maggots.'

Gilly shrugged his shoulders. 'Being dead tends to have that effect on you.'

Lucy giggled in response.

There was a long period of uncomfortable silence as they regarded each other. To a bystander, unfamiliar with their history, the friction, anxiety and apprehension in the air would have been as clear as crystal. Their relationship one of animosity but, bubbling under the surface, an explosive chemistry; chemistry which was impossible to deny, impossible to be left undetected. It was as if they had completed a round of foreplay and were waiting for the other to make the next move. It was one of those twisted relationships where those involved derived pleasure from pain — an almost supernatural S&M session.

'Why haven't you joined me, Gilgamesh? We could have fun together, and you know I can do away with all this being dead nonsense. You could be that strapping young man again,' said Lucy. 'It is only a matter of time before I succeed, so you might as well. You are only delaying the inevitable.'

Gilly shrugged his shoulders. 'I know, but what else am I going to do. There aren't many jobs out there when you're dead.'

A broad smile crossed her lips.

They had met on many occasions over the millennia, and she enjoyed every one of their encounters. She motioned for Gilly to sit. He shook his head and gestured at his legs, indicating they were not as supple as they had once been.

Gilly considered the puddle of blood and gore. He looked at Lucy then back at the carnage. 'Let me guess? Richard Steel?'

'Unfortunately. He really was a bit of a scallywag, but he knew too much, and you can't trust men like him.'

'Nothing to trust now,' said Gilly.

'So, dear Gilgamesh, what do we owe the pleasure of your presence?' said Lucy.

'Oh. Right. Yes. I was having this chat with a fellow you might know, Gordon McBride. He really is not a nice person, and self-absorbed.' Gilly raised his finger to his chin as if remembering something. 'I don't think I was meant to tell you his name. Never mind. Anyway, he happened to mention you were in town, so I thought I would stop by and congratulate you. I must say, I am impressed with your planning this time, and your execution has been simply brilliant; nothing short of masterful. I knew you were up to something, you've been far too quiet lately, but this exceeds anything you have done before. Far subtler than your normal fire and brimstone approach.'

'Why thank you, darling,' Lucy momentarily blushed. 'I knew you would appreciate my understated approach. And congratulations to you too, darling. I didn't think anybody would uncover my plan, but you did. Such a pity you are too late though.'

'I'm definitely not a pretty face.' Gilly's face contorted and scrunched as he unsuccessfully attempted to wink. 'Of course, there is a chance I might not be too late.' Gilly noticed Lucy's eyes narrow and her body shifted nervously in her seat. 'Perhaps you have forgotten something, some little detail that could turn everything around? It would be rude of me if I didn't offer you one last chance of redemption before it's too late. So, if you leave Duncan alone, I'll forget all about this and you can continue your mischief until our paths next cross.'

Lucy laughed gracefully, before snorting not so elegantly. 'You have such a delicious sense of humour. I'm afraid, you are too late. It is a fact, a mathematical certainty. I have planned everything to perfection.'

'It's your choice. What do I know? I'm just a corpse,' he shrugged his shoulders.

'How is Purgatory? And dear old Balthasar?'

'The same. If I didn't know any better, I'd say he has something shoved up his you-know-what. Such a pain. If you ever want to take someone to Hell, I could recommend him. He does need to get out more often.'

Lucy smiled knowingly. 'Well, the offer to join my team stands. We do have fun in Hell, it's not all work, don't we, Oliver?'

Oliver nodded his agreement.

'Don't get me wrong, I appreciate the offer, but I don't like killing people. It's a bit anti-social.'

'You do know, the offer won't be around forever, and I would hate for you to find yourself in Limbo, plucking maggots from your shrivelled body once I win.'

A smirk crossed Gilly's lips. 'I can think of worse fates, but who knows? Anything can happen. Sometimes, people can surprise you.'

Lucy and Oliver convulsed with laughter. 'Gilgamesh. Your optimism knows no bounds. I assure you everything has gone according to my plan. You may as well face it: Tellus Limited will soon be mine, and my investors and I will start to realise the enormous inert value stored within Tellus. We'll start by stripping its assets and selling them one by one. By the time I'm finished, Tellus Limited will be nothing but a hollow shell of a company.'

Gilly sighed loudly. 'Okay then. I better get going. No rest for the wicked and all that!'

'Come back soon. Don't be shy,' smirked Oliver to the retiring figure.

Gilly looked over his shoulder and smiled without humour. 'You take care, Baal.' He turned, waved his hand and padded out of the room.

34

Duncan's car stopped at the top of the car park ramp. Yet another gloomy, overcast London day. The type of weather that drives people to reconsider their purpose for living, except in Duncan's case, he was far too preoccupied contemplating his lot in life and whether death would be a preferable option.

His spirits sank to the bottom of his being where they promptly sat down and proceeded to go on strike.

A little over a week ago, his life had been far from exciting; it had been in an entirely different universe to excitement. It would have been apt to describe his life as a bunch of Mondays strung together, which was a whole lot preferable to the overcooked, collapsed soufflé it now resembled.

Duncan shivered, not from the cold air outside but from a pervading feeling of terror which had slowly slithered into his inner being and made itself at home.

Despite the cold weather, Duncan flicked a switch on the dashboard turning the air-conditioner on; catching a cold was the least of his concerns. He peeled the sweat-drenched shirt from his skin; the cool air a welcome respite. He let his shirt fall back and flinched as it slapped against his skin.

His mind raced as he quickly analysed the various possible scenarios available to him. All of them ended badly. He was the proverbial rat caught in a trap.

***

Two hours later, Duncan was no closer to deciding what to do, though he had realised he only had four options.

His first option required him to go to the police and tell them everything that had transpired. They would promptly arrest him, charge him with murder, and then call in a team of psychiatrists. Undoubtedly, he would be locked up in a secure facility for life whether found sane or not.

The second option dictated he bury his head in the sand, do nothing and hope the problem miraculously disappeared. Of course, it wouldn't, and it would most end the same way as the

222

first option.

His third option was to flee the country and go on the run. Again, it would inevitably end the same way as the first option.

The final option involved him accepting his new reality and joining Lucy's side. He would have all the money and fame his newfound position brought with it. Though he knew, it might have sounded perfect, but it would require him to be evil and do things he couldn't even bear to watch in a movie.

In his despair, he even briefly considered suicide but dismissed it out of hand. Even though, he knew everything was lost, he couldn't help but be faintly optimistic.

Then, just when he resigned himself to the first option, a thought popped into his mind. An intelligent thought, that made no sense. He might as well have decided to go to Las Vegas and bet his entire life on a spin of the roulette wheel. This idea made no sense, it had to be the worst possible idea he could have possibly thought of, but most importantly, he had no other idea.

'*He gave people the right to vote, he wants us to make up our own minds, and to decide accordingly. I sure hope he knew what he was doing.*'

His foot slammed on the pedal and the Roadster screeched out into the road, causing cars to swerve. He sped through a red light.

From the shadows of the Towering Innuendo hobbled Gilly, he tilted his sunhat lower on his face but, from the shadows of the brim, it was easy to see a wide smile on his face.

35

'Mr Bottomley, you're a mess! Makeup!' bellowed this woman with a large padded earpiece over her right ear with the attached boom mike jutting out at chin level. She must have been the producer.

'Makeup! Makeup!' she hollered.

Another woman jogged towards them, grasping a large case by her side. The producer grabbed Duncan by his forearm and pointed at the two directors' chairs bathed in bright lights on top of a raised platform. She forcefully guided him in that direction.

Duncan staggered to the chair on the right and sat down. His body wilted under the intense light.

The woman appeared next to him, laid her case down and sprung it open. It was like a portable cupboard filled with concoctions, pastes, creams and powders. She grabbed a paintbrush and delicately slapped it across his face. Seconds later, armed with a pencil she began to scratch it across his face, Duncan was convinced she was playing a game of noughts and crosses. She then extracted a large ball of fluff, which resembled a rabbit's tail, dabbed it into a pot of powder and daubed it across his face.

An attractive woman with layered short brown hair and asymmetrical flicks which curled outwards at the ends, sat in the chair opposite. She wore a dark grey suit with a short skirt which moulded around her bottom and thighs. Her lips a darker shade than her flawless olive skin complexion. She extended her neck upwards while a man fixed a microphone to her lapel and handed her a flesh-coloured earpiece, which she duly screwed into her left ear.

She leaned forward and reassuringly, almost dismissively, patted Duncan's leg. 'There's nothing to worry about, Mr Bottomley. Don't be nervous.'

The scene before him was a whirling dervish of activity. People wearing headphones ran in multiple directions, seemingly going nowhere in particular but shouting and waving clipboards as they did. Large cameras on wheels shunted from side to side. Lights flashed. It was all a blur.

The producer advanced and sunk to her knees before Duncan.

She squinted at him and clicked her tongue to get his attention. 'Okay, Mr Bottomley. Thank you for your time today. The camera with the red light above is the camera being used. If you look at a camera without a red light, it isn't on. In that situation you should slowly turn to face the camera which does have the light on. There are only two cameras so it shouldn't be difficult to work out which is on and which isn't. This is a two-minute interview and is the usual glossy questions concerning your appointment, your background, and your thoughts and feelings surrounding your role. All straight forward and nothing to worry about. Remember to smile and follow Stephanie's lead. Christ, you shouldn't be worried, you work for Sheol Trading, they probably own this station!'

Duncan, mentally numb, acknowledged the producer's spiel with a curt nod.

She backed away until she stood between the two cameras, a clipboard clutched to her chest. 'Okay, people. We're live in 5… 4… 3… 2… 1…' The producer pointed at the presenter next to Duncan. An annoying jingle, a cross between a typewriter and a badly played guitar, filled the air.

The presenter's head assumed a jaunty angle and a smile spread across her face. The music faded.

'Welcome to "Business before Lunch?" with Stephanie Puppét,' said the presenter.

The first ten minutes of the show were spent recapping the latest financial news, the movement of the FTSE 100 index that morning, and some pointless banter between Stephanie and a chubby man, who stood before a large plasma screen and a plastic London Stock Exchange sign. It was meant to appear like he was actually broadcasting from the exchange but, in reality, he was ten feet away in the same studio.

'Today,' said Stephanie, as she turned towards the camera. 'We have an exclusive: The first interview with Duncan Bottomley, the recently appointed Chief Financial Officer of Sheol Trading, arguably the world's largest and most respected hedge fund. Good morning, Mr Bottomley. Thank you for joining us this morning. This is a privilege.'

The camera panned out, allowing Stephanie and Duncan to be seen together on the screen. Under the heat of the lights, Duncan's hurriedly applied makeup started to drizzle down the side of his face, staining his collar. To the viewing population, it appeared his face was melting.

'Good morning,' said Duncan.

'I guess if you had to use one word to describe your appointment it would be "WOW!",' mused Stephanie.

'That would be one word. Yes.'

'I understand before your appointment you were an auditor with Wollenwal & Wollenwal?'

'Yes, that's right.'

'What was the deciding factor that made you decide to join Sheol Trading? Was it their industry-leading working conditions or the opportunity to be at the forefront of financial services?'

'Um. Neither. They asked me.'

'Sheol Trading is renowned for being an energetic and leading company. A real adrenalin rush. You must be enjoying working at Sheol Trading.'

'No. I'm definitely not.'

Stephanie glimpsed at the producer, surprised by his answer. She raised her finger to her ear, as if she suddenly had an itch but in reality, she was waiting for further instructions as to how to respond.

'Of course. I guess you have more responsibility now you are CFO, and this makes it difficult for you to enjoy yourself as you might have?' She gave him a look of feigned interest.

'No. Not at all. You see … And this is the truth, I know it might be shocking: It was for me when I discovered it. Some people won't believe me, but it is completely true. You see… Sheol Trading isn't what it seems. It is Hell.'

The presenter tittered. 'It must be extremely hard work there.'

'No. You don't understand. The CEO, Lucy Smith, is really the Devil. Satan. As in Lucy-fer! She wants to take over the world which, in reality, is a massive company. Because that's the other thing, you see, Earth is like a big corporation, and God is the Chairperson, an entrepreneur, just like Richard Branson!'

Once he started, he couldn't stop. It was cathartic. The words flooded out quickly and left him with little time to contemplate what he was saying. He went into greater detail about the hostile takeover which Hell had launched before veering off into a lengthy discussion on the off-balance sheet partnerships on Sheol Trading's accounts which he suspected were hiding nefarious activities. He enlightened the viewers on Lucy's involvement in the murders of Harold Wilson, Detective Malloy and the recent devouring of Richard Steel. He also suspected, although he admitted he had no proof, she was also involved in the previous CFO's death, and the head traders last year. Not content with his diatribe to that point, he finished by telling the story of how he had met Gilgamesh, who was dead but actually alive, caught the Tomb everywhere, and while he wasn't exactly sure what his job was, he was some sort of trouble fighter helping the Earth to fight this takeover.

There was a long silence as he concluded his theory. You could have heard a pin drop.

Stephanie grinned, unsure how to respond, her earpiece absent of any voices. Out of the blue, she grabbed her ear and winced. To the general public it would have appeared she had spontaneously suffered an acute earache but, behind the scenes, the producer in the control room alerted to the dead air started to scream profanities to attract her attention.

'That was… truly… interesting. So, what else can we look forward to from Sheol Trading? A new acquisition?'

Duncan reciprocated her question with an incredulous stare. Did she not hear what he had confessed? This company was inherently evil, and the danger they were all in from this company didn't seem to have registered on her radar. Live on air, with thousands of people potentially watching, he suddenly realised it was hopeless. Nobody would believe such an incredible story. His desperate machinations had doomed him. His decision to throw himself on the mercy of the people had backfired.

The annoying music started again. The lights above both cameras went off. Stephanie rose, removed the earpiece, and limply mumbled her thanks to Duncan for the generosity of his time. She stepped out of arms reach and regarded him as you would a crazed man, though listening to her voice you would have thought she found him fascinating.

Duncan, bleary-eyed and feeling sorry for himself, skulked out of the studio.

***

'This is a disaster. Do you want me to instruct the PR department to combat this? There is bound to be negative publicity from this,' shrieked Oliver panicked. His face lined with worry.

Lucy looked sharply at Oliver. 'Don't be silly. This is a small-time television show. It garners an audience of a few thousand. Besides, nobody will believe him; you saw how the presenter reacted. All he has succeeded in doing is demonstrating how insane he is. He has done us a favour. He now realises he has no choice but to join us.'

'The police will investigate this,' insisted Oliver.

'I wouldn't have thought so; he is hardly a credible witness: A blithering idiot spouting far-fetched tales of his boss being the Devil. It is hardly anything to concern ourselves with.'

'I wish I could be as confident as you are. This vexes me.'

'Oliver, we have nothing to fear. Remember who we are, we are Sheol Trading: The world's most powerful company. We have the world by the balls. If anybody challenges us, we will destroy them! It's simple. Straight forward. We have nothing to worry about.'

'And Duncan Bottomley?'

Her eyes narrowed. 'Well, that, my dear Oliver, depends solely on Mr Bottomley. His choice remains the same — he will join us or go to prison, where he will eventually beg us to free him and happily join us in exchange for his release. Who needs eternal damnation when you have prison?'

36

The atmosphere in the flat was depressing. Duncan spent most of the time curled up on his sofa, nursing his head as if hungover, and groaning in an infantile voice. Gilly, who sat on an armchair by the wall, had spent his time Tuesday morning replaying the interview from yesterday, interspersing his viewing with regular cackles and thigh slaps.

'You really should see this newsreader's face when you tell her about me. It's priceless.'

Duncan groaned. 'You're not helping.'

'Oh, come on. You have to laugh,' and laugh he did, hysterically. 'This is hilarious. Look at you. Your face looks like its liquefied. At least I'm dead, what's your excuse?'

'How can you possibly laugh? My life is over,' lamented Duncan.

'You really are a cup half-empty person, aren't you? You should look on the bright side, at least you aren't dead.'

'Yet,' Duncan interjected.

'That's the spirit!' Gilly's attention returned to the video and he continued to guffaw.

'Do you really need to be here?' asked Duncan deflated. 'Where were you when I needed you?'

'I was busy.'

'It's only a matter of time until the police turn up. Just, leave me alone.'

'Well, I could go but I am here for your protection. You know, fighting off demons and so on. Trust me when I say, I take no pleasure from this,' twittered Gilly, before bursting out with laughter at the television.

'I don't understand why you are happy. She is not going to be happy after she sees what I have done. She won't be happy at all.'

Duncan rose from the sofa and stomped down the hallway, then returned with a can of air freshener which he sprayed around the room, particularly the airspace near Gilly. He took a deep sniff. Satisfied the room's odour had appreciably improved, he dropped the can by the sofa.

'It's not my fault. You should try being dead. Smelling like a daisy isn't easy,' remarked Gilly.

Duncan threw himself backwards into the sofa and despaired loudly. 'What are we going to do?'

'We? What's with this "we" stuff? Last week you wouldn't even speak to me!'

'What do you mean? You've got to help me?'

Gilly guffawed. '"What are we going to do?"' Gilly parroted. 'We're going to do absolutely nothing! Honestly, Lucy couldn't care about this. You made a fool of yourself on television. So what? What does she have to worry about? Nothing. But, on the other hand, if you were to die, then people would get suspicious and start to think there might have been some truth to what you said and start digging around. Which is, of course, the last thing she wants. No. She isn't going to do anything to you, not yet. I imagine she will want to speak with you, make a display of forgiving your escapade, and then offer you one final chance. If you turn her down then the police will find the evidence, and shortly afterwards, you will find yourself locked away in an asylum somewhere.'

'How can you be so confident?'

'Everything I have told you is true. Trust me, I'm a dead man. Have I lied to you before?' said Gilly cheerily.

'Why is this happening to me?'

'Cheer up. I thought being dead was depressing but it's nowhere near as bad as your company is.'

Duncan groaned. His despondent silence punctuated by the occasional bout of laughter from Gilly.

'So, Lucy gets away with this? Nobody can stop her. Is that the bottom line?' asked Duncan despairing.

'That's not strictly true. You could stop her,' said Gilly.

'Me? How?'

'Well, I did say that if you were to die then the police would begin to suspect that there might have been some truth to what you said and start to dig around. They are bound to turn up something.'

'You want me to die?' sputtered Duncan.

'What's wrong with that?' asked Gilly indignantly.

'I'm dead!'

Gilly shrugged his shoulders. 'Oh well. It doesn't matter, it will work out. Anyway, there is no point worrying about it now. What is done is done.' Gilly slowly eased himself to his feet, using his arms as leverage to crank his rigid body from the chair. He rocked slightly on his feet and gazed down at Duncan. 'Let's go to the pub.'

'Why? You can't drink.'

'You are definitely a cup half-empty person,' Gilly frowned. 'Call me masochistic but I like hanging around watching other people drinking. It reminds me of when I used to lie in gutters with a reed bucket of sweet wine by my side. I don't mind going to pubs now, you can't smoke anymore. You have no idea how hard it is to remove the stench of smoke from my shrivelled skin!'

37

It had started yesterday, Monday morning in New York, a few hours after Duncan concluded his first and probably last television interview.

It was a small spark on the Internet that had been diligently tended, nurtured and coaxed, by unseen hands, until it burst into a feisty flame: A flame that quickly spread.

People bored with their work, hungover from their weekends or simply trying to look busy on a Monday, logged on to the various social networking websites in search of something to distract themselves.

Their eyes were attracted to a video entitled 'Sheol Trading's CFO on-air breakdown'. It was the innocuous words 'Sheol Trading' which acted as an immediate attractant.

An anonymous individual, who went by the moniker 'Rigid boy', had posted a video of the interview and within a few seconds of posting, a few hundred people had viewed it, then a few thousand. The numbers exploded as word spread, rapidly climbing the popularity rankings.

The laughter of those watching the video was infectious and attracted those surrounding them: In their office, in the Internet cafes, wherever they were watching. Emails sharing the video were distributed at a frenetic rate to colleagues, friends and family. In a happy and uplifted mood, people phoned their friends and regaled them with a description of what they had seen.

As other cities woke up and logged online, the flame was fanned into a fire. It developed an impetus of its own, like a stone thrown into a pond with the ripples extending outwards — ever growing and reaching further across the surface.

The momentum continued to grow. Those with time on their hands delighted in watching the public meltdown of such a senior member of the world's most feared hedge fund. There was only one thing people loved more than a little person beating the odds and succeeding, and that was a successful person failing.

By the time Tuesday morning ascended on London, the video had made the jump and escaped the Internet. Media outlets started to convey the story, initially reporting it on their 'other side'

232

pieces, the segment they normally reserved for the stories of a dog water skiing or a monkey dressed as a cowboy riding the family cat. By the time the morning breakfast programme had finished, it had grown further and was being included in the main news.

When the London Stock Exchange opened for business, the share price for Sheol Trading immediately fell ten percent; the largest one-day fall in the history of the company — and the day had only just begun.

Journalists were stunned by the extreme, unprecedented scale of the fall. When they were asked for an explanation for the dramatic fall, they explained how investors were questioning leadership at Sheol Trading for appointing Duncan to the position of CFO, they then duly replayed the clip for those who had not yet seen it.

No longer was it an amusing anecdote but a story about a company which had lost touch with reality and was making catastrophic mistakes. The world and its media looked on, questioning the company's integrity: If they could hire such a man to fulfil one of their most senior and important positions, then what other mistakes were they making? Where were their checks and balances? If they did have controls in place, then how thorough were they? The shame of hiring Duncan Bottomley cast a dark shadow, and everything was brought into question.

By lunchtime, the share price had fallen thirty percent. The story continued to snowball. Already, multiple press interviews had been conducted with partners from Wollenwal & Wollenwal. Its partners, fearful of the repercussions and the effects it would have on their beloved firm, conveyed the same story: Mr Bottomley had been dismissed from the firm and they were staggered to learn Sheol Trading had appointed him to the role of CFO, especially as he had never been appointed as a partner within their own firm and had no relevant experience.

The afternoon newspapers, not known for their shyness, grabbed the passers-by by their eyeballs and impaled them with its headlines — 'Sheol Trading Meltdown'.

The sale of Sheol Trading shares gathered apace. It became a vicious circle, quickly spiralling out of control. As the story gained momentum and consumed an increasing amount of airtime, it led to people fearing the worst and instructing their brokers to sell. Everybody wanted to sell, and nobody wanted to buy, not even if they threw in a free knife set.

The share price plunged.

Nobody wanted to go down with the sinking ship, and a blood bath descended on the share market.

It was only a matter of time until the authorities involved themselves in the day's events. Their reputation had previously been smeared, and they were worried another corporate scandal was brewing. This time, they would be seen to act swiftly, to act decisively, in the best interests of the public.

***

'What do you think you are doing?' Lucy roared into the mouthpiece of the phone, her face bright red. 'If you don't tell your customers to buy our shares, you'll make sure you never work in this city again! Even better, I will make sure you spontaneously combust in your overpriced suit.'

There was a pause. She lifted her eyebrow as she listened.

'I don't care! We're Sheol Trading! I look forward to seeing you in Hell!' She slammed the phone down and spun to face Oliver, who cowered on the other side of the desk.

'Should I instruct our PR team to take action?' asked Oliver in a voice of some concern.

'Do something! Anything! You fat tub of lard! This is preposterous.'

A voice hesitantly sounded out from the phone. It was Wesley, her assistant. 'Um, Ms Smith?'

'What do you want?' she growled.

'There are officers from the Financial Services Authority and Serious Fraud squad here. They have a warrant and would like to speak with you.'

'Whaaaaaaaaat?' screeched Lucy.

The doors to her office burst open. A tall man with neatly cropped dark hair wearing a long dark coat led the charge through the doors. His aftershave preceded him into the room. His hand, held out in front, carried a folded piece of yellow paper, which he deposited on the table before Lucy. He flashed his identity card and advised her he was an officer from the Serious Fraud squad.

An army of people followed him into the room carrying large boxes, which they set down and immediately started to fill with any papers they could lay their hands on.

'What is the meaning of this?' asked Lucy in her most commanding timbre.

'Ms Smith, we have a warrant here to commandeer all company records on the suspicion of corporate fraud. Our teams are currently throughout your offices, performing similar operations.'

'This is insane. Do you know who we are? I hire solicitors who earn more in a week than you do in a lifetime! They will eat you and your warrant for breakfast! I will have your head on a platter before the day is out!' She visibly reddened, biting her bottom lip as she stared defiantly at the officer.

The officer smiled wryly and turned to his colleagues. He ordered them to remove all documents, no matter how trivial or insignificant they appeared to be. He told them to leave no stone unturned and to seize all laptops, desktop computers and hard drives. He smiled at Lucy and told her if anybody interfered with their work, they would report the person to one of the large teams of police officers on the ground floor.

Lucy's entire body throbbed with indescribable anger. She raised her hand, her fingers poised ready to click. Oliver coughed, and he frowned in Lucy's direction. She lowered her hand and stormed from the office.

***

Shortly after 2.30 p.m., the news of the raids leaked to the market and this, in turn, spurred the analysts from the banks to start their own investigations into the allegations of off-balance sheet partnerships. It was obvious to all, the deeper they dug, the murkier the financial records became. Of course, the information had always been there, but nobody had ever bothered to investigate; they were all far too busy making money.

Concerned with what they were uncovering, the banks immediately changed their recommendations to sell, and hurriedly began to unload securities, shares and anything related to Sheol Trading. In the operation departments of banks, the

235

world over, the grinding sound of shredders worked overtime. The firms, fearful of the reverberation of Sheol Trading's collapse, subsequently ordered their staff to destroy all documents containing any reference to the company.

When the New York stock market opened, prompted by their cross-Atlantic cousins' actions and the knowledge of the raids, they too joined in the bloodbath, accelerating the descent of the share price.

Sheol Trading's share price haemorrhaged as if somebody had sliced its arterial vein.

The journalists had all left their studios and were all now actually based at the stock exchange where it was felt they could cover the story best. They huddled around the one shiny sign which boldly proclaimed: 'London Stock Exchange'. Each and every one of them without exception sweated profusely, burdened by the heavy workload thrust upon them. They had grown accustomed to a few live crosses each day which only lasted a couple of minutes; they certainly weren't used to having to make a report every hour for ten minutes. This type of workload was usually reserved for the gossip reporters.

Staff at Sheol Trading, with the exception of Lucy and Oliver, started to plead with their friends within the financial services fraternity for assistance in finding another job. Their previous allies, the banks who until that day had pandered to their every whim, ignored their pleas for help and advice, and viciously turned on them. They plucked at their remains, like vultures at a carcass in the desert.

The banks all knew how to make money on both good days and bad. Even when a company was spectacularly imploding, it was possible for them to make money out of it. The banks, without reservation, leapt at the opportunity.

A few minutes before the London market closed, the London Stock Exchange intervened and stopped the massacre by suspending trading in Sheol Trading's stock. The share price stood at five pence. Billions and billions of pounds in shareholder equity had vaporised in one day. Numerous personal fortunes, pension funds and investment trusts were wiped out. It was the biggest single day's loss in the history of the share market, and the bulk of the loss attributable to one company which had, up until last week, stood as a colossus astride the world.

38

On Wednesday morning, Duncan and Gilly attentively studied the television. They had maintained this position for all of Tuesday and throughout the night until the morning.

Duncan should have been at work yesterday for his confrontation with Lucy but, as the news of the collapse filtered out, he found himself entranced by the increasingly frequent news bulletins. As the day progressed, he had anticipated hearing the limp and flaccid toots and beeps of his doorbell, and to be greeted by the police or, worse still, Lucy or one of her demons. Despite the anxiety, all remained quiet.

Gilly and Duncan observed the news in flabbergasted silence. Duncan struggled to comprehend the chain of events leading to Sheol Trading's demise; one minute it was a behemoth and the next little more than rubble.

A news report showed the exodus of staff from the building at the end of the day, each carrying boxes containing their personal possessions. Clearly stunned employees consoled one another outside, and the occasional interview with staff interspersed the story. Suffice to say, everybody was in dismay at the swift downfall of the company. Much to the chagrin of Duncan, some placed the blame firmly on his 'crackpot' shoulders, while others remained knowingly silent. The story finished and the newsreader, with the graph of Sheol Trading's share price displayed vibrantly behind her, advised they were crossing to their reporter live from the London Stock Exchange.

The screen split into two, the newsreader on one side and the journalist on the other side.

'It is another day of confusion and mayhem as people stop to actualise the events of yesterday. It is understood the regulators and authorities have swarmed over the Sheol Trading's records and accounts, but we're hearing word their investigation has been hampered by the mysterious overnight shredding of documents. Despite the building, deemed by police to have been empty, secure, and under guard,' the journalist paused to allow his words to sink in the viewing audience. 'The fallout from this spectacular collapse is not only confined to London. We understand

238

investment banks from all points around the globe are being summoned to appear before hearings and tribunals with a view to answering countless allegations of their implicit cooperation in Sheol Trading's activities. We anticipate numerous arrests to follow in the days ahead,' said the serious reporter.

'And what about the enigmatic leader of Sheol Trading? Have there been any further comments?' The newsreader in the studio angled her face, allowing the camera to capture her best profile.

'Not a word. For all apparent purposes, she and the other leaders at Sheol Trading have vanished off the face of the earth. We understand borders throughout Europe have been put on alert and Interpol is investigating their disappearance.'

'And how is the rest of the market reacting this morning?'

'Judging from the people we have spoken to today, they expect there to be several tremors throughout other financial companies, particularly those with close ties to Sheol Trading. They, too, are expected to fall in value. The fear now is that we may now be witnessing the beginning of a financial crisis which has the potential to engulf the world.'

'This is a shocking development. The question on all of our viewers' lips is. "how could such a large company implode this quickly?"'

'Well,' the journalist had been preparing for this question all night. This would be his moment of glory. 'What was once a billion-pound company, seemingly unstoppable and monopolising the financial markets, is now worth less than a crisp packet. The irony is that Sheol Trading died by the hands of their own weapon, the stock market, that and their bumbling CFO.'

Gilly chuckled to himself. 'Bumbling,' he muttered.

Duncan glared at him.

The newsreader suddenly grabbed at her ear, the split screen disappearing. She immediately sat bolt upright. 'Our apologies for this interruption, but we have some breaking news in this ongoing saga. We are now crossing to our reporter, Manendra Ramprakash, live from the offices of Wollenwal & Wollenwal, where Duncan Bottomley was an employee before his spectacular breakdown.'

Duncan glared at Gilly, daring him to say something.

'Yes, thank you, Jennifer. In what is an extraordinary twist in the tale, we have learned this morning a letter dated Monday, the day this saga began, has been found in the desk belonging to Richard Steel, a partner from Wollenwal & Wollenwal, who is also missing. You might recall during Mr Bottomley's on-air meltdown, he claimed Richard Steel had been working for, and murdered by, Lucy Smith, the CEO of Sheol Trading, or "the Devil" if you happen to believe Mr Bottomley's ramblings.' The reporter smirked. 'We understand this letter was uncovered by an aggrieved former employee of Wollenwal & Wollenwal, who had gained entry to the premises to search for evidence to support her claim of unfair dismissal against the firm.'

'That is quite a coincidence,' said Gilly.

'We have been reliably informed within this document Mr Steel admits to his involvement in last week's murder of Detective Superintendent Malloy, and that he had acted on the instructions of Lucy Smith and Oliver Baal, the CEO and COO of Sheol Trading. We have also been told this letter also states Lucy Smith ordered the death of Harold Wilson, another of Wollenwal & Wollenwal's partners. The police are treating this letter with the utmost seriousness and severity, and have issued an arrest warrant for Mr Richard Steel, as well as Lucy Smith and Oliver Baal, who are also wanted for questioning by the authorities concerning the collapse of Sheol Trading. We will bring you updates as this story continues to unfold.'

'Who would have thought,' smiled Gilly. 'Lucy's fall from grace is complete. You would think she would be used to falling from grace!'

There was a moment of silence.

Gilly scratched as his ear, his fingers squirreling around. Duncan's eyes flared in disgust. 'Don't you dare.'

'You must be feeling fairly pleased with yourself?' said Gilly.

'I can honestly say no,' lamented Duncan.

'Why not? You saved the world.'

'I'm thirty-seven years old. I have a six-pound haircut. I am single and now unemployed. To top it all off, I am hanging out with a corpse. That says it all!' riposted Duncan drily.

'Ah, that reminds me. I have some good news for you!' said Gilly cheerily.

'Great. I could do with some good news.'

'You can cross unemployment off your list because I have got a great job for you.'

'And what's that?' Duncan enquired. His curiosity piqued.

Gilly slid his arm around Duncan's shoulder. 'Ah, well, you see. If you remember, since the first day we met, I have been trying to talk to you about something quite pressing.'

'I thought you wanted to tell me about Lucy?'

'Oh no. Not at all. To be honest, I wasn't even aware Lucifer knew about you. Actually, this is quite funny. You see, Purgatory determined you are the best candidate to take my place, when you died of course. And this is the funny part, Lucy found out you had been appointed my replacement. There was a mole in Purgatory, leaking information to her. Anyway, she decided to corrupt you. Thought if you were showered in wealth and so on, you would switch to her side. When that failed, she resorted to old-fashioned blackmail.'

Duncan sat dumbfounded and stared blankly at Gilly.

'You see, there is only so long a rotting body can survive. I have to retire soon. And this is the good news for you, Purgatory has decided to hire you. Lucky you!'

'I don't understand.'

'You say that a lot, don't you?' Gilly shook his head, maggots rattled around inside. 'Lucy learned you were to replace me and hatched this plan to convert you to her side. If she succeeded, then once you started to do my job then nobody would have been able to stop her hostile takeover. You would have voted with her, taken her side. It was a brilliant plan; you really have to give her credit. She outdid herself this time. Even if I found out you had been corrupted, switched to her side, before you started the position, there would have been nothing I could have done. Once a decision is made in Purgatory, there is nothing you can do to change it; that's bureaucracy for you. Whether the decision is right or wrong, fair or not, it doesn't matter. Once it's made, it's made.' Gilly's tone brightened considerably. 'But, as luck would have it, everything worked out fine and now you are free to take on my role.'

'You mean… Everything that has happened to me, is because of you and Purgatory?'

'That's one way to look at it, not the right way, but one way. I don't know why you're upset. You should be happy; you've got a job when you die. That's much better than a job for life.'

'You can't be serious. I would rather be dead... than dead! You know what I mean. No way. This isn't happening.'

'You're being deadist again, you really have to stop that. Besides, it's not like anybody is going to hire you now. You were the CFO of the biggest bankruptcy in corporate history. Were you planning on listing it as one of your achievements? Trust me, it won't look good on your CV. You may as well take the job.'

'This is all yours and Purgatory's fault.'

'There you go again; the cup is half-empty. You need to lighten up, look on the bright side. Come on, let's go hang out in a pub and watch people drink. Let's celebrate!'

'I don't understand how this all happened?' said Duncan.

'What's there to understand? All we needed was a bit of faith. That and a video of you making a fool of yourself on television, and a few million shares being dumped on the market to help push the share price down. Once the market saw the share price fall, they were bound to panic and — hey presto! — you have a global meltdown. Now, what about the pub? I can hear it calling our names.'

'Did you know I would make a fool of myself on television?'

Gilly shrugged. 'No, but I knew you would do something stupid. I find people who are inherently good, when faced with an Earth-shattering event of this magnitude, tend to do something stupid. Noah and the whole ark thing.' He smiled, exposing his lack of teeth. 'The point is, I knew you would do the right thing.'

'I really don't like hanging out with a corpse.' Duncan despaired, rolling his eyes, his expression at once one of pain and exhaustion. His shoulders slumped.

Mind you, not that he would admit it, the thought of a beer at that moment sounded perfect and, if there was a bright side to going to the pub with a dead person, it would be the pleasure he would derive from being able to constantly remind Gilly how good a pint of beer tasted.

He sighed, nodded his head and frowned.

'And after the pub,' Gilly said, interrupting Duncan's thoughts. 'We can pop into Purgatory and remind Ballsy how wrong he was. Yet again! I never tire of that.' Gilly slapped

Duncan on the back and guffawed as he lumbered to the front door.

'Before we go anywhere, can you … spray on deodorant. My eyes are watering.'

- THE END -